JAY TINSIANO AND JAY NEWTON

White Horse

Acknowledgement

We would like to extend huge thanks to everyone who helped craft this book. Your contribution helped us make White Horse the best story we possibly could.

Firstly, special thanks to our editor, Jason Whited, for beating White Horse into shape.

Also, thanks to the following beta readers:

James Newton
Mr Maff
Nick Stuart
Diane Velasquez
Dorene A. Johnson
Lynn Hallbrooks

We would also like to give out a shout out to the following for their support.
Ronald Carr
Adam Chilvers

Join the Jay Tinsiano Reader Group

Free Thriller Starter Library
Books and stories
Previews and Sneak Peeks
Exclusive material

To join the VIP Jay Tinsiano reading group, head to:

www.jaytinsiano.com/newsletter

Revelation

"The horseman on the white horse was clad in a showy and barbarous attire. His Oriental countenance was contracted with hatred as if smelling out his victims. While his horse continued galloping, he was bending his bow in order to spread pestilence abroad."

The Four Horsemen of the Apocalypse, by Vicente Blasco Ibanez

Chapter 1

11.40 AM, March 11
Three miles outside Madrid, Spain

Vibrations shot through the toilet floor, followed by a high-pitched metallic grinding that sounded like a demonic scream. A rush of force violently threw Hugo Reese's whole body into the mirror, fracturing the glass into a spiderweb of cracks.

Panic flashed across Hugo's mind; the carriage shook, and then he was in free fall. The world turning upside down.

Time slowed, senses went into overdrive as his body pumped adrenaline and he felt himself curling into a fetal position, waiting to die.

Inevitable impact.

The railway carriage was turning, metal crumbled by an unseen force crushing it up like a foot on a tin can. The small window darkened as the ground quickly filled the space.

A vicious crack.

The smell of sticky, stale urine filled the air before Hugo's body slammed against the window. Then, as if someone pressed play again, the moment jumped back into action.

Blackness.

Just like an earthquake.

His mind spiralled in the darkness, consciousness slipping through the cracks. Then he was standing in Firestone, LA, and the buildings, the concrete under his feet, all began to move like nothing he had ever known. Senses playing tricks on him.

One weird feeling. No control.

Like free-falling into a volcano, the heat of the lava burning his skin. Steam surrounding him, making it hard to get air.

Hugo pulled at a mask that wasn't there, as if something was there to stop him breathing. No matter how hard he tried, it would not shift, and his time was up.

No air, no life. *Adios.*

He almost jumped back into consciousness, head springing up as if physically gulping for oxygen. As his vision slowly returned, he saw smoke forming all around him.

Then he realised he was still on the train, still in the familiar surroundings of the toilet cubicle. Nick Batchman's lifeless body was juxtapositioned into place as if arranged like that by an unseen puppeteer; his back curved in a U shape, limbs flopped by his side. Dead eyes stared ahead in frozen fear, just as Hugo had first discovered him. His round glasses still hanging around a bruised neck.

An overwhelming silence followed that seemed to draw on for an eternity. Then, slowly, the screaming began—a child crying, panicked cries for help from someone trapped, and moans from children, men and women alike. All barely audible, all in extreme pain.

Hugo realised he was in a similar position to Batchman on the other side of the sink. He tried to move, but a sharp pain shot through his neck, making him wince, and he cried out like he hadn't done since he was a kid.

And then the blackness returned.

***

Kem and Droops were hanging out on the sidewalk, leaning against the wall of a yard and arguing about which recent Narcocorrido tunes were best.

Narcocorrido was narco music, a subgenre of the Mexican norteño-corrido northern ballad music genre, traditional folk music from northern Mexico. The lyrics usually centred around *cholos*—tough gang members—or the killing of rivals. Either way, it helped audiences be the *narco* gangsters that they aspired to. Narcocorrido had a massive following in the Latino communities on both sides of the border, so much so that chains like Walmart eventually overlooked the violent nature of the lyrics and stocked the various albums.

Kem, nicknamed for his panache for ketamine, preferred the raw, homegrown Mexican talent called The Kommander, who came from the Mexican side of the border in Juarez, near El Paso.

Droops growled that only the Stateside singers were any good.

Hugo was trying to tune out the banter as he had that feeling again. He rubbed a hand over his shaved head and spat onto the sidewalk. He was stocky, brown arms covered in tattoos that depicted alliances to Florencia 13 followed by their own *clique* markings. A feeling of uselessness and numbness beset him. There should be something more than this. There must be.

It was a tapping thought that nagged at the fringes of his consciousness and one that frustrated him as he could never put his finger on—whatever the fuck it was—and now it was eating at him again, just like it always did.

Their clique was a subsect of the much wider Florencia 13, the gang that had dominated the Florence-Firestone district of South Central LA for decades and now stood at over three thousand members. It was like a corporation. All the cliques paid allegiance to F-13, who took orders directly from La Eme—the Mexican Mafia, a prison gang that had higher connections. La Eme, or M, was also the thirteenth letter in the alphabet, a respectful nod to F-13.

Their business was extortion, drugs, arms dealing—anything that made money, and they would go to any length to hold on to that power. Hugo refocused on the present situation. Their clique was small in size. Although they were part of F-13, they were on the edge of the territory, and beyond it was enemy turf. He could see the corner no more than one hundred metres away to the east, controlled by Chinos, and they were a ten-minute walk from South Watts and the Crips. Hugo had spent a few days mulling it over. Their clique needed a lot more green coming in.

More green, more members.

The Chinos were no friends to him or any other Latino gangbanger, but he was shrewd enough to know it was about doing business, nothing else. Hugo and his clique could supply the powder, and he knew full well they would undercut the Crips' own operation. It was the longball game. Eat away at the Crips. That would take the heat off Hugo's crew while the Crips would have to defend against the Chinos. It would also make their clique look good with F-13 for shifting so much product.

So, Hugo had set up the meeting, but his car had died a death.

Now Tonio, the only other guy who was available in their clique with a vehicle, had just called. Couldn't make it. No show. His mother was just taken to the hospital, and he was pretty upset about it. What was Hugo supposed to say? Fuck your mother?

Droops and Kem were too young at fourteen to have wheels, and the useless fucks would probably crash anyway. It was a shame he couldn't rustle up more *vatos*, but everyone else had let him down at the last minute with some shit. Besides, they weren't too enthusiastic about Hugo's plan and the low profits involved.

If they didn't turn up for the meet, they'd lose any kudos that Hugo had managed to front so far. No, they had to be there, and time was ticking. They needed to hoof it and skirt Crips territory to get there on time.

"I'm not sure, vato. They got Scott this way, remember?" Droops said warily.

Hugo remembered only too well. Scott had been another close amigo whose grave he now had to pour bourbon over every month, the standard gang ritual when respecting passed compadres. He had been loyal to Scott, who had a vision for the gang's growth and had taken the first steps, but he had made a mistake, got himself caught in a sticky situation, and then boom! Adios, Scott.

Scott had always looked out for Hugo, taking him under his wing in the clique, like the father he never had, and they had gunned him down near Florence Avenue right on their own turf.

Forming the new gang had been a challenge as members often saw the formation of a new clique as divvying up the turf, but Scott had a good standing with one of the F-13 senior members and got the nod after arguing it would bring in more members and strengthen their position in the area.

Scott had led the clique, with Hugo being his numero dos, but they had struggled to turn it into a high-money operation, and their numbers were still way too small. Not only that but because their territory dangerously bordered the Crips' zone of influence, it often sparked shootings or fights-on-sight.

His death had hit Hugo hard.

Drinking liquor until he was stumbling, Hugo wandered the streets with a Glock 13 held tight in his thick hand, trying to find the scumbags who did it. The truth was he had no idea and somehow ended up back home without being spotted by the feds or any other gangs.

"Yeah, course I remember, Droops. 'Course, I fucking remember. You think I would forget that?" Hugo said bitterly, fixing him with a deadly stare.

Droops looked away, shrugged, and mumbled something that might have been an apology. Hugo immediately felt bad for talking to Droops like that. That's what he loathed about all the bullshit of this life. You had to be the Big Man, full of hate at all times; otherwise, you'd soon be hung out to dry. Droops was a good guy—his friend.

Hugo waved a hand nonchalantly and fixed his compadre with a smile. "Hey, Droops, if we see any of those fuckers that got Scott, we can take 'em down."

Droops grinned at the thought. "That would be sweet."

The three figures—all donning long white shorts, vests, and expensive trainers—moved confidently across the baked tarmac that split the Florence-Firestone district with South Watts. Stolen Beretta 92s or their *gats* were tucked into their belts, hidden by long vests and baseball shirts. They headed along Ninety-Second Street, past numerous backyards, ignoring fearful glances from the residents, and then walked down Compton Avenue towards South Watts, their demeanour becoming more alert the deeper they moved into enemy territory.

Hugo spotted an F-13 tag that he had sprayed on a house wall that had been crossed out, indicating Crips had been back in the last twenty-four hours. The three young men threw each other a casual glance but said nothing.

As they reached East Century Boulevard, Hugo could see the cafe on the far side of the busy street. The sound of a whistle pierced the air, and then he saw a young black kid, no older than eight, start running away from them down the avenue.

"Keep your eyes open, amigos, and let's do this quick," he said. He guessed the kid was a lookout, and they had already been spotted. It would be easy to turn back and run to Firestone, but Hugo was too pumped up to abort now. They crossed the street, playing leapfrog with the traffic until they reached the far side and regrouped outside a liquor store.

"Kem, keep checking behind us. Droops, stay on me, a few paces behind, OK, Bruh?" Both nodded, and they started strolling along the sidewalk past a line of stores before a barren car lot appeared on their left.

"So, this is good biz fer the clique, huh, ese?" asked Droops, turning his head to glance at Hugo.

Hugo nodded and jerked his head as if shooing Droops ahead. A few hundred metres in front of them was a dilapidated café that hadn't served food for years, the windows shuttered by blinds.

One of the Chinos leaned against the wall—thin but toned, bare arms covered in gang tattoos as was the norm. He exhaled a cloud of smoke from his joint, gaze raising to meet the figures coming towards him.

Droops stopped in front of the man without acknowledging him, turned, and nodded at Hugo, who also stopped.

"We're here to see Tony Yong," said Hugo.

The Chinese guy appraised Hugo and dropped the roach on the pavement before grinding it with the heel of his trainer.

Without saying anything, he swung back and knocked on the glass with a rap of his knuckles and then turned back to face them with cold, unsmiling eyes.

The door opened, and another guy peered out at them, checking them each out in turn.

"Tony Yong?" asked Hugo.

"Who's asking?"

"I'm Howzy," replied Hugo, using his gang call sign.

The Chino jerked his head, indicating they should come in.

Hugo turned to Droops and Kem, who were both looking up and down the street.

"Stay here, keep an eye out. This'll take two seconds."

They both nodded, but Hugo could tell they weren't happy about it. Inside, the dark room that used to be a buzzing café was now trashed. A crate serving as a table was in the middle, and three heavily tattooed Chinese men dressed in vests, long shorts, and trainers were hunched around it. They looked up at Hugo with a nonchalant, stone-faced casualness that half threatened to explode into violence at any moment. One muttered something in Chinese, which Hugo ignored. He needed to focus on getting them to do the deal.

A stocky, muscular man stood up from the crates. He could have been any one of the gangbangers that Hugo hung around with; bald head, tattoos, basketball vest. The only difference between them was race. Yong jerked his head slightly. It came across as a half greeting, half command to follow him. They walked into a small room at the back of the derelict café that had another table and chairs, a slashed sofa, and more debris scattered on the bare floorboards.

"So, what have we got?" said Yong, eyeing Hugo with razor-dark eyes.

Hugo took out his sample and threw it onto the table-top—white powder wrapped in plastic. Yong unwrapped it and proceeded to rack up a line on the table. He rolled a twenty up and snorted up the coke within a second.

"What are you looking for?" he said, pinching his nostrils with his fingers.

"Fifteen for half a key, amigo."

The Chinese snorted harshly and slammed his hand onto the table. His snorting slowly turning to a laugh as his eyes reddened, focusing back on Hugo with veiled contempt.

"Fifteen? I was paying that for a whole key less than a year ago. I can get this same shit for less, much less. Bounce already; we're done."

Hugo dismissed it as bravado. The Chino knew it was good shit and was just playing hardball.

"You know that's the real deal; there's five hundred ounces you can turn into crack and easily cut out the Crips on their own turf."

Yong shook his head. "I sell at whatever price I want, vato." He rasped the last word between his teeth like a snake and fixed Hugo with a stare.

After a few seconds of staring back, Hugo shrugged.

"OK. You miss out, and I'll take the deal somewhere else."

He started to walk towards the door, and the Chinese tutted behind him.

"Ten...and we got a deal."

Hugo smiled and turned back to face him. The snake was negotiating at last.

***

An hour later, they moved back across the street towards the beginning of Compton Avenue and safer streets. Hugo felt relief. Yong had agreed to $12K per half key, which was around what Hugo had hoped for. A small profit but enough product to fuck the Crips. He hated having to deal with all this drug shit. But now, at least, they could start doing the drops and focus on business while the *Wah Ching* did the dirty work of eating away at the Crips territory, which would only strengthen their clique. Hugo started going over the figures in his mind as he watched a blue-grey Ford van turn onto Compton Avenue just ahead of them. It pulled over sharply, and Hugo felt a spike of adrenaline surge through him. He whistled to get the others' attention and reached under his shirt, grabbing the handle of his gat. The van had blackened windows, so he couldn't make out who was inside, but his instinct was screaming at him that it was a trap.

"Hey! Hey!" Hugo shouted, turning back and gesturing with his hand for the others to follow his lead.

"The van, the van..."

Droops glanced across the avenue and seeing the vehicle Hugo was frantically gesturing at made a grab for his piece.

"Well, let's take 'em, vato."

"We don't know how many..."

A series of loud cracks pierced the air around them. All three dived onto the ground through pure instinct. Hugo kept his eyes trained on the van, confirming he was right. It was a trap. The side door was open, and Hugo could just make out a couple of Crip boys in khaki-green trainer tops aiming directly at him. Hugo fired in their direction; the first bullet punctured the side of their van. The Crips quickly slid the door closed as a shield, not that it would really protect them any better. Hugo turned his head back to the others.

"Get back the other way!" he shouted.

Droops and Kem didn't hesitate and jogged back down the street. Somewhere across the block Hugo heard a scream and caught a glance of people taking cover behind cars. Drivers raced past to avoid the escalating incident, and one screeched to a halt in the middle of the lane, blocking the road. Hugo turned back and fired another shot towards the van before making a run for it back in the same direction as his friends. There were a series of gunshots ahead. Hugo watched in horror as Kem and Droops both fell to the ground in a volley of bullets. Four black guys suddenly appeared, stepping out onto the sidewalk from behind a wall.

Shit!

They had been trapped in a classic pincer move. Hugo stared in disbelief. Droops was gripping his stomach, crying in agony as he rolled around on the sidewalk. Kem was facedown, his body unmoving. One of the Crips casually took aim at the dying boy's head and fired once, and Droops was still. Hugo froze, and every fibre of his being wanted to run at them, guns blazing. A bullet whistled past Hugo from the other direction, barely missing him, shaking him out of his fixated state. The gangbangers were out of the van, taking cover at the corner, taking pot shots.

Hugo felt surprisingly calm as he returned a series of shots, hitting one of the gang in the chest as they mistimed a run across the sidewalk to take cover behind a parked car. As he caught a snapshot of the body, he realised it was a kid; no older than nine or ten. His lifeless eyes stared in Hugo's direction, mouth caught open in frozen horror.

Dios perdóname. A kid!

Hugo swung around looking for escape routes. He was almost surrounded. The only option was a wooden fence directly ahead. Vaulting over it, Hugo was running fast, through backyards and over more fences. An old man cowed back as he ran by, hearing another gunshot behind him. As he ran, he was already replaying the scene in his head, as vivid as the trees blurring past him. Suddenly, he was in the middle of a nightmare, all recent feelings and misconceptions about his life morphing into one spearhead that struck him once again in the pit of his stomach. Distant shouts and screams carried across the road, drifting through the neighbourhood. In that moment, he knew he was out of the conflict. But his amigos, his compadres...

Shit.

Dead on the sidewalk.

And that little kid, lying in his own blood, his lifeless eyes forever imprinted in Hugo's mind.

Chapter 2

Shafts of bright light. A loud, grating sound, like sawing through metal.

Voices.

"Can you hear me?"

Hugo flickered his eyes open to see the kind face of a woman asking him once again whether he could hear.

"*Sí, si,*" Hugo managed to whisper, and then the pain shot through him as if slapping him to remind him it was there.

"OK, don't move. I'm going to give you morphine for the pain and put this neck brace on you, and then we're going to strap you to a board and get you out of here. Si? You've been in a pretty serious accident, so it's important you stay still; you may have suffered trauma to your spine."

Hugo shifted his eyes around, noticing he was still in the toilet cubicle. Batchman's body was still there, and then he remembered again. Finding him dead. Before the accident. The paramedic stuck a needle into Hugo's arm and then shouted back to a colleague to prepare a stretcher. He could see that they had cut a hole in the side of the carriage, which was above them, and the paramedic must have climbed through. Faces of rescue workers peered down, their faces obscured by shadow, and then a winch lowered towards them.

He noticed Batchman's iPad had fallen and wedged itself next to the sink, still zipped up in its green leather sleeve. A pattern of memory tapped away at him. It was important. The prof had been scared of someone he had seen. The shit he was talking about had sounded serious. Exactly why he did not know, but Hugo grabbed the iPad and held it close to his chest.

****

March 11, 8.54 AM
Córdoba Train station

Hugo Reese had leaned down and hugged his aunt goodbye. She was four-foot-nothing and almost as wide and grabbed his head with two powerful arms, the kind of arms that were used to working all day. She kissed him twice, once on each cheek.

"Vaya usted con dios," she said, looking up at him with warm eyes.

He grinned at her with genuine affection, clearly glad that he had come the distance to reconnect with these distant relatives. The last few months had been just what he needed, the contrast from his old life in South Central to the travels in between and, finally, the dusty village of Pozuelo de Calatrava in Spain.

He turned to his cousin, a slender lad with a mop of thick dark hair, and extended his hand.

"Until next time, Cuz, and that is an open offer for you to come visit me. Not sure where I'm going to end up, but you are always welcome."

"Gracias, Hugo, it has been a great pleasure to meet you. Hasta pronto," his cousin said with a little smile.

Lifting his rucksack up and slinging it over his shoulder,

Hugo turned towards the waiting train; the sleek modern carriages succumbed to dirt and dust. Things somehow seemed simpler here, an easier way of life that had helped recharge him, yet he couldn't hang around forever. Besides, he had restless feet and yearned to look around more of Europe. Why the hell not? He was here and had green in his pocket. All that waited for him at home was possible prison or death. There was nothing there for him now, only a vague alliance with the ghosts of dead compadres who wouldn't be able to help him anymore.

He stepped up onto the train and scanned the carriage for a free seat. Si, the country life had been good, different. Although at the heart of it he was a city vato. Could he really give up the hustle and bustle for the quiet life? The inside of the train reminded him of what he had been missing: the hustle of the Metro Rail, the life of the big city.

Walking down the aisle, Hugo spotted an empty table seat opposite an old guy working on a tablet device. He swung his large black-and-blue rucksack up onto the storage shelf that hung from the ceiling and slid into the plastic moulded seat. After a few moments, the train rocked, gently swaying into motion as it slowly pulled out of the station. Through the window, he could see the dry Spanish landscape, plants struggling to stay green as the sun beat down upon the dusty ground. The air-conditioned carriage offered an almost alien environment in comparison, and he was glad of the cool air.

Hugo's gaze lingered out the window as his mind wandered, and then he realised how dry his mouth was. He remembered seeing a cafeteria coach towards the front of the train and fished around for his wallet. He caught the eye of the elderly man who was sitting opposite, a Panama hat resting on the empty seat beside him. His grey hair was swept smoothly back, and his blue blazer and crisp white shirt clearly gave him the look of a teacher of some sort. Eyes that sparkled with intelligence shone behind a pair of round gold-rimmed glasses as he glanced up at Hugo from his iPad.

"Excuse me, *señor*? If you're going to the bar, could you get me a tea?" he asked in perfect Spanish as if reading his mind.

The old guy pulled out a euro note and handed it to Hugo. Hugo paused for a moment and then took the note.

"Sure. A tea."

"With milk," the man added in English. He smiled courteously and returned to typing on his iPad.

Hugo made his way down the train carriage to the refreshment coach and ordered a beer and tea. As he waited for the steward to prep the tea he wondered about the old man. Usually, strangers took one look at his shaven head and gang tattoos and avoided eye contact at any cost. This stranger had started a conversation without a hint of fear in his eyes. Not something Hugo was used to. Was he on the train to keep an eye out for people like him? Maybe he was pulling up Hugo's details right now on some fed database? Or was Hugo being too paranoid?

The steward handed over the tea in a cardboard cup, and Hugo paid and made his way back down the carriage. As he neared the seat from behind the man, he made a point of checking his screen. There was a lot of text and some diagram on it that Hugo didn't understand, but it didn't look like anything for him to worry about. Whatever. He'd play along for now, and if his suspicions were confirmed in any way he'd deal with it.

"Thanks very much, young man," the professor said, taking

his paper mug.

Hugo nodded and put down his beer.

"*Sin problema.* I don't know how you can drink hot tea in this country."

The man smiled benignly. "Hot drinks can keep you surprisingly cool," he said.

"How so?"

"If you take a hot drink, your body compensates and makes you sweat more—which is your body's way to help you cool down. It's not an exact science, but it works for me."

Hugo stared blankly at the old man and then grinned.

"I see, Prof. You're having a joke. That's OK, man. I'll stick to my ice-cold cerveza. You stick to sweating it out."

He opened the can, making a loud *psst* noise, and took a long gulp, savouring the cold, malty brew as it slid down his parched throat.

The old man smiled and nodded. "I don't blame you at all. I enjoy a cold one once in a while."

He held out his hand to Hugo. "I'm Nicholas Batchman, by the way, but please call me Nick."

Hugo reluctantly shook it and nodded.

"Hugo."

Lapsing into silence, both men gazed out of the carriage window. The view of the Spanish countryside flashed past them: rolling hills and valleys blanketed with the dead sunflowers left to dry in the heat and dotted white buildings with terracotta-tiled roofs nestled behind olive groves. They could see the slow-spinning turbines of the giant windmills, ghostly grey silhouettes in the distance, lining the landscape as far as the eye could see. As their great blades turned in unison, the shapes reminded Hugo of a line of ballet dancers moving gracefully through their performance. He turned his attention back to the old guy.

"So, what is it that you do, Doc?"

"I'm a professor of virology. That is the study of viruses."

Hugo raised his eyebrows slightly. "Viruses? What kind of viruses?"

"Well, it's usually any that are fatal to the human body. When it comes to finding cures, there are a lot of bloody options. Most of my time is spent on H1N1 virus. You may have heard of the Spanish flu?"

Hugo thought for a moment. "I have heard of it, Doc, but I have to admit I don't know shit about it."

With a benign smile, the old man went on. "Without boring you to tears, it was a vicious form of the flu that broke out in 1918. It infected five hundred million people across the world and killed fifty to one hundred million of them."

Hugo stared at Batchman in genuine surprise. Although he vaguely remembered hearing the name, he had never heard of this number of fatalities before.

"That's one badass virus. Why Spanish? Is that where it started?"

"Not exactly. Nearly every country's news outlets at the time barely covered the virus because it might be bad for 'morale,' except in Spain, where the media had fewer qualms about reporting the deaths. So, it appeared to be worse there, but in actual fact, it affected most countries with the same devastating end."

Batchman paused to take a long sip of his tea.

"And it was most devastating on young, healthy adults rather than juveniles, the elderly, or already weakened patients, which is contrary to what you would normally associate with flu. It was a problem that initially stumped doctors. That's partly why I'm going to Madrid. There's a conference on virology where I'm presenting."—Batchman paused and cleared his throat—"and will be revealing some new information on the virus."

"What kind of information?"

The old professor, pleased to find such an attentive audience in Hugo, continued with genuine warmth in his voice.

"This might sound strange, but one of the things I've spent my life working on is finding out what makes the perfect pathogen."

Hugo said nothing and carefully placed his beer on the small table between them. Batchman focused on the passing landscape before warming to his theme.

"It would have to be easy to catch and cause a high mortality rate."

"And difficult to cure, I guess?" asked Hugo.

"Yes, absolutely. When a new strain of virus emerges, as there has been no previous contact within the human race, there is no immunity. Our bodies simply don't know how to defend themselves from it. The most common way for this to happen is for a strain to jump species, for example, a virus like the Asian bird flu that has only been found in birds, and then it comes into contact with a human. That virus would have to mutate to be able to survive in its new host."

Hugo brushed a hand protectively over his arm as if imagining a rampant mutating virus forming inside him. "'Nice....'"

Batchman clasped his hands together and gave a satisfied sigh.

"Now, viruses mutate all the time; it's quite normal. Look at the common cold or flu. Each year small mutations occur, changing it in some way. We call this 'antigenic drift.' Our bodies learn to recognise the new mutation and defend themselves. In the case of the flu, the vaccines need to be constantly modified because small genetic changes can accumulate over time. This would mean that the vaccine would no longer match the current form of a virus, and so the body's immune system might not be given the opportunity to recognise the viruses."

Batchman leaned forward on the table, taking note of the blank look on Hugo's face.

"One way to get your head around it is to think of influenza as a deck of cards. The flu has fourteen genes, and antigenic drift is when there is a gradual change in the genome and the flu shot from the previous year is partially effective. Antigenic shift is when the deck is completely reshuffled with parts of different flu viruses—avian H1N1, swine flu—then the vaccine is totally ineffective. This means that, in effect, there is a completely new virus, and worldwide pandemics can occur."

Subconsciously, Hugo leaned towards Batchman.

"I like the deck of cards. Seems clearer."

Batchman continued. "So, we can almost fully expect for a virus to mutate, but imagine what the odds are that the virus mutates in such a way that it picks every single one of those key traits to make it so deadly?"

Hugo raised an eyebrow. "You tell me...sounds like crazy shit."

"Well, that's what I'm working on. My latest paper looks at how viruses mutate and how we can manipulate them to mutate. I carried on the research that my old lecturer, Ljungborg, had begun so long ago. He was on the literal frontline of the 1918 pandemic. Lost his family to it..."

Batchman paused for a moment and glanced out of the

window as if replaying a memory. He turned back to Hugo, who waited for him to continue.

"We need to understand this virus and how it acted the way it did. If we are to be better prepared, then we have to understand the mechanisms and identify the key mutations. The only way to stop another mass pandemic is to educate ourselves on such things. Crazy as the idea sounds, knowledge is the key to our survival here."

The old man settled back in his seat with a look of determination on his face, and Hugo could see he was passionate about this shit.

His suspicion of the old man had slowly waned. Certainly, no fed. *Still, be careful.*

Batchman made a dismissive swoop with his hand.

"Anyway...enough about me. I don't mean to bore you. So where are you from?"

Hugo leaned back in the seat and sighed.

"LA, man. I lost *muchos amigos* in that place...bad mems all the way and a lotta pain, but I'm turning a new leaf—things are gonna get better. I always wanted to see those places you only ever see on the TV, you know, man? I already saw a lot of places across America. Amazing places...but I still got shit for these..." Hugo brushed a hand over his tattooed arm.

"Sounds like you're doing the right thing, Hugo—and I'm sorry about you losing family members and friends."

Hugo nodded slightly, but his mind was far away as his eyes turned again to the passing hills. He thought about his friends who died on the street. And the young kid. A Crip for sure, but still just a kid, shot by his own hand.

"When you got nothing, you got nothing to lose. You see the other gangbangers wearing top-line Nikes, gold shit, driving nice wheels, so you go out guns blazing and take what you can. It was like a rainbow on the horizon, the greener fields on the other side of the fence. The cool thing to do. Be respected and feared; every guy's dream, but it always ends the same. Death or prison. I knew I had to get out."

Batchman appraised Hugo with considerate eyes and closed his iPad, returning it to a zip-up cover before placing it on the seat next to him. He leaned back against the padded headrest, evidently giving up on any work he was doing.

"I can't pretend to know what you've been through. I had the opportunity to study, become a doctor, follow my dream. It's not been an easy road, but a very different struggle from what you've been through, my friend. Tomorrow, I have a conference where I will present my findings, almost a decade of work. I can tell you I'm more than a little nervous about it. Still, at least I will have a chance to catch up with a few old colleagues, some like my old lab assistants, Paul and Eduardo. Others, sadly, have succumbed to the passing of time, the biggest killer of friendship when you reach this ripe old age," he said with an ironic grin.

"Well, that's good—I mean you did it at least—not just sitting around wishing it would happen." Hugo shook his head. "Like so many of my homies," he added.

Batchman held up the disposable paper cup of tea and looked directly at him.

"Let's drink to absent friends then, Hugo, alive or otherwise."

Hugo smiled and lifted his can of beer.

"I'll drink to that, Doc. *¡Por los amigos ausentes!*"

Chapter 3

The train pulled up at Puertollano, and the two men fell silent; Batchman was tapping into his mobile phone as Hugo watched groups of passengers disembark, and new ones get on. A trio of young travellers walked down the platform, laden with weighty-looking rucksacks, a tall man with a ponytail in a dark suit passed by, as did an elderly local man walking with the aid of a stick. Hugo crushed his empty beer can and slumped back into his seat, allowing himself to drift off to the reverberating clanking of the tracks as the train began to move off.

Soon, he remembered walking slowly along the sidewalk, and he saw the stains of blood first soaked into the dusty concrete. Then he saw the familiar British Knight trainers on the lifeless corpse of his friend Kem—the white shorts, still bright and vivid, strangely untouched by any blood. Then there was Droops writhing in agony; his hands clutched close to his stomach, the dark red flowing from his wound. He stooped down and tried to comfort him.

"Droops, vato. You'll be OK. It's cool." Meaningless words. It was nowhere near cool.

Finally, there was the young black kid, his body contorted in the horror of death, lifeless eyes staring right at him, penetrating his soul. A continuous scream carried on the wind, approaching sirens, and there was the familiar rush of adrenaline before Hugo opened his eyes wide with a start. He found himself looking at a pale-faced Batchman who was staring at something farther down the carriage, deep concern etched on his face and fear in his eyes. A fear Hugo recognised from his gang days like the eyes of the young boy looked just before he had shot him.

The doctor got up, grabbing his bag from the overhead rack before making his way back towards the front of the train without a word or even a glance at Hugo.

Was he getting a drink? But why take the bag? Why not say something?

A moment later, a tall man with a ponytail brushed past Hugo as he followed in the same direction as Batchman—a sliver of recognition like a distant memory stirred in Hugo.

A bell for the public address system sounded, chasing the thought away, and a metallic male voice came on: "The train will be arriving at Cuidad Real, the next station, in ten minutes."

Hugo contemplated grabbing another beer but then wondered if he should see if the doctor was going to come back. He felt a mild irritation at the man's sudden departure and tried to dismiss him out of his mind.

What the hell. He was just a stranger.

Hugo returned to gazing at the passing landscape. After another ten minutes, the train began to slow as it came into Ciudad Real. A stream of passengers got off, and he watched them pass his window: flashes of tourist shirts, Panama hats, a dark suit, a gaggle of Spanish women talking loudly. No sign of the doc. The train moved off again.

The doctor was going to Madrid so why would he get off

here? A sense of unease washed over Hugo. Something didn't add up. And that's when he saw the iPad in its dark green leather sleeve, placed flat on the seat where the doc had left it. Hugo got up and grabbed it, and purposefully strolled down the train carriage to find him.

He walked through two carriages before he got to the end of the train. As he reached the final row of seats, he stopped and looked back. No sign of the professor here. He asked the guy behind the counter in the buffet car if he'd seen him. No, he had not. Hugo frowned and headed to the only place he could be if he were still on the train.

When he arrived at the toilets, the soft glow from the yellow engaged sign told him someone was inside. Rapping his huge fist on the door, Hugo stood patiently. No response. The prickly sense that something was wrong increased, and wouldn't let go.

"Doc, are you in there? You OK?"

Still no response.

A train conductor edged past.

"Hey, *señor*." His deep voice stopped the man midstride. "I think my friend went in here. I'm a bit worried; he's not responding."

The train conductor paused and eyed Hugo, glancing down at the tattoos and back again. A look Hugo was now well used to. The guard sighed and rapped on the toilet door himself, loudly asking for a response in English and Spanish. After a further lack of response, he took a bunch of keys from his belt and shifted through them until he found the one he required and unlocked a panel next to the door.

He shook his head, looking at the bent edge of the access panel.

"This has been tampered with," he said, unlocking the override mechanism.

He pressed a button, and the door slid open with a swishing sound.

Doctor Batchman stared right at them, his head twisted slightly at an acute angle, giving his frail body the appearance of a rag doll that had been broken. There was a gash across his forehead, stained blood on his shirt as well as all over the compact sink.

"Jesus! Doc!" Hugo stepped inside the cubicle to look closer. He was dead; there was no doubt about it.

And then the train shook, and the world turned upside down.

Chapter 4

7.05 AM, March 10

The chauffeur closed the car door behind them as they walked towards the entrance of the Centro Nacional de Inteligencia, the Spanish colours draped overhead. Jamall Salazar didn't even consider saying thanks; it just wasn't in his nature. The only sound that followed them was the crisp patter of their shoes on the concrete. The wave of heat hit them. It was coming up to midday; soon, it would be unbearable outside.

It had been a long flight over from the US, and Jamall was keen to get to work. Even the relative comfort of the hotel had not helped him rest; a small handful of sleeping tablets had taken care of that duty. It was his work that offered true solace; that was all that motivated him. His sense of purpose. His sense of completion.

Jamall slowly cracked his knuckles and glanced up at the grey block building, another architectural disaster of the 1970s. The day in the hotel getting over the jet lag had his mind racing with all the things he should already be doing.

Time is short. There is prey to find.

They rounded the corner of the building, Zara Zimmermann stepping into pace beside him, her heels clicking rhythmically along with his. The warm Spanish breeze hinting that it would be another clear and beautiful day. They walked in silence; Jamall's clean-shaven and angular face matching his attitude, efficient and to the point. He had darker skin than most Latinos, which made him look almost Indian in appearance. A dark merino wool suit hung on his frame, keeping him cool in the heat.

Zara was slightly shorter, athletic, black hair pulled back into a neat ponytail and a folder tucked under one arm. She lacked the curves that made some women but walked with the same determined purpose that Jamall did. They had been a team for a while now, a bond formed in their days of training.

As they drew close to the main entrance, Jamall looked up at the sculpture that was in front of the building. One large cube made up of a series of smaller ones.

Jamall shook his head in bewilderment. He could appreciate real art, but modern pieces like this were lost on him. Where was the skill involved in creating that? He liked to think of his work as art; it pleased him somewhat to think of it that way. Jamall had little say in what he did, just take the orders and follow them. How he followed them was his choice, though, and he prided himself on being quick and efficient. His reputation for getting the job done was one of the main reasons they had sent him to Madrid.

The glass front doors to the CNI opened, and a portly man walked out. His jowly face supported a thick-set mustache; his ill-fitting suit looked like it had been slept in. As he descended the steps to meet them, it was clear he was a man used to carrying weight yet still kept himself active.

"Mr. Salazar?" he asked, extending his hand towards Jamall and raising an eyebrow, without a smile.

Jamall shook it with a curt nod. "Secretary State Director Ortez. Good to meet you. This is my colleague Zara Zimmermann," he said, introducing Zara with a slight movement of his hand. Ortez mumbled a greeting and kissed Zara on both cheeks, as was the European custom, before leading them inside the building. The secretary at the front desk looked up as they entered and smiled. Leaning over the front desk, Ortez picked up two security passes and handed them to Jamall and Zara. He gestured with his hand towards the lifts.

"So, it was late last night that I received word to expect you today. I'm not exactly sure why you are here, but I've been told to extend you every courtesy of my office."

Jamall gave a dry smile as he passed through the metal detectors.

"I realise it's short notice, State Director. As explained, we are here as part of the SSEUR agreement."

Ortez nodded. He was well aware of SIGINT Seniors Europe or SSEUR and its purpose of coordinating the exchange of military signals intelligence amongst its members. Originally, the Five Eyes intelligence sharing network had only included the US, Canada, the UK, Australia, and New Zealand but had now taken the European state under its wing. He also knew Salazar and Zimmerman were really CIA, working under the banner of the SSEUR. Spain was obliged to open its doors to agencies like the CIA to assist with intelligence gathering, specifically in relation to terrorism and any other threats to the status quo.

"We've been on the trail of a UIS cell, possibly here in Spain. We hope by pooling our intel, we can stop a major attack here in Europe," said Jamall.

Ortez purposely masked his surprise with a stony face. It

was the first he had heard of any imminent threat, and he hated nasty surprises, especially involving the United Islamic State.

The doors to the lift opened, and the three of them stepped in. Ortez pushed the button marked 6, and the lift rapidly moved skyward.

"I've set you up with your own space in a conference room and can give you access to a couple of workstations, but they'll be in the main control room."

"Thank you," said Jamall with a curt nod of his head.

They stepped out into the corridor that had seen better days, with peeling paint and unclean floor tiles, and followed the director as he led the way. Multiple doors led off the hallway, and despite its shoddy appearance, the building felt alive with activity, the sound of fingers tapping on keyboards and footsteps echoing around the concrete shell.

They stopped by a door marked 281. A quick swipe of his security pass over the pad, and the door clicked as it unlocked. Ortez pushed it open, revealing a good-sized office within. A large circular table filled the middle with a dozen chairs around it; the far wall was mostly taken up by a large window overlooking the Spanish suburbs. A small fridge was tucked over a pine unit under the window.

"Make yourself at home. You'll find refreshments in the fridge. If you need anything else, call reception and they will be able to help. Our cafeteria is located on the second floor. We'll have our briefing in half an hour if that works for you both?"

Jamall glanced at Zara and then nodded at Ortez.

"Yes, the sooner, the better."

There was a knock at the door, and Ortez let a petite, smart-looking woman into the room.

"Now let me introduce you to Dana Amador, our operations manager. She will be heading up your monitoring team and will help you with anything you need."

Amador walked over to Jamall and Zara and shook hands. She had black curly hair and large glasses that hid a natural attractiveness. Her eyes fell on Jamall, and she flashed him a warm smile.

Chapter 5

Ortez put down the phone in his office and sighed. His wife of fifteen years still struggled to understand that he needed to be with his team, especially when there were threats to the nation. Of course, he couldn't tell her that. His work could not be discussed in any detail, and to be fair, she never asked. She had been focused on family, their young son's birthday party arrangements. The roof that needed fixing on the car garage; when was he going to get up the ladder and see to it?

He smiled to himself as he leaned back in his chair, the leather creaking under his weight. He couldn't blame her. Family time came at a premium nowadays. The work life had changed so much. Siestas were history, part of the old days. Days when you could smoke in the office, or at least outside the front doors, were long gone. Now you had to go to a designated area to stand at least ten metres from the building like lepers being kept at a distance from "normal" people.

Placing his coffee mug on the desk, he gently spun himself to look out the window. With an office on the sixth floor, his window offered a good view of the Madrid cityscape. The summer sun had claimed most of the green vegetation except for the well-watered lawn of the Centro Nacional de Inteligencia, which remained vibrant, green, and fresh. Ortez could already see the first heat shimmers of the day gently warping the light. It was going to be another hot one.

Looking out of the window, he saw Jamall walking towards his car. Those dead, cold eyes. Was there any kind of soul behind them? The American leaned inside and took something out of the glove compartment. Ortez realised he was simply getting a pack of cigarettes, which made him want one as well.

Ortez sat back down at his desk and sighed.

He could understand the idea behind intelligence sharing, the pooling of resources. But it was usually a one-way ride: the Yanks barging in and demanding intel. If he were to go to them for any kind of information, he'd bet his entire collection of Cuban cigars the door would be slammed in his face. With that thought, he flicked a finger across his monitor to wake it up and logged into the highly classified SSEUR network that only he and a handful of assistant Directors at CNI had access to. He searched for Jamall Salazar, but the results page came up blank.

It was unlikely to be his real name anyway. He tapped his fingers on the desktop, his mind ticking over the question in his head. Not being listed on the SSEUR network didn't necessarily mean much. It could have been that he had been seconded into the organisational structure very recently, and they were just slow at making updates on the system.

But he doubted it.

The one thing that had happened in recent years was the step up in efficiency inside the EU, with the rise in the international climate of fear driven by increasing terrorist activity from UIS, both physical and online. This meant all Western-aligned governments had passed numerous laws for increased intel sharing in a move towards a more competent system.

What good was he really going to do here? Could they not have just sent the UIS intel and let the CNI work through it? Did the Yanks really think Spanish forces were so incompetent they needed some hotshot American babysitting them? One thing being in this business had taught Ortez was that no one did anything for nothing. You had to play the back-scratching game. The order from on high had come to offer his full cooperation, but he would keep a close eye on him. Something didn't feel right.

Chapter 6

Twenty-five years earlier
Mexico City, Mexico

Renata was only fifteen with jet-black hair tied into a ponytail. She wore a simple dress and sandals, but tears streamed down her face as she clutched her newborn baby, willing it not to leave her breast.

Despite his being born from a loveless encounter with a stranger, she loved her son with every fibre of her being. He was the jewel in the dust dunes that was their world of poverty. The one remaining prospect of a better world; a better life, if only sometime in the future.

A faint hope, but hope nevertheless.

Her pitiful wails were almost drowned out by a gaggle of angry voices from her mother and father as they waved their arms around, bitter disagreement growing louder until a slapping sound cut through the air. The mother stepped back, holding her face and moved away from him quickly. Renata began to wail even louder as she weakly chastised her father through sniffling sobs.

"Enough! There is no chance we can keep the baby. No Chance!" he shouted.

From the stony glare on his face, it was clear to all he had made up his mind and was digging in. The mother looked up at Renata, defeat in her eyes. In return, a pleading look from a desperate daughter spurred her to try once more. But as soon as she opened her mouth, her father's hand came crashing down upon their makeshift table, causing a plate on top to crash to the ground.

"I said enough!" he bellowed.

Her mother, cowed and submissive, stopped arguing.

Sometimes provoking her husband was akin to prodding a lion with a sharp stick. Unwise unless you were well out of range. She came over to Renata to comfort her and then escorted her out of the cramped, cluttered room that housed the family's meagre possessions.

Mother, daughter, and baby stepped out into a tightly arranged courtyard from which a sea of shacks made from concrete blocks with rusty corrugated sheets for roofs could be seen. A mere ten metres away from those roofed shacks of Mexico City were the bright white wealthier condos with manicured lawns, swimming pools, and newly built carports that were hidden behind high walls.

Soon, there was a sound of a female voice and a knocking from the front of their shack, and both mother and daughter froze. They could hear the father had changed his voice to a respectful tone as he greeted the stranger, which was followed by the murmur of conversation.

The young Renata cradled her silent baby boy, who had fallen to sleep after his feeding. With tear-filled eyes, she gazed at her son as she whispered over and over. "I will never forget you. Your mother loves you forever."

***

"So, it has been agreed?" the woman asked Señor Garza. They stood outside the front of the shack, keeping their voices low. Renata's father was a big man for a Mexican. Over six feet and referred to by those who knew him as *El Oso*—the bear. Although big and strong, he was uneducated and gravitated towards the pursuit of money, alcohol, and gambling. His neighbours, while fearing him, quietly despised him.

He leaned his hand on a pillar of rotting wood that served as part of the doorway and eyed the officious-looking woman from the orphanage in front of him. She was middle-aged and had the look of a South American with prominent cheekbones and tightly tied back hair, wearing a plain but smart suit.

"You have the money?" he asked in a quiet voice.

"Yes, as agreed. As I explained to you before, *Señor* Garza, this is a special government program. Your grandson will be well looked after, be assured."

The woman took out a clipboard, and the man signed the document where they stood. She then handed over an envelope, which he immediately opened. There was a wad of large-denomination *amero* notes; the recently released currency of the North American Union.

Once satisfied that he had the agreed amount, *Señor* Garza led the woman through the shack to the rear yard, where his wife and daughter stood waiting. They both shrank back in fear, the young daughter clutching her baby even closer to her chest. She burst into tears at the sight of the woman who she knew had come to take her baby away forever.

***

Flashes of memory.

Pain. Fear. Confusion. They all felt it, although they were much too young to comprehend the meaning of these feelings.

None of the children had ever known love or any kind of normality. The boy had never known a mother or father. The concept was completely alien to him. Only Doctor Red, the figure that brought him up in a warped vortex of pain, fear, and orders, served as any kind of surrogate figure.

The boy, or *Child 459*, from Mexico City, his only identity a number, was packed inside a steel shed with dozens of other children. None of them had seen each other before, and none were older than six years old.

It might have been in the afternoon as it was hot and humid inside; dust and the smell of sour sweat and human excrement hung thickly in the air. Shadows moved slowly across the floor, the gradual passing of another day in the cage. All of them were stripped of clothes but knew enough to try to huddle together for warmth as the night sapped away the heat from the day. Scared eyes searched each other for help or some kind of hope. But hope was a scarce commodity where squalor and cruelty reigned supreme.

As the dusk lengthened, with the increasing darkness, the rats came in their droves, pouring through portholes near the ground, sniffing the air in eager anticipation. Then the screaming began. Their rancorous squeaks grew louder and increased to a frenetic pitch as more of the rodents kept coming, spreading across the shed floor like a black puddle; their worm-like tails sliding behind them.

Soon there were hundreds of them, and they skirted around the children, occasionally biting at their toes and feet, causing shrieks of horror. They tried to kick them away, but the tidal wave continued. Their screams grew more intense as the rats attacked them, ripping at their flesh with their bare teeth.

A girl, face masked with fear, began clambering up onto the back of a skinny boy to get as far away from the creatures as possible. The boy couldn't hold her weight and fell onto his hands and knees, and they both tumbled to the ground. Several rats circled and went for their faces.

The boy from Mexico City grabbed the girl and hauled her up before the boy was lost under the sea of rodents. He rolled around screaming, but no one helped. Eventually, mercifully, his screams subsided, and blood pooled around their feet on the white-tiled floor.

After what seemed like hours, the doctors pulled the children out of the cage one by one and sent them back to their huts where there were no rats. A place where the boy could dream and escape to another place. A place of safety, if only for a short time.

****

One day Doctor Red came to the delta hut and spoke to the house leader, a boy not much older than the Mexican boy. They stood in the doorway of the large wooden structure that housed around twenty-five children; the hut was one of fifty or so that had been built in rows within the complex.

The house leader came over to Child 459 and told him to go with Doctor Red, who led him by the hand towards the large aircraft hangar that dominated the surrounding camp.

The boy looked up at his father figure with confusion, but they walked towards the building where he knew only pain and horrors lay waiting. The doctor tightened his grip as they got closer, but the boy did not resist or pull away. Any capability to resist had long been burned out of him.

Over at the hangar doors, they stopped, and Doctor Red spoke to the guard, but the boy didn't hear their words, his eyes squinting as they adjusted to the dark, eerie light inside and ears straining to block out the whimpers and echoing sobs that drifted through the vast space.

Inside, the harsh smell, like a sewer, hit the back of the throat, making him gag. A stink he would never ever forget in his entire life.

His eyes rose upwards towards the dark metal cages stacked up on top of each other like a grid system. In the centre was a stairwell surrounded by a metal framework for access to the different levels. A series of walkways gave access to the cages and the children that huddled inside them. The boy felt their eyes on him, staring in silent fear.

Child 459 looked up and saw the doctor was now wearing a gas mask, which only added to the horror swirling in the boy's mind.

The doctor's hand guided him by the shoulder, walking him through a side door, into a brightly lit room with tiled white walls and floor, in huge contrast to the rest of the darkness of the hangar. Two other doctors stood waiting, both also in long white coats; a short man with a beard and a woman with blonde hair tied back into a bun.

In the centre of the room, there was an examining table.

"Lie down on the table," the male doctor said. The boy did as he was told.

Then the woman walked over and wiped a wet solution onto his temples.

Securely tied down, the boy started to struggle. "Let me

go," he pleaded. The white coats ignored him as the woman proceeded to force a thick wedge of rubber into his mouth.

"So you don't bite off your tongue," she said.

The boy began to cry softly in small gulps, his body stiffening.

A sudden firing of thousands of volts into his body made him think his skeleton might rip out of his skin. An intense rush of the worst feeling surged through his small frame. No matter how many times he has been given the treatment, nothing ever prepared him for it.

The body contorted, jerking at the rush of electricity firing through him. A pitched screech like a fatally wounded fox echoed mournfully off the walls.

Less than a minute later, it finally ended, and the boy felt his flesh had tightened. He struggled to move, and the taste of burned flesh coated his entire tongue.

He was untied and carried back to the hangar area and up the stairwell by both doctors. His mind completely numbed, as if wiped away from a chalkboard. One of the cages lay empty, and the whitecoats pushed him inside and locked the door.

They headed back down the steps, leaving the boy holding himself, shaking uncontrollably. A sound like a long sigh converged into sobs.

Inside the cage, not high enough for him to stand up straight in, a dirty blanket was strewn on the floor. Child 459 slowly pulled it up and around his shoulders, his whole body still shuddering.

An hour later, a rush of fear and his heart beat faster as the sound of steps echoed on the floor below.

They are coming back!

Doctor Red began to climb the stairwell and walked slowly

along the grated floor towards him. He crouched down and peered inside. Pale grey eyes inspected him from behind wide spectacles. A smile appeared on his face.

"Please, no..." said the boy quietly. "Not the white room again."

"Don't worry, not that."

Something moves in his hand, a creature.

"I've brought you something," he said. "A kitten."

459 had never seen a kitten before. Its little green eyes looked at the boy as it opened its mouth and made a mewing sound. He had never seen anything so beautiful.

Doctor Red opened the cage door and placed the kitten inside.

"You have to look after it. You're responsible for it for a little while," he said.

The Mexican boy took the kitten, immediately stroking its soft fur, enchanted by its small green eyes as they studied him. Another mew came from its mouth, and the boy held it against his chest, feeling the soft fur on his palm and the light purring against his chest. He smiled fondly at his new companion, eyes watering with an unfamiliar emotion.

After a few weeks, the boy had grown extremely fond of his new companion. Its affection for the boy, rubbing its tiny head against his hand and softly purring, brought him a little comfort with its little eyes, fluffy fur, and strange sounds. It was the only thing in the dark, rank hellhole that was wholesome. The only thing capable of bringing the boy happiness into this world of pain and suffering; some kind of love. All from a tiny animal that responded to his touch, something capable of returning the stirrings of affection that have been awakened within him.

Occasionally, Doctor Red came and gave the boy food and milk so that he could feed the kitten himself.

After another month or so, the doctor took him and the kitten into one of the white rooms. The boy felt a familiar sickness in the pit of his stomach as if he knew with awful dread what was coming next.

Doctor Red gently took the kitten and placed it on the table, his emotionless eyes falling on the boy, who slowly shook his head, chin wobbling as the tears welled up.

"No, please..." he muttered.

Within his tiny frame, there stirred a swelling of resistance against the awaiting horror. He wanted to be defiant, to save the animal. To look after it and shelter it from harm.

Doctor Red's large hand swiped quickly, slapping the boy across the face, hard and fast, almost knocking him to the ground.

"Kill it..." he rasped, and then more softly, "for Daddy."

The boy, his mind a maelstrom of confusion, picked up the tiny animal. Expectantly it snuggled into the familiar touch of his hand, waiting to be petted and adored. His fingers caressed the little animal's head, a soft purr vibrating softly. As his hand moved down the neck, the little kitten arched its back expectantly...

"I said kill it...!" screamed Doctor Red. The boy's last shred of resistance was pierced by the final demands of the doctor.

Slowly the boy's fingers encircled the little animal's neck and tightened slightly. The purring gave way to a frantic mewing as the little animal fought for air, twisting and scratching at the hands that had once caressed it.

Convulsive scratching and twisting became weaker and weaker as the boy, with tears streaming down his face, relentlessly continued to squeeze. As he choked the last remnants of life from his little friend, it seemed to the boy that he was choking out a happiness and compassion he had only just begun to understand.

He stared down at the lifeless form of his little friend, the tiny eyes stared back without seeing. Without life.

***

The boy peered through the metal grid of the cage down towards the floor of the hangar. A sliver of daylight in a far wall gave some shape to the vast black void. Above, below, and on either side of his metal enclosure were more cages that housed the other children. Somewhere, there was the sound of a slow drip and low whimpers that provided a continuous soundtrack on the edge of the boy's consciousness.

In the blanketing gloom, he could see a smear of blood across his hands. Deep scratches arched across his wrists. Tears formed and rolled slowly down his cheek.

What had he done? His friend killed by his hand. The thought rocked him to his core, and he dropped to his knees, head in hands, as anguished sobs escaped his lips through ragged breaths.

Why did it have to die? Because Daddy wanted it that way.

The boy nodded to himself and felt better, if only for a second.

A series of coughs punctured the air from alongside him; it was a girl he saw once on the way to the *treatments*.

He could sense her looking across through the grid, even as he stared straight ahead towards the light. Her face was smudged with dirt and black hair, matted and stringy.

"Hello? You awake? I'm *Triple 3*. I've seen you before," she said.

"Shhh," the boy hissed.

There was silence for a while. At first, the boy sensed rather than saw a fluttering near his cage, and then the whiteness of the wings became clear even in the deep gloom. The creature settled on the wire lattice, wings slowly spreading wide for a second before closing together.

"Butterfly," he whispered. Straining his eyes to see as much detail as possible, he slowly moved his cupped hands towards it. The small creature stayed still on the wire for just a moment and then, without a sound, was gone.

"What?" the girl asked.

The boy sighed and leaned his head back against the wire mesh.

How did it get in here? Where did it live? Did it come to visit him and say hello?

He hoped it had. Maybe it would come back and say hello again.

"459," he said, finally.

"Huh?"

"I'm Delta 459."

Chapter 7

Present Day
CNI Headquarters, Madrid

Ortez punched in a series of numbers into a keypad next to the chrome door frame, the door swishing open, revealing a large operations centre. Jamall and Zara followed the director inside the windowless room that buzzed and hummed with the latest technology for intelligence and surveillance.

There was a low hum from fans that had been placed on most of the desks, which were arranged in rows. Figures were hunched in front of dual monitors, each telling a different story through covert footage, none of which concerned Jamall. His mind was fixed on his mission. He and his colleague just had to go through the motions, but his fingers twitched in his coat pocket, eager to get on with it.

"Unfortunately, the central air conditioning is down again, so it's a bit uncomfortable at the moment," Ortez said. He wondered if Coal Eyes was going to remove his jacket, but the guy didn't flinch at the thick air.

A high-resolution flatscreen covered the entire back wall, showing live drone footage from above the sprawling metropolis.

Ortez strode purposefully into the centre of the room, followed by his guests, and loudly clapped his hands, demanding attention from his subordinates. He rolled up his sleeves, revealing large hairy forearms as all eyes turned towards him.

"Everybody! This is Jamall Salazar and Zara Zimmermann, working with SSEUR. We are to assist them in any way we can in their investigation," he said loudly, the tone authoritative yet brusque.

"Mr. Salazar, would you like to brief the team?" said Ortez, crossing his arms as he stepped back to allow Salazar to address the assembled personnel.

There was a moment of silence as all eyes fell on Jamall. Only the sound of the humming fans and gentle radio crackle from operatives on the ground filtered around the room.

Jamall lifted his dark eyes and looked around at the CNI operatives, and spoke slowly and evenly.

"We have been tracking a terrorist cell. An active and very dangerous one, and there is a high possibility of an attack here in Madrid. We have a list of suspects as well as possible targets. We have to get ahead of this threat so any help on 'chatter' from these suspects would be *muy apreciado*." Jamall paused and took out a thumb drive from his pocket, and held it up between his thumb and forefinger.

"Is that the list?" asked Ortez.

"It is, Director," Jamall replied.

Ortez took the thumb drive from Jamall, and they walked over to where the operations manager, Dana Amador, was standing.

"Ms. Amador, can you run this please?"

Taking the thumb drive, she plugged it into the main console and twirled around to face the big screen on the back wall for all to see. An image appeared, and she proceeded to open the folders until she was prompted for a password.

She turned to look at Jamall, who reeled off a password, which Amador typed in. A list of names with covertly taken photographs alongside them appeared on the screen.

Zara cleared her throat and stepped forward. "Each name has further information and personal details, including logged phone calls, web history, and travel movements that we have managed to collect."

"Any information that the CNI can add to this pool is greatly appreciated," Jamall added.

"Do you know where any of these suspects are right now?" Ortez asked sharply.

"Not exactly. But we have some addresses that they're known to frequent. Perhaps you and your people can help?" asked Jamall.

Ortez nodded.

Amador clicked on one of the names on his screen: Akil El-Hashem. The photo showed a bearded Arabic man in his twenties getting out of a Mercedes in a crowded street somewhere in Europe. She clicked through with taps of her forefinger, and another wealth of information popped up. Addresses. Phone transcripts.

"What have we got here?" asked Ortez, still feeling increasingly out of the loop.

Jamall jutted his head at the screen.

"That's Akil El-Hashem, a UIS lieutenant photographed in France," he stated.

"UIS, huh? We'd better warn the French authorities."

"He left France, and everything points to him heading here," said Jamall flatly.

The United State of Islam was the group that had risen out of the ashes of ISIS after it lost its power and influence following a sustained bombing effort by the Russians and, to a lesser extent, the West.

Ortez shook his head, unsure of who was to blame. Most worrying was the fact his own agency had not picked up this major threat to Spain. Not only would the agency look like a bunch of amateurs, but he would lose his job, and if this terrorist succeeded in striking on Spanish soil, countless innocents would probably die.

"And the others?" Ortez gestured at the screen, a young man with a shaved head and a woman in a hijab head dress.

Zara cleared her throat. "Fariq and Afya Bashar, a married couple from Iran. Both trained in the UIS–held areas before popping up in Europe. Almost certainly connected or part of the same cell as El–Hashem."

"Sounds like they're planning a fucking party," growled Ortez, his concern now evident.

"One or all of them are about to strike on your soil, State Secretary. You're looking at dead Spanish civilians any day now," said Jamall.

Ortez looked at him with distaste; the tone was almost as if he were willing it. He crushed an empty paper coffee cup and threw it into the waste bin, suddenly fuelled into action by the prospect of bombs going off in his city.

"OK, let's get on this," Ortez growled to the whole room. "Each one of you pick a name. Look for any signals in the previous few days. Any communications they may have made. Any face recon, any sightings? We need to know where they are. I'm not having our city attacked by these *putas*."

The analysts turned back to their monitors and got back to

work with renewed determination. The hive reactivated. Zara sidled over to Jamall and whispered in his ear.

"So far, so good,"

Jamall remained tight-lipped, his eyes never leaving the big screen.

Chapter 8

Fifteen years earlier
Area 71 Base, Colorado

The Mexican boy stopped running, took two deep breaths, and carried on moving in a staccato rhythm, totally focused on the targets. Ten years old, he moved with purpose, raising the pistol in his hand and firing at the first target on a tree eight metres away.

He hit the bull's eye with ease, then swung his aim and fired again at a second target with the same result: a rush of splintered wood flying off in all directions.

The boy moved like a well-oiled robot, closely followed by a man clad in black fatigues, who monitored the boy closely to add up the final score.

The boy's feet scuffed lightly on the dusty ground as he deftly grabbed a double-barrel shotgun from a rack and approached a series of smaller orange-coloured targets clustered in the bushes and around the woods. He aimed left at one and fired, shredding it into oblivion in a cloud of smoke. Immediately swinging to his right, he fired and hit another target. Moving up the path, he continued the action.

Crouching by a low wall, he stopped and took a deep breath,

small beads of sweat slowly rolling down his forehead, glistening in the early morning light. A few beats of the heart later, and the boy moved again, zigzagging up the path, firing, moving, firing until the series of targets were history.

Once finished with the shotgun, he threw it to the ground, eyes focused on the flat board human target ahead. In one fluid motion, he unclipped the pistol from his belt, pointed it, and fired three times in rapid succession. The board swung around from the impact, leaving three large holes in the target's head.

"Ten seconds!" the trainer shouted. Another few small steps revealed two more targets, and the boy focused, firing off two rounds apiece to complete the circuit. The boy hit the magazine release button, and the clip slid smoothly from the pistol. He pulled back the slide to eject the last round from the chamber and looked up at the trainer with dulled dark eyes, a blank, unreadable expression.

"Good work," the trainer growled. "Clean up the weapons, and return them to the rack. Next, we're going to the pit."

On the mention of *the pit*, the boy felt a shrill of sickness that gnawed at his stomach. He hated the pit but did as the trainer asked and reluctantly walked back through the woods, along the track to the far side. There was an occasional shout or cry from the other children through the thick trees; whether through fear or pain, he could not tell, nor did he care.

The boy stripped down the weapons and proceeded to clean them as the trainer watched, occasionally barking at him to hurry up. He replaced the weapons in the rack and moved off towards the pit area, where the screams slowly grew louder. Sunlight streamed through the trees giving a tranquil setting to the horror film soundtrack. The woods opened up, revealing a clearing with a typical army training course.

There was a group of children lining up as they waited to crawl down under green army nets into a long trench, their heads drooping in fearful expectation of what lay ahead.

What awaited them at the end? Would this be the day they die?

For some, it would.

The trainers, dressed in black fatigues, wore pistol belts, and some brandished the dreaded cattle prods. Child 459 caught sight of the girl that sometimes trained with them.

The same girl housed in the cage next to his. Triple 3.

There weren't usually any girls with their group; most of them were housed somewhere else for other training.

The girl had pretty green eyes and straight black hair and looked at the Mexican boy briefly and then to the ground. Talking to each other was not allowed in the training area. The boy wished he could speak to her again and regretted being snappy with her before.

Despite his previous exhausting run, Child 459 joined the children as they followed each other, falling down onto their chests one by one as they crawled downwards into the pitted trench that was thick with muddy sludge. The green netting hung oppressively close over their heads, closing them in like the lid of a coffin.

The trainers walked casually along the pit edge, swinging their cattle prods like batons as they barked aggressive commands at the little soldiers crawling through their collective hell.

A scream farther down the trench, followed by a shout from one of the trainers who was leaning over the trench with a cattle prod in his hand that he pressed down through the net.

"Keep moving!" barked the command. A smell of metallic burning wafted through the trench.

Delta 459 shuddered at the sound of a light gunshot and looked up. One of the training masters had pulled a pistol and fired into the pit. The boy soon arrived by the still body of another child, facedown in the mud, a bloody chasm punctured into the back of his head from a .45-caliber bullet.

459 wondered whether the boy was dreaming now that he was dead, and if so, what about? Dreams seemed so real until awakening—that was the worst part. Waking up.

What if there were a way to stay in his dreams forever? Was death the way of escape for him?

The boy sped up, digging his elbows into the mud to slither past the corpse as quickly as possible, holding his breath to avoid vomiting. The sight of brain tissue mingled with streaming blood in the muddy water, however, made him retch and heave.

Glancing ahead, the boy watched two metallic canisters hit the mud; the hissing grew louder as a snake of green smoke escaped and drifted across the ground like a fog. The boy coughed, squeezing his eyes shut to avoid the stinging mist, and crawled onwards.

The trench widened into a pit, which was just enough room for them to stand. Five tunnels led off from the pit—a Russian roulette of fear and pain. The Mexican boy dragged himself into one—a trench filled with excrement making him gag again—but he continued through the ten or so metres of the foul-smelling shit as fast as possible.

As he emerged at the other side, he could see the end of the trench, rope cargo netting covering the slope. After a few minutes, he reached it at last, his little hands stretching and clasping at the rope. Using all his remaining strength, 459 hauled himself up inch by inch.

As he pulled himself over the edge, he rolled over onto his back, completely drained of any strength, and just listened to his wheezing breath as he sucked in fresh air. He wished he could go to the dream place, just for a while, but the moment was soon gone. Massive hands grabbed the side of his upper arms and pulled him upright, lifting his feet off the ground and shaking his entire body. 459 could no longer feel his legs and immediately collapsed back onto the ground in a heap.

The trainer laughed, clicking his stopwatch.

"Delta 459. That's twelve minutes and thirty."

The trainer then turned his attention to another skinny boy crawling out of the swampish pit and gave him a swift kick in the ribs, causing a shriek of pain.

"Alpha 325. Fourteen minutes and sixty."

He checked his watch once again and strolled along the ridge, watching as other small figures struggled up the net rope.

***

The boy, slightly older, although he didn't really know his exact age as birthdays were forbidden, walked through the delta camp slowly. He deliberately did not hurry.

He was on the cusp of becoming a man, shoulders and biceps much more defined, yet his tall frame still wiry and agile. His dark hair combed tightly back. Across the encampment, a harsh northerly wind rattled some of the wooden building's slats. It was winter, and the young man felt the cold surround him but did not flinch or shiver.

Ahead was a line of concrete buildings, square slabs with no windows, and the prisoners' quarters.

He walked around the building to a small guard house tucked

alongside the blocks and knocked on the closed steel door.

The trainer opened it and ushered him inside, where Doctor Red was sitting behind a desk. The doctor adjusted his cufflinks that glinted from the bare lightbulb above them—Rose gold with the engraved symbol of the Baphomet.

The doctor smiled as he caught the boy looking at them. He reached under the desk and pulled up a baseball bat, caressing the fine lines of the maple wood for a moment before placing it on top of the desk. The soulless eyes of the doctor glanced from the boy to the bat for a moment, and then he nodded an unspoken command.

Without hesitation, the boy picked up the bat.

He was led to one of the windowless cells, where the trainer swiped a card to open the door. The doctor pointed at a young man wrapped in a dirty blanket, crouching on a bare concrete floor.

The man, frail and bony, looked up at them with wide, terrified eyes. Delta 459 noticed they were blue, like the sky. His arms held his knees together, and he rocked gently, back and forth.

There was no bed or furniture, just a bucket in the corner, the stink of human waste that hit them like a wall.

"Complete the mission. Kill the man with the bat." Doctor Red's voice low and banal, as if asking him to open the door.

The boy did not hesitate.

For to hesitate shows weakness and a certain unwillingness to serve. It shows the fragile human state.

The doctor told him that in classes.

The bat swung fast.

Screaming, the man scurried back along the wall. A cracking wet thud echoed around the cell as the bat hit the man's skull, eyes turning white, followed by a strange animal-like sound drifting from his mouth.

His body began to shudder.

The Mexican stepped forward in sharp, aggressive movements to get closer, hammering down the hardwood maple on fragile bone and flesh. He hardly noticed the blood and brain tissue splattering his clothes.

The pampered population had become spoiled, needing to be clothed and sheltered like children, useless to the world.

The wet, methodical thuds continued like a drum beat long after the cries for mercy had stopped.

***

The next day, 459 was called by Doctor Red.

The boy walked into a bare-walled office where the doctor was sitting behind a large mahogany desk, staring at him through thin-framed glasses. There was a large leather couch in one corner, a large plant in the other, and the distinct smell of air freshener.

The boy's eyes stared down at the floor, a sense of dread in the presence of the doctor, for it usually meant something bad.

"I'm pleased with your progress, 459." Doctor Red peered down at a report on his desk for a moment before fixing his stare back onto the boy.

"You have made me proud."

The boy's heart quickened. Praise was rarely given and extremely hard to earn.

"I like to see my children do well. You are all my children, after all. Some don't make the grade, and on this earth, the weak must be culled. I am going to reward you, and I really hope you don't let me down. I would hate you to disappoint me in the future and have to take away your reward. One that you worked so hard for." The doctor spoke evenly, without emotion, leaning forward with the bony fingers of his hands steepled.

The boy shook his head quickly and spoke for the first time. "I will never let you down, Daddy."

The voice was quiet yet underlined with confidence. The doctor nodded in satisfaction and continued.

'The pit, the shed and the cage will all be a thing of the past. It pains me to see my children go through all that, but it is necessary to make you strong enough for the life you will live. Now begins the second part of your training: advanced military tactics, communications and explosives training. We will sharpen your skills to make you the best you can be. Now are you happy with my gift, 459?"

The small Mexican boy looked up from the floor and nodded, a flicker of pride swelling in his chest for the first time in his life.

*****

That evening they took him to a different part of the camp, an area that he had never been to before. Several rows of small wooden porta-cabins were surrounded by neat little gardens, and 459 was escorted into cabin number 16 and left alone.

Inside, it was clean and comfortable. A small window let in the light: a table, a clean-stripped floor, and a bunk bed with a blanket.

459 sat down on the bed, sinking slightly into the soft

mattress. He had never known such comfort and looked around in wonder. He slowly ran his hands over the soft fabric of the sheets.

Is it a trick? Will he be hauled back into the white room?

Standing up, he slowly walked over to the small wardrobe and opened it. Inside there was a rack of clothes, all seemingly his size. All dark or black.

He picked up a neatly folded hoodie and felt the material in his hands. There was a sense of happiness that felt strange to him and a thrill in his stomach that he was able to please Doctor Red. 459 placed each item of clothing on the bed, neatly lining them up as if he were building a puzzle: black socks, black underwear, black T-shirt, jeans, and hoodie.

The door to the cabin swung open, and one of the trainers walked in.

"I see you've found your new clothing," the man said. "Everything should fit you, although it can be hard to judge. Now quickly, get changed. We have to be going."

459 hurriedly slipped on a pair of jeans, a zip-up top, Nike trainers, and a baseball cap. He had never worn these types of clothes before and relished the feel of them on his battered body.

The trainer handed him a Glock 13 pistol. "You'll need to pack supplies for your task. Basic supplies are in that chest of drawers. Keep it light, though, as you need to stay mobile."

459 took a small thirty-litre backpack from the bottom of the wardrobe. He placed the Glock in the front pocket and walked over to the chest, grabbing a small first aid kit along with some basics: a water bottle, some food, and a pager and placed them all inside the pack.

The trainer then unfolded a map and placed it on the table.

"Come here," he ordered and proceeded to brief the boy.

Ten minutes later, Doctor Red walked in wearing a black suit and stood in the middle of the room. The trainer left.

"Are you ready to make me proud?" Doctor Red said as he looked down at the boy. The boy nodded once and lowered his eyes to the floor. From his pockets, Doctor Red brought out a small piece of paper and handed it to him.

"Call this number when the mission is complete."

459 looked at the number and then immediately handed back the paper. He was good at remembering things. He was told he had a photographic memory, one of the reasons he excelled so well in his training,

"Have you ever heard of people having names?"

The boy looked confused for a moment.

"With a name, you can live in the outside world, and become part of society. Would you like that?"

The boy nodded. He did very much.

"But first, you need to earn your name. Complete today's task, and afterwards, you will be given your very own name."

Child 459 smiled and felt a slight quicken in his heartbeat at the prospect of leaving the camp.

***

A black SUV turned off a main street and cruised at a slow constant speed like a shark patrolling through the water looking for prey.

Pulling slowly to a stop, the young Mexican boy slipped out the rear door with his backpack and walked away from the vehicle in the direction he had been told to. Soon he found himself on the main street, where afternoon shoppers were browsing the stores. The boy purposefully strolled to the next block and checked the street sign before turning right onto a less busy road with office blocks on either side. He had seen a street view in the briefing and knew exactly where he was going. Another right down a back alleyway led onto the street toward his objective.

There was only one task on his mind: He had to achieve it and earn his name. No distractions from the stores that sold exciting toys, games, or candy that would have reeled in any other ten-year-old boy from a mission. Looking at his watch, he saw that the target would be entering their office in less than ten minutes. That was when he had to strike.

"Hey, li'l fella. You lost ya, mom?"

Looking up, his dead black eyes took in the man, his weasel-like face and wolfish grin smiling down at him. He seemed to have come out of nowhere and was standing in between him and his objective. What to do? Item 23 on mission protocols flashed into the boy's brain: when encountering members of the public interfering in mission directives, then either take evasive action or terminate.

"No, I haven't lost anybody," the boy said, deadpan. He tried to go around the man, who suddenly grabbed his arm.

"Hey, kid, I'm talking to..." Weasel Face barely finished his sentence before the boy kicked his shin, hard and fast, before running down the alleyway. The man cried out and swore at the kid, trying to hobble after him.

Child 459 lost him easily, but doubling back and taking a different route had cost him valuable minutes. By the time he arrived at the Cryostone office block, he was running late.

He could clearly see the target, a tall man with a bald head, already entering the swivelling doors. Instructions were to take him down outside the building; ambush him where there were fewer witnesses.

He had failed before he had already started. Failed his first real mission.

No name for him now. No privileges. Just back to the hangar or the cages.

459 did not like the thought of that. Maybe he could still redeem himself. He would kill this man today.

Yes, kill the man by any means.

The orders didn't say *not to pursue* the target, did they? Or enter the building?

Just remember: no witnesses.

The boy sprinted up the steps to the revolving doors, his hand holding the Glock tightly in his hoodie pocket. Inside, there was a large reception area. Child 459 quickly scanned the space.

Directly in front was a long reception desk where two female staff members were sitting and staring at him. Alongside them was a turnstile, a security entrance to the stairs, and elevators set farther back behind them.

A big security guard looked at the boy and frowned.

Behind the guard, having just cleared security, was the target. The Glock appeared in the boy's hand as he walked over towards the security point. He lifted his arm, and the guard's eyes widened in surprise. 459 fired, hitting him directly in the forehead.

An eerie silence fell after the gunshot as all eyes turned to face the small boy.

Then the screaming began.

He could clearly see the bald man standing within a group of suits, frantically tapping the button to the elevator.

Running fast, the Mexican boy cleared the turnstile in one easy jump, the sound of his Nike trainers squeaking on the polished floor. There was a ping from the elevator as the doors began to open, a safe haven for the terrified people waiting.

459, still moving, closed the distance. The bald man leapt for safety inside the elevator just as the boy fired. The bullet hit another office worker in the head; a plume of red splattered onto the wall behind, and the lifeless body then slumped to the ground.

The metal doors began to close, but an arm of the fallen office worker prevented them from shutting. Those inside desperately tried to kick the arm out with their feet, but it was too late. Skidding to a halt outside the elevator, the Mexican boy looked inside, his cold dead eyes taking in the terrified huddled group as he raised his weapon once again.

Chapter 9

Present Day
CNI Madrid

Jamall stepped back into the ops room, glad to see a wealth of additional information appearing on the main screen.

Dana Amador walked up to him and gave him a broad smile.

"I can get your workstations set up...this way."

Jamall followed her to an alcove near the back of the room, where she took out a laminated card with a series of numbers printed on it.

'This is the access for the computer itself, and I'll remotely set you and your colleague up with access to the system."

He grabbed the card and scanned his eyes over the numbers before placing it in his pocket.

Ortez appeared with another paper cup of coffee, gently sipping at it. He wiped his moustache and peered over at Jamall.

"Three suspects have been found inside Spanish borders. One in Barcelona and the couple in Madrid. Armed units are ready to apprehend them."

Jamall nodded. "Good. Fast work."

"Si."

A tall Afro-Caribbean man dressed in a dark military uniform with an insignia on his left pocket of a yellow eagle with a snake wrapped around its talons appeared next to Ortez.

"This is Kurt Coleman, inspector of the GEO operative section. He'll be commanding the teams on the ground," said Ortez.

The inspector quickly shook hands with Dana and Zara before moving to Jamall, who shook hands with him with a tight grip.

"You have the subgroups in place?" Jamall asked.

"Yes. Two subgroups, each with five men. Our usual mix of specialists." Coleman cast Jamall with a curious eye, who in return flashed him an eerie smile.

"You're not Spanish?" Jamall asked.

"I have served many different clients. It's the way of the world nowadays."

"It certainly is," Jamall said knowingly. "Good luck, Inspector."

Ortez showed Coleman to his station, where he slipped on an earpiece and began testing the communications.

Dana Amador swiped through a series of windows on her screen as she set up the live feeds from the simultaneous *Grupo Especial de Operaciones* missions throughout Spain. The large eight-foot-high screen split into six separate windows displaying altered angles of the same location from the operatives' cam feeds; a team of the GEO, hunched and waiting in the back of their vehicles. All the men wore balaclavas under their Kevlar helmets and clutched MP5 submachine guns.

The images were crystal clear as if the people in the control room were watching a movie.

Coleman did a last comms check with each sub-inspector

and then turned to Ortez, who stood nearby, hands on hips.

"We're all good to go here, sir."

Ortez looked around the control room as if mentally checking a list.

"Please, State Secretary. We're eager to see the show," said Jamall slowly and coldly.

Ortez nodded at Coleman. "Alright, Inspector, it's all yours."

A series of instructions flowed down the pipe of communications; a splutter of radio commands came from the speakers hidden in the dark corners of the room.

Team Alpha in Barcelona.

A blur of movement through the helmet-mounted camera on the squad leader, a flash of parked cars as he jogged towards the front doors of an apartment block.

The leader turned towards two officers holding a battering ram. A quick nod, and they sprang into action. There was a loud thudding until the door finally gave way with a squeal of protesting metal, and several uniformed figures rushed into the dark corridor.

For a moment, there was a brief image of one of the men holding a shotgun. His body jolted as he fired. The blast aimed at the locking mechanism left the door looking like smashed tinder wood.

They reached another interior apartment door, and the shotgun appeared again, making short work of the obstacle, the bang puncturing the air through the radio.

"Hostile sighted!"

"Gun! Gun! Gun!"

Automatic gunfire filled the airwaves, an overwhelming reverberation in the confined space. The captain's head cam jerking from side to side as he ducked into an alcove in the hallway.

"Team Beta. You're good to go," Coleman said, turning to another screen.

A cam feed burst into action, revealing a suburban Madrid street. The team moved fast up a flight of stairs and then down a corridor towards a steel door.

The team stacked up on the door, every man touching the next on the shoulder, a simple way of knowing the team is ready without having to look or talk.

Coleman shifted an eye back to Team Alpha.

Creeping forward, the captain moved up behind his two lead men, his hands signalling quick and clear movements. The man with the shotgun responded, his hands doing the talking.

"Two men, both armed. In cover!"

The captain gave a quick nod of understanding, his hands quickly signing his orders.

The lead man nodded his understanding and removed a stun grenade. Pulling the pin, he then held it ready for deployment. There was a short nod from number two that told him he was ready, and the grenade was thrown in.

Seconds later, a blast shuddered the entire floor, and the cam fuzzed for a moment, the quality suddenly degrading to nothing but static noise.

Jamall's posture stiffened. "Can we get that back?"

Dana Amador typed commands on her laptop for a few seconds. "Negative. It's an equipment fault."

Just as she finished talking, the picture returned to normal. The target, Akil El-Hashem, suddenly appeared from behind a wall, and started firing off a round.

A rapid report from an MP5 9mm responded immediately,

hitting the target's arm as he dove for cover.

Bullets sprayed the wall, and one of the GEO men pounced around the corner, holding his weapon up and firing downwards at the unseen target. Interference clouded the screen for a few moments.

The next shot in the control room was of El-Hashem lying in a pool of blood, his body riddled with bullet holes, still clutching his AK-47.

After several confused minutes, a low voice came over the radio: "Area secure."

The focus turned back to Team Beta in Madrid. A loud blast shook the camera slightly as the leader stormed into the studio apartment.

A naked woman quickly covered herself with a sheet from the bed, a frozen look of terror on her face. The man next to her, reaching for the bedside table, wore a grim look of determination on his face.

"No te Muevas!"

A rapid burst of MP5 fire reverberated around the CNI control room like a frenzied woodpecker.

"Hold fire!"

The room went silent as all eyes focused on the couple riddled with bullets and clearly dead, dark blood patterned across the wall and the crisp white bed sheets.

"Shit!" said Ortez. "We needed them alive."

"It was Fariq and Afya Bashar?"

"Confirmed," said Coleman as he listened to his earpiece.

Idle chatter filtered through the air as the tense, adrenalin-fuelled raids gave way to a general sense of relief in the control room. No GEO men had been hurt or killed, which was always going to be a high possibility when dealing with fanatical terrorists.

Ortez shook hands with Coleman.

"Be sure to congratulate your men, Inspector. It was a difficult situation for them, I'm sure," he said, his tone clipped.

"I'm sorry we couldn't keep them alive for you. We'll search the apartments to try and find any clues or evidence of what they were planning. I take it you'll be wanting some of your people over there to work with the police department?"

"Yes, yes," Ortez replied before walking back to Jamall and Zara.

"Well, thank you for the information, Mr. Salazar," said Ortez reluctantly. He leaned in, lowering his voice.

"How did you get that intel?"

Jamall smiled, something Ortez had rarely seen; the smile of a viper about to strike.

"The CIA has rapidly advanced in overseas intelligence gathering. Closely working with our partners." He brushed a hand on Ortez's shoulder. "Our friends."

Jamall and Zara slipped back to their terminals at the far side of the room that Dana had set up for them, giving them limited access to the CNI database. The operatives in the room glanced over with more respect now as opposed to the mild hostility set by Ortez. They had shone a spotlight on the rats and allowed the Spanish to deal with the vermin. Those men and women from the CNI would be perceived as heroes.

Jamall adjusted his dark jacket, sat down at his station, logged in using his temporary access code and began tapping the screen, navigating to the train manifests where any pre-booked passengers would show up. He typed the words Nicolas Batchman into the search bar.

Zara silently slipped into one of the black office chairs and stared at Jamall with a questioning expression on her face. She glanced around briefly and spoke quietly.

"What happened there? Why did we just waste two valuable cells?"

Jamall concentrated on the screen, his fingers tapping the mouse to rapidly move back and forth across each segment of footage from a train station.

"They served their purpose," he said flatly, almost uninterested.

"Served their purpose? They just got wiped out." Zara was looking at him closely as if trying to figure out the missing piece.

"They made a nice little distraction for this whole operation and for getting us access to the CNI network."

Jamall's dark eyes flashed wide at the screen, and he checked his watch.

"He got on the eight o'clock Malaga train. Check the CCTV so we can confirm. I think we have him."

With a time and location, it didn't take long before Zara paused the video and pinched her fingers on the screen to zoom closer to a figure on the platform.

Jamall leaned forward and stared with satisfaction at the figure of Batchman standing on the platform. It was him, alright. The game was in play. Maybe now he could get on with completing his mission.

"Get everything prepared. We need to get going and intercept that train."

Chapter 10

Fifteen years earlier
Area 71 Base, Colorado

"The programming can't be right. We must have missed something. I think a reassessment is needed, possibly running another repatterning sequence." Doctor Black leaned forward on the leather couch in Doctor Red's office, looking across the expanse of the Colorado mountain range through the ceiling-high windows. Doctor Black wore a dark suit and tie that contrasted with his pale skin and dyed jet-black hair that was swept back.

"In his mind, he followed the protocol we gave him to the letter. He achieved his objective but left a huge mess. For him, the only consequences come from not following our orders. What's the difference between one body or five? If we want to contain this behaviour, we must be clearer with our protocol," said Doctor Red.

He cracked his knuckles, sighing heavily, tired from his flight from his headquarters in Denver. It had been a routine visit to the facility in China Lake that turned into a crisis. A simple mission that had somehow spiralled out of control.

Of the twenty-plus years Doctor Black had overseen *Project*

Monarch, the system had always been flawless.

As the "stock" arrived, it was processed, and the babies were checked into the nursery building. The babies were fed and looked after by a small team of specialist nurses who kept them in the nursery block—a huge house that had five floors, each containing several hundred cots, a number of kitchens, bathrooms, staff quarters and "play" areas.

Each baby was assigned a number, stamped onto the arm and displayed at the bottom of the cot. As the months passed, the nurses spoke to the babies in English, Spanish, Russian, and Mandarin as they brought them up into a strict world of routine. To the nurses, this was the normality of their existence. It was the world they had themselves been brought into.

The doctors would come by and visit, checking on their progress. Occasionally, they would get security guards to wheel trolleys of the babies to the control and behavioural sector in the converted air hangar.

Here the dark art of behaviour therapy would be unleashed. A torrent of chemical and electro-shock therapy referred to as "de-patterning": rape, torture, and the breaking of the young minds.

For the mind to be completely controlled, it must first be broken down. And in Doctor Black's opinion that breaking must begin early in life. Before, the mind had a chance to grow, to become its own entity.

Basic schooling would come for them in time. After all, they would need to not only learn the basic curriculum just like any other child in society—languages, math, science—but excel at them. Their young minds then needed to be moulded to the will of their masters, for they were the slaves of the *cabal*.

At six years old, they were thrown into combat training combined with a continual de-patterning treatment, and after ten years, the exceptional ones received another assessment to decide what direction they should go in. Some would become assassins, politicians, CEOs, and even generals. All would be puppets with roles to play in the new paradigm.

Doctor Red was behind the desk, his large glasses reflecting the newspaper reports on his screen that covered the shooting and the deaths of innocent office workers at the technology company Cryostone.

"First, we need to kill this story as quickly as possible. We need to feed them, someone, to wrap it up," said Doctor Black impatiently.

"Not 459. He's becoming a valuable asset. He did the job, not the way I wanted it done exactly, but I'd like to work with him, mould him. We'll find another boy to take the blame."

Black didn't seem convinced. "He killed three people; he was only supposed to kill one. It draws unnecessary attention to that company and our operations."

"You know we can tidy this up. We have done it hundreds of times. I just need to readjust some of his treatment, that is all," said Doctor Red, with an underline of irritation.

"Let's talk to him then?" said Black.

Red picked up a phone on his desk. A few quick words were spoken before he replaced the receiver. Ten minutes later, 459 stood in the middle of the office. His eyes firmly fixed on the floor. A memory flickered in his mind. He had seen the black-haired man who was sitting on the couch before—one time in the cages, strolling around with a cattle prod.

"This is Doctor Black. So, 459, you carried out the mission, but the window of opportunity passed. Why did you not abort?"

The boy did not take his eyes off the ground.

"Look at me, and answer the question."

Delta 459, the ten-year-old Mexican boy, unknowingly torn from his true mother, looked up at Doctor Red with an unreadable expression.

"I wanted a name," he said flatly. "And the objectives were completed within your parameters."

Doctor Red smiled thinly, revealing small teeth that reminded the boy of a shark.

"So, you killed all those innocents to complete the task and earn your name?"

"Yes. Complete the task and earn my name," the boy repeated.

Red looked beyond the boy towards Doctor Black, who was cross-legged on the couch, watching the proceedings silently. Doctor Black nodded, and the man behind the desk leaned back, still smiling.

"So, what will it be?"

The boy looked confused.

Doctor Red repeated the question.

"What first name would you like?"

The Mexican boy looked up at the desk and pointed to the newspaper.

"Who's that?"

Doctor Red picked up the paper and glanced at the advert on the front page for a movie; emblazoned with the title *End of Days*. The image was of a Samurai warrior, sword strapped to his back, standing stoically on a hill as he looked down on a desolated cityscape. There was rising smoke from burning buildings, black helicopters buzzing overhead, and a general sense of chaos. The whole scene was bathed in an orange-reddish tint that gave it the feeling of a world in ruins.

At the bottom of the advert was the bold typeface of the lead actor: Jamall Stone.

Doctor Red looked at the boy with an expression of mild affection.

"Jamall Stone's latest movie? You like the name Jamall, do you, 459?"

The boy nodded eagerly.

"Fine. It's your choice, and you have worked hard to earn it. Your name is Jamall, then."

Looking up at Doctor Red, a small smile spread across the boy's face for the first time in his life.

Chapter 11

Present Day
CNI Madrid

Zara pulled the black SUV back into the CNI car park after flashing her ID at the security gates. Pink-hued clouds crisscrossed the darkening sky.

Jamall checked for any chatter on his smart device; news was filtering through of an incident south of Madrid, near Parla.

On entering Puertollano Station, Zara had a neat little tech device that interrupted the CCTV feed signal, effectively freezing it for a period of five to ten seconds. It was a rough and ready option that would just display as a technical error, but it meant neither of them should be on any footage.

They had boarded at Puertollano, and Jamall had spotted the target at a table seat. Zara had then discreetly planted the plastic explosives under two seats in the quieter carriages, each with their own fuse that would trigger from her mobile after their departure from the train. Amazing how diplomatic cover could help get certain materials into the country.

Unfortunately, Batchman had seen Jamall and tried to escape. It had been a few months before when Jamall had paid him a "friendly" visit to attain how far his research had come.

Jamall soon caught up with him. As Batchman opened the toilet door, Jamall shoved him hard into the toilet cubicle. The Mexican quickly moved inside, shutting the door behind him as Batchman fell against the sink.

The doctor turned, eyes wide with fear, as Jamall came at him. A hand grabbed his head and smacked it hard against the edge of the basin, instantly knocking him unconscious.

The Mexican then quickly wrapped an arm around the old man's neck, fingers gripping his chin. Pulling sharply, he twisted with one swift movement.

A dull crack filled the space.

Picking up the doctor's bag, he left the toilet and pressed the door close button on the way out. The door slid smoothly back into place as Jamall walked over to an access panel in the wall. Pulling out a small penknife, he slipped it into the small gap and jimmied the lock open. The small panel controlled the emergency override for the toilet door. Reaching in, Jamall pressed the lock button before pushing the hatch shut again.

Stepping off the train, he merged with other passengers, making his way to the exit, where he met Zara, who had stepped off at the opposite end. They drove the hired SUV under an alias to just outside Madrid and then switched to their CNI-supplied vehicle.

Zara took Batchman's bag straight up to their office on the sixth floor as Jamall headed to the ops room. There was a buzz of conversation and orders being shouted as screens showed the columns of smoke from news channels around the world.

Ortez, ashen-faced, turned around from leaning over one of the desks to face Jamall.

"Salazar! There must have been another cell. Something we

missed, something you missed!" Ortez was struggling to hold down his anger with Jamall.

"As I said, it's a fast-moving situation, State Secretary. There must have been another cell we were unaware of. Have you got anything?" Jamall's voice was calm, bordering on deadpan.

Ortez stared at him hard for a moment, the bags under his eyes more prominent in the artificial light and shook his head.

"No, not yet." His voice was quieter now.

"They hit us again, to the day. To the fucking day!"

Jamall looked at him, unsure of what he meant and then realised with a mild interest he was referring to the multiple bombs that had ripped through the Madrid trains on March 11, 2004.

"It was near the military base at Getafe. Could there be a connection?" Jamall said, his eyes held Ortez's for a moment, who nodded slowly as if in thought.

"Si, Mr Salazar. We're already on that," he replied gruffly.

"I'll be back in a minute, Mr. Ortez, to give you any assistance or help you need."

Ortez turned away from him and, without a further word, disappeared towards the sea of monitors.

Jamall headed up to join Zara, grabbing two coffees from the machine in the corridor before stepping into the lift.

Inside their assigned office, Zara had emptied Batchman's belongings onto the large table and was looking at an old laptop screen.

She tucked a string of long dark hair behind her ear and tapped at the keys.

For a brief moment, Jamall pictured her from a memory a long time ago. The dirty face and matted hair, staring at him from the cage next to his.

"What have we got?" Jamall placed the coffees down and began sifting through the items: a notepad, travel book, and money belt with his passport, bank cards, and various other personal effects.

He looked back to the screen.

"Nothing," she said. "It's not here."

Chapter 12

Present Day
Zafra, Southern Spain

A low voice from the radio drifted through the kitchen, seemingly ignored by the whole family who gathered around the table for breakfast.

Elsa reached over and grabbed another sugary churro from the basket to add to her plate and grinned at her mother, who smiled back approvingly.

"I really shouldn't, but..." Elsa said.

"Don't be so stupid, *mi vida.* You eat your breakfast. You have a long journey ahead, and they'll only sell rubbish on the train," her mother replied.

Elsa chomped away with a contented look on her face and looked over at her father, whose focus was on his smartphone as he sipped sweet, black coffee.

"Are you going to take me to the station, Papa?"

Juan looked up at her expectant expression and felt a twinge of remorse. He glanced back at the time on his phone and pushed the feeling away.

"Ahh, I'm sorry, Elsa, I have to work. Your mama will take you." He looked at his wife, who nodded and smiled at her daughter.

"Si, of course, I'll take you." She glanced back at her husband with a slight frown. "What is so important at work that you cannot see your only daughter off, hmm?"

Juan shook his head with regret. "There's so much paperwork, my petal. The gangs are still active, despite the crackdown. We need to track every single one of them down; you know that."

The previous few years had seen a shocking deterioration in the standard of living, not just for the inhabitants of Zafra but the whole of the country. He had read it wasn't much better in the rest of Europe either. As more people's lives became desperate, they turned to any means to make money, usually at the expense of honest citizens. Those who knuckled down and worked harder were usually their targets.

The rats and cockroaches.

It was the younger ones who were most vulnerable. They had no work, no hope, and so fell into the maw of poverty, drug abuse, and alcoholism. Juan had seen it too many times, and it was a story retold across the nation.

His department was in the middle of a manhunt for a hardened criminal gang preying on the poor and the weak.

Juan stood up, pocketing his phone. He held out his bear-like arms, and Elsa stood up, beaming at him. They hugged for a few seconds, and Juan kissed her forehead.

"You'll be back again to visit us soon?"

His daughter shook her head. "It will probably be Christmas when I can visit again, Papa."

Juan looked at her with a mock frown. "Not before? We have to wait so long?"

She smiled regretfully.

"University is busy. I'm already behind with all the assignments and essays."

He nodded, understanding. He was so proud of her, immensely proud. She had gone to the big city and university with a determination to be a doctor. She was his and Mia's only child, and they could not have hoped for any more from her.

"Goodbye, mi vida. We'll call you at the weekend, si?" he said.

"Si," she smiled.

Juan kissed his wife on the cheek and disappeared through the side of their modest casa to the garage and then drove to work.

***

Juan Cerezo sat in his unmarked vehicle, his hand resting on the steering wheel, tapping impatiently. He was parked in his usual spot down the street from Plaza del Alcázar, spending time watching the crowds ebb and flow through the market.

The low drone of the police radio provided the background noise he always craved. No matter where he was in his house, he had to have a radio or a TV switched on. It drove his wife mad but somehow gave him peace of mind.

On the passenger side seat was a loaded Glock pistol. Ever since he heard that there were drug dealers preying on the town's youth, he kept his eyes wide open, even if it was on his own time.

He yearned to drag those little leechy fuckers into a dark alleyway and give them a pistol-whipping they would never forget.

And no, he wouldn't be in his police chief uniform when he cracked their heads open.

It was the only way to handle them. Hard. Unforgiving. Especially at his age. He didn't have the patience anymore. Blood easily pumped to his temples. He could hardly control it.

The last time he had lost his temper, he hammered some little puta's face in. Dropping him into a dark side street after he had sold powder to a twelve-year-old. Juan couldn't stop thinking of how it could have been his child.

The thug had grinned at him.

Big mistake.

A flurry of fists, and Juan had found himself with blood-covered hands and a whimpering figure on the ground. He spat on him and gave him a warning in low, guttural tones.

When his daughter, Elsa, had moved to Madrid, he had truly been relieved for her and glad that she was out of this shithole that seemed to be getting worse by the year.

Si. Madrid was a little far away and impersonal, the way big cities were, but it had its class, its culture, too, and he knew Elsa would gravitate towards that. He was truly proud of her growing into a confident young and beautiful woman, grabbing life and making the most of it all. She had visited over the weekend and was now heading back to Madrid and her new life.

Good for her.

Thinking of his daughter calmed the police chief.

It had been a quiet day at the station; very little was coming through, and Juan had expected to be called in by now. He reached into his back pocket and pulled out a folded silk handkerchief, wiping off the sweat on his glistening forehead and then took out a stick of gum before flicking through the pages of *El País*.

Something came through the radio. Juan upped the volume.

Emergencia...a train accident has been reported north of Parla, south of Getafe. All available units move out immediately. We need all emergencia personnel at the scene.

Madrid? A shiver rolled up his spine.

He switched on the engine and eased ahead through the sun-baked streets, the realisation growing stronger.

Elsa! Was that the train she had taken? Or did she get on a later one?

He couldn't be sure. Hadn't really paid attention to the conversation at breakfast. He racked his memory for details as a cold rush streamed through his body, the hair on his back spiking.

Chapter 13

The CCTV monitors were clear with high resolution giving the operator the ability to freeze footage and zoom in for more detail. There were crowds of people going about their lives, streaming off the train and onto the platform while others waited to embark, mostly unaware of their surveillance and the events to come.

Jamall and Zara were back in the operations room, studying one of the screens. At the other end of the room, the CNI operators ran footage from different stations around the time of the Malaga-Madrid train.

The same train that was now the centre of world news.

The main screen showed footage in live breaking news mode. Emergency teams were all over the scene like little green ants, crawling through the twisted wreck of jackknifed carriages that would feature in most global newspapers the following day and already on hundreds of websites.

Batchman's briefcase and laptop had not given up their secrets, and it seemed like they were back to square one. There was always the possibility he had stashed what they were looking for in a different location, but Jamall didn't believe this to be true.

He needed it for the conference and must have had it on him.

Jamall's mind quickly ticked over. Was there something he may have seen at the time, tucked away in his subconscious?

"We missed something. Another device he took onto the train at Malaga Station. It's either still on there somewhere, or he gave it to someone else," he said.

"Are you sure it wasn't on him, and you just didn't see it?" asked Zara.

Jamall shook his head dismissively.

"No, it wasn't. I don't make mistakes," he said deadpan.

"Was he speaking with anyone on the train?" asked Zara.

"I don't know. I sat down a few seats away to double-check that it was him. Then he spotted me and took off down the carriage."

Jamall suddenly stopped talking; his eyes had drifted to the main screen where footage displayed a stretcher with a shaven-head Latino, half-conscious and clutching a green leather sleeve against his chest.

"Check the CCTV again at Malaga," he said tightly. He didn't need to see it because he remembered seeing Batchman holding it under his arm. But he needed to be sure.

After a few moments, Zara retrieved the same footage and zoomed in on the green iPad sleeve. They both stared hard at it.

"It looks to be the same," she said.

"It is the same."

Jamall stood up and walked closer to the back of the room towards the news item.

He slipped into a spare chair next to Dana Amador and flashed her a smile, his dark eyes settling on her with a well-practised look.

"Hello, Dana." The voice deliberately warm.

Dana smiled back and paused the CCTV footage on her monitor. "Oh! Hola, Mr. Salazar. How are you?" she said, brushing a strand of hair behind her ear.

"Could be better. A grim day for us all." He gestured only with a movement of his eyes towards the large screen. "The news footage. Can you isolate it for me? I'd like to take a closer look myself and perhaps run facial recog on it. Do you think you can do that?"

She looked up at the monitor.

"Si, si, of course. Have you seen something?"

The news had returned to the drone aerial shot looking down on the epicentre of chaos.

"It's probably nothing. Thank you, Dana." He slipped off the chair and walked back to his desk. Five minutes later, he was staring at the footage again on his own screen. The shaven-head Latino on the stretcher must be in a hospital somewhere in Madrid.

"Keep running the face recog. Find out who this guy is," he said in a low voice. "And check the CCTV blocking device worked. That would take a lot of explaining."

Zara kept her eyes peeled on the footage, her fingers tapping the screen occasionally.

"I already checked. Just some flashes of static that shouldn't be noticed, and we're nowhere in sight in any of the footage," she said slowly.

Jamall nodded, and they continued to stare at the images of the Latin guy clutching the green-sleeved tablet holder. Jamall was convinced it was the missing piece he was looking for.

"Is this one a suspect, Mr. Salazar? He's not on the list you gave us earlier."

A voice behind him. Ortez.

Jamall swung around a veneer of calm on his face.

"Possibly. If this is who I think it is, then we need to get confirmation of his identity quickly to make sure," Jamall replied, picking out a smartphone from inside his jacket pocket. His fingers tapped an icon and opened up the map app.

"Any idea what hospital the victims will be taken to?"

Ortez thought for a moment.

"It could be any of them. Most likely Hospital Gregorio Marañon or Hospital Doce de Octubre. The last time this happened, there were five or so hospitals involved."

Ortez looked sombre at this thought and shook his head. "I cannot believe it has happened again. Another train bombing in our city."

"Call the hospitals and find out which one he's at, and as soon as you get a positive ID, let me know," Jamall said, looking at Zara before making his way to the exit door.

"Wait a minute. Are you going after the suspect alone? I don't think so," said Ortez, a look of indignation on his face.

Jamall turned his head.

"I'll deal with this. It's what I'm here for."

"If that *hijo de puta* has bombed and killed our citizens in my city, you can be bloody sure the CNI is going to take some credit in this thing, *Mr. CIA man*." He almost spat the last part in a sarcastic tone.

A thin smile appeared on Jamall's face, and he stopped walking.

Treading on toes was one thing; stamping on them was another.

"Mr. Ortez." He fully turned around to face the state director. "Let me apologise. As I said, a fast-moving situation often gets me fired up. How about I take some field guys or a unit? I'd be happy to babysit them for you."

Ortez fixed him with an icy stare and slowly crushed his empty paper coffee cup in his fist.

Chapter 14

The radio continued revealing more information. Sounded like some kind of explosion on the train.

Juan Cerezo grabbed his mobile and dialled his daughter's number.

No answer.

Then he tried his wife.

No answer.

She never had got used to using a mobile phone.

The driver in front had been idling for what seemed like an age. Ortez leaned out of the window and shouted an insult. "*Venga cojones, vas pisando huevos!*"

The driver swore back and pulled over, allowing Juan to rush past, heading north towards the outskirts of Madrid, towards the reported accident scene.

Pulling off the A-42 at speed, Juan continued heading east into an industrial estate. There was no need to ask for directions. A towering black column of smoke, like the finger of god, showed him where to go. Navigating his way through a maze of roundabouts and narrow dusty roads, he was soon confronted with a sea of blue and red lights.

As he drove closer, a group of ambulances blocked the way, where the road curved parallel with the train track. Behind them, Juan could see the twisted carriages of a train, lying bent like some great deformed serpent.

Juan could feel the blood pumping through his temple, anxiety rising. He tried his daughter's number. Still no bloody answer. He left a message, calmly asking her what train she had caught and then hung up.

Please, god, make sure Elsa is alright!

Juan slammed the door of his car and hurried over to a field gate where an impromptu police checkpoint had been set up. One of the young officers held up his hands to stop Juan in his tracks.

"What happened back there?" he shouted, trying to break away from the undertow of people searching for their loved ones.

"An explosion," said the officer standing next to him. "It's like a war zone down there."

Juan stared at the scene for a second and then tried to push past, focusing his energy on chewing the gum tucked into his cheek. The young officer held his ground.

"Let me through! Are you seriously going to stand in the way of a chief of police?" he asked, still chewing.

He reached inside his back pocket and, in one smooth action, pulled out his police ID.

The two officers looked at each other.

"Chief Cerezo, I'm sorry, sir," one of the officers mumbled. Juan ignored him and began to jog up the narrow road that led to the carnage.

The narrow road skirting the edge of the industrial estate was jam-packed with emergency response vehicles: a mix of ambulances and fire engines. A continuous wail of sirens came in waves as more arrived at the scene of chaos. On one side, there were a dozen or so news vans, the reporters giving a running commentary with the very little information they had. A constant hum of news helicopters, feeding live pictures to the masses, buzzed overhead.

Juan ran along the road, dodging emergency vehicles that were attempting to leave the area with the injured.

A team of firemen jogged towards the train with the equipment needed to save lives, seemingly unaffected by the heat of the day. The long fence that separated the train track from the estate had been ripped down; a bunch of water hoses snaked across it, pumping water to where the fire raged. The explosion had happened near the rear of the train, and the firemen were putting out the flames.

A few metres from the train, paramedics worked on a seriously injured woman, strapping up her head with bandages; the dark red blood had soaked into the front of her dress.

At the opposite end of the train, a stream of lightly injured passengers were being led out by paramedics, their emergency foil blankets crinkling in the afternoon breeze.

"Sir? Were you on the train?" A voice from behind. He turned to see a young police officer eyeing him with suspicion. Juan flashed his badge again without a word, and the officer nodded.

"Chief. How can I help?"

"Do you have a manifest of the dead and injured? Who's in charge here?"

The officer pointed farther up the line to a car park towards which glimpses of green-suited medics carried the injured.

"That area is the immediate holding area for victims. Best ask someone up there," he said.

Juan jogged as fast as he could along the scrub that was

parallel to the train. A section had jackknifed; several carriages lay twisted on their side while the emergency crew worked their way through the side with hydraulic cutters. Farther along, another team were pulling out a victim on a winch, the process slow and methodical.

At the car park, crash victims from all walks of life were laid out on the ground.

A woman screamed as two medics hunched over her, and Juan could see why. She had lost an arm, and they were desperately wrapping up the stump. An ambulance crew member hurriedly gave her a shot of morphine. An old man, pale-faced, wrapped in a foil blanket, stared ahead as if in a trance. A boy no older than ten had his shirt removed by a medic who treated deep bruising across his ribs.

Juan saw a harassed medical officer hunched over a fold-out table, talking into his radio as he stared at a clipboard in his hand. Juan felt his hands sweating and heart pumping in his chest, the reality of the situation falling over him like a blanket of desperation.

The medical officer finished his call, and Juan stepped up quickly in front of him.

"Do you have a victims list yet?"

The man, in his thirties with a neatly trimmed beard, barely looked up from his clipboard—a list of emergency numbers that, at first glance, didn't look like what Juan was looking for.

"There's not much of a list. I'm afraid you'll have to wait. I'm very busy, as you can imagine."

Juan held his temper in check; his temple was throbbing again.

"Sure, you're busy, but my daughter was on that train. Can I see what you have?"

"Just give me one minute."

"Did you not hear me? My daughter was on that train!"

The officer looked up at Juan for the first time and seemed to recoil from his hard stare.

"One moment. I'll get it for you." He walked over to another ambulance crew and came back a moment later with a clipboard.

"That's it, that's the manifest?" asked Juan.

The man nodded, and Juan grabbed it from his hands, eyes scanning the words in quiet anxiety, but he couldn't see her name. Was that hope? Yes, he was feeling hopeful and immediately scrubbed it away from his thoughts.

"Not the train manifest; we haven't received it yet. Just names of the conscious victims that we've seen. There are bodies that we haven't been able to identify..." Juan felt a sharp tug in his stomach as he mentioned bodies. The officer continued. "We haven't had time to make any progress with it right now. There are still many victims stuck in the train."

"That's not good enough. Who the hell is in charge around here? I need to look for my daughter now!"

A young female in ambulance crew attire came over and touched Juan gently on the arm as if to calm him down.

"Let's check over here," she said in a soft voice. Juan followed the direction of her pointing arm and saw it led to a line of bodies at the far end of the car park, covered head to toe in white blankets. The anger suddenly washed out of him, the fear returning to claw at him within several long seconds. His baby girl could be right there, now just a Jane Doe waiting to be claimed. He merely nodded and followed her lead, walking reluctantly over towards them.

They went along the line, one by one. The nurse lifted the

blanket of the first victim.

"I'll just show you the females, sir. Take your time with each one."

Cold, pale, washed-out corpses. Some were encrusted with dried blood. One girl with a cracked skull must have been quite an impact. In his line of work, Juan had seen many bodies. He simply shook his head with relief as each one turned out to be someone else's daughter, mother, or sister. They came to the last body, and the blanket pulled back to reveal a young girl. A blonde in her teens. So like Elsa. Possibly the same age. Finally, Juan shook his head. "No, that's not her either."

"I'm sorry I can't help you any further. If you leave her name, I'll keep a lookout."

Juan sighed. His world was spinning, and he was struggling to keep control of his emotions. Should he be happy that his daughter was not one of the dead or still worried that her fate was unknown? They began walking back to the fold-out table and the bearded medical officer.

Juan mopped his forehead with his handkerchief as the late afternoon sun beat down mercilessly. His gaze wandered back to the train and the dotted green of the emergency service crew members moving amongst the chaos. Two figures carried a stretcher from the train towards the car park. A distant grinding sound of machinery drifted through the air as emergency rescue teams cut through the mangled metal of the train carriage.

The two men carrying the stretcher came nearer, and Juan caught a glimpse of blonde hair on the victim.

He walked faster, eyes transfixed.

The female officer was talking to him, but the words evaporated into the air like a dandelion in the wind.

The face so like Elsa.

And as the stretcher came nearer, Juan found himself staring at the unmistakable corpse of his daughter.

Chapter 15

The Hospital Doce de Octubre was a hive of activity, rushing nurses and doctors, shouts of agony and raised voices. Hugo Reese watched through a morphine-induced haze as the double doors flew open and a nurse pushed a stretcher through towards the main accident and emergency section. There was an unconscious woman with an oxygen mask covering her face; an old man in a wheelchair getting pushed past by an ambulance crew member.

A nurse's face appeared in front of him. She smiled.

"We're going to get you to a bed just for observation. Do you understand? You had a nasty hit on the head and cut your arm, but otherwise, you are fine."

Hugo nodded and smiled. "Sure, sin problema, bonita. Muchos gracias."

The nurse helped him get into a wheelchair and pushed him through a seemingly endless corridor.

"Guess you're having a busy day today, huh?"

"Si, it's mayhem. I don't remember anything like this. Every hospital in Madrid is overwhelmed, apparently."

They turned right and entered a nurse station consisting of a desk with a computer monitor. Beyond was a long ward with rows of beds on either side. She pushed Hugo near the end of the ward and stopped at a bed; bending down, she gently started to help him onto it. He waved her off and pushed his weight from the chair.

"It's OK, bonita. At least I'm still alive, right?" Hugo slumped onto the bed. "Do you know what the hell happened out there?"

The nurse puffed up the pillows behind his head. "A terrible accident. That's all I know, I'm afraid."

Hugo frowned and laid his head back. The nurse began to pull the curtains around the bed and turned at a shout for assistance from another nurse at the main desk.

"I have to go. I'll be back to help you get undressed, and a doctor will be round to check on you a little later."

"OK, thanks. I'll miss you," he said. She flashed him a smile and strolled quickly back down the ward.

Hugo took the tablet in its sleeve and placed it on the bedside table. His forearm had been heavily bandaged, and apart from the fogginess from the morphine, he didn't feel too bad. Then, perhaps, the morphine was why he didn't feel so bad? He adjusted himself in the bed to sit up better and tried to piece together the previous events.

It came back like a creeping bad memory. The doc. His twisted body, staring eyes. It sent a shiver down Hugo's spine even though he had seen his fair share of corpses.

The old guy had been murdered on the train. No doubt.

And then the bomb. Now the memories came back, and he knew he had heard it. A violent bang and rush of energy.

Yeah, it was a bomb, all right. No fucking doubt, Bruh.

A murder and a bombing. Was there a connection? Or was it all a freakish coincidence?

Hugo drifted in and out of sleep. Visions of Batchman's

staring eyes and the fear that lay behind them. The kid he shot back in LA, hitting the deck with a look of shock on his face—faces of death.

His eyes focused on the nurse station through a gap in the curtain.

The nurse. He shoulda asked her name. *Bonita.*

A tall figure appeared. Dark suit and black ponytail. Leaning forward on the desk, questioning the nurse. Familiar, real familiar. That dude from the train again.

A memory flashed into his brain. The station at Puertollano, walking past in the crowd. Walking past on the train after Batchman had taken off down the carriage.

He recognised the type; he was a player—a killer.

Why hadn't it clicked before? Then he knew why.

After weeks of relaxing with family, his street sense was off.

The nurse pointed, and ponytail glanced down towards Hugo's bed.

Mierda!

Hugo suddenly knew he had to get out of there. Right now! Something from his past? Some fucking Crip assassin? No. It had to do with the doc.

His eyes fell on the green-sleeved iPad case on the bedside table.

That fucking thing. It was important. Important to that guy. That's why he had grabbed it in his semi-conscious stupor on the train.

Smart, Bruh, smart.

Hugo was already moving, his hand grabbing the tablet, his body shifting off the bed out of the opposite side of the curtained cocoon.

Goodbye, bonita. Some other time, maybe.

As his was the last bed, Hugo was able to go to the far door without stepping into ponytail's line of sight. Pushing through the double doors into a busy corridor, Hugo turned right, his eyes darting around at the overhead signs until he saw the exit.

Out in the corridor, his senses sharpening, Hugo quickened his pace. A group of nurses rushed across his path into a ward. Another gurney with an injured man being pushed by hospital staff passed by.

The sound of the ward doors slamming open echoed down the corridor, and all heads turned towards the noise. The dude was in the corridor, looking around. Their eyes met, and in a heartbeat, Hugo was running down the stairs. Taking the last steps two at a time, he came to double doors and barged through, almost losing his footing. Hitting the next set of steps as fast as he could, the staccato drum of his footfall bounced off the walls as he raced downwards.

Another slam of doors above him.

Fuck!

He had reached the third floor, according to the sign, and he was breathing deeply now and pushed on. There must be more than one of them, the clicking footsteps closer, snapping at his heels like a rabid dog.

Glancing up, he saw ponytail looking down over the edge, dark eyes that told him one story: things were not gonna end well.

He was on the second floor in no time, slipping through the doors and into another hectic corridor. Things were getting busier now as more patients were ferried in. Frantic loved ones added to the noise as they tried to find their relatives in the chaos. The stress was thick in the air as exhausted hospital staff worked tirelessly to return some kind of order. No one seemed to notice Hugo as he skirted the edge of the ward.

As he made his way through, he passed a middle-aged nurse who looked at him suspiciously.

"Señor?" She confronted him, but he brushed past her without a word. "Excuse me, Señor? Are you a patient?" she persisted.

"Just leaving!" he shouted back, picking up the pace. She was about to go after him when Hugo's pursuer appeared at the doors, and she turned to face him.

Hugo focused on the doors ahead.

Got to get ahead of this guy enough to give him the slip.

Reaching the doors, he pushed through, ending up in yet another corridor. Heart pounding, he had completely lost track of where he was.

Beads of sweat ran down his forehead, and he was feeling faint. The crash had made him weaker than he thought, with the extra exertion draining his remaining stamina. His forearm was throbbing, a constant ache grinding at his resolve, the white bandages now showing the blood was seeping through. The strain had reopened his wound.

This corridor, like the last, was a hive of activity. Hugo's eyes darted around, trying to find the best route, and then he pushed on at a half jog.

Rounding the corner ahead of him came two guys in suits; from the way they were moving, he could tell they were looking for him.

He stopped short and froze, unsure of what to do.

Both men spotted him at the same time and reached into their jackets, pulling out standard issue gats, their faces contorting into a vision of rage and fear.

"*Al suelo!* No te muevas!" the closest one bellowed down the corridor.

Hugo slammed a shoulder hard into a side door, tripping from the momentum, his body falling forward, and he hit the hard ground with his right arm.

Pain shot through his entire body as he smacked into the floor—another bruise he'd forgotten about.

Cursing to himself, Hugo willed all his strength and pushed himself up, shouting at himself in a mix of anger and pain.

"Get up, Bruh. They ain't messing around. Get up!"

On his feet, Hugo pushed forward and down more steps, the frantic footfall billowing off the walls once again.

He was nearly on the ground floor, escape from the building teasing him now.

Above, the doors smashed open, followed by a hail of thudding gunfire aimed down at him through the handrail gap. Dust flew up from the impact on the floor, spreading slowly up into the air.

Silencers on those puppies thought Hugo. He knew that sound.

Footsteps growing closer, so one of them was rushing down the steps as the other guy was firing.

Where was the ponytail?

The thought had barely passed his mind as he went rushing through the doors at the bottom of the steps, and he found himself in an expansive space, a waiting room now serving as a triage centre, another frantic scene with a stream of victims being ferried into the hospital.

Glass doors at the far end let in a kaleidoscope of light; the dust floating within it was all Hugo could see for a moment. The chaotic scene was a mere backdrop in some kind of dream where time suddenly slowed.

Beyond the dark blur of rushing figures that cut out the light in perfect sequence, Hugo's eyes focused and immediately clocked a tall, dark figure standing still like some kind of robot while the mayhem ebbed and flowed around him.

It was the ponytailed bastardo, luckily looking in a different direction.

Wasting no time, Hugo ducked down and moved behind a pillar, out of sight, heart hammering in his chest, his lungs burning from the effort. Any second, the gunmen would appear from the stairwell, and it would be game over.

All of a sudden, the room started to swell with an influx of people; their cries and rapid Spanish soon told Hugo they were relatives who'd descended on the hospital, hoping to find their loved ones safe.

Hugo cast a glance around the pillar and took his chance. Keep low and keep moving, he told himself, the people in the room shielding him from view. Moving across the space and around a corner, he saw a steady flow of masked doctors coming and going through a set of swinging doors.

Hugo was practically crawling now.

An older man, father to some child, no doubt, glanced at him for a moment but was too preoccupied with his own grief to care.

Energy was low, lower than it had ever been.

Glancing behind him, he saw a group of turning heads face the doorway from the stairwell with an audible gasp. The gunmen must have come through packing their pieces.

Ponytail glared at them, his face a picture of frustration and then a controlled mask before walking off in the opposite direction.

Hugo crawled along the waxed floor and poked his head around yet another door, this time an empty office with three desks and a ceiling fan that threw the humid air around the confined space.

Rolling inside, he pushed himself upright and stood up on a crouch, which caused his head to spin. The pain in his arm was something else. He could quite easily curl up under one of the desks and sleep. His body didn't have much left to give, but now was not the time to give up.

"Come on, Bruh...keep going!"

Raising his weary head, he focused on the window. He shut the door behind him and moved over to it.

Outside there was a small car park and, hopefully, freedom from his pursuers, who seemed determined to hunt him down like a dog. He felt the small tablet that was still tucked into his belt, more for reassurance than anything, and slid the window open.

He pulled out the tablet from in front of his stomach and slipped it behind his back so that he could ease himself out, feet first.

As he sat on the windowsill, the door to the office burst open, and the ponytailed one stood expectantly, dark eyes assessing him as he drew out a pistol with a silencer attached.

Hugo dropped down on the other side, landing on a row of flowers, crushing them into the earth.

Glass from the window above him shattered, showering him with fragments as he crawled away. Forcing himself up and staggering, Hugo skirted along the wall of the building, moving as fast as his legs could carry him. He rounded a corner and felt the whistle of bullets fly inches away from the back of his head.

Motherfucker was trying to kill him, no doubt.

No wounding shots. Death or glory.

Hugo moved fast, spitting onto the ground as his chest heaved and the breathlessness returned.

Adrenaline had kept him going so far, but it was draining fast. Now was not the time to stop. A quick glance around the next corner told him it was clear; he set out at a jog about all the speed he could muster. Crossing a small road within the hospital complex, he ducked down behind a low wall.

He checked around a corner and, seeing it was clear, moved quickly.

Hugo made to move around another corner.

A sudden bolt of pain coursed through his forearm from an unseen force, and he heard his own shout echo across the car park.

A bullet had gone through his forearm, and for a moment, he could see the hole that had ripped out his flesh.

Fuck!

Hugo gritted his teeth as he fell around the corner away from the line of fire. Slumping to his knees on the concrete, he clutched his arm, blood dripping freely through his fingers, splattering on the ground.

For a moment, he was only aware of the sound of distant traffic, the city rolling on through its daily routine, bombs and shootings or not.

Hugo forced himself to get off his ass and ran hard and fast to a line of palms. The near-death experience gave him access to a new energy reserve. It was move or die.

Taking refuge behind one of the trees and checking he was out of any firing line, Hugo tore off his short-sleeve shirt and wrapped it around his forearm as tightly as he could, tying up the ends to form a bow. It was far from perfect, but it was all he could do.

He sneaked a glance across the car park, and the ponytail had rounded the corner of the building and stood looking around. The two men appeared and stood next to him. Ponytail pointed at one of the exits across the far end, and the two men began jogging across. He then glanced towards Hugo, and together with the woman, they began walking in his direction.

Hugo began running again, covered, he hoped, by the trees and shrubs. There was a busy six-lane road, and he ducked around the slow-moving traffic and across to the far side lined with cafes and stores.

People were going about their daily routine, browsing the cafes and chatting idly. Hugo slowed down, held his arm close to his body, and made his way through the crowd.

Those guys were feds or with some kind of agency, no doubt, and he would have all his fed friends out looking for him.

How the hell was he going to get out of this? And what the fuck was going on?

Chapter 16

Hugo kept walking, keeping in the flow with the people, his head continually turning to check behind him.

Soon enough, they'll find it, no doubt.

A helicopter roared overhead, out of sight but menacingly close. Hugo walked quickly, not wanting to run and draw attention to himself but also needing to establish where he was and where he needed to go.

Walking past a row of stores, cafes, and bars, he realised he desperately wanted a drink. His head was pounding, body screaming in protest.

Rest and water. Fast.

Reaching into his pockets, but no dice: The wallet was gone. Probably dropped it when he was running. He had lost everything; his rucksack had probably been burnt up on the train, and all he had now was the doc's tablet computer tucked into his trousers.

The afternoon heat shimmered through the air; a continuous crowd of office workers were filling up the bistros and cafes for their lunch.

Hugo took one last look both ways and, on not seeing his pursuers ducked into one of the cafes, his hand clutching his arm.

Slowly moving past the office workers, he went straight into the men's bathroom. He locked the door behind him and unwrapped the shirt from his arm. As he took the dressing off, the spike of pain made his head spin.

Bending down, he rinsed his arm in the sink, a steady flow of blood swirling down the drain. A glance in the mirror told him what he already knew: he looked like shit.

Pale and exhausted. A hunted man.

Looking down at his arm, he cleaned the wound as best he could. It appeared the bullet had passed right through near the surface, just clipping the muscle near the cut from the train wreck.

Taking a small handful of paper towels, he placed them on the wound, rewrapping it with his shirt, taking longer this time to make sure it was tight. The bleeding had not stopped, and the pain had intensified. Leaning down and putting his mouth on the tap, he drank deeply, the cold water soothing and offering him mild comfort.

We'll get out of this, Bruh. Fuck them. Go out fighting. Need a weapon. Get a knife from the kitchens? Yeah, that was a good idea, Bruh. Better than nothing.

He opened the door and found a booth right at the back. A young skinny black girl around his own age was sitting on one side. She had dreadlocks tied back in a bun and those geeky glasses that students wore.

Hugo slumped down opposite her and, ignoring her curious glances, went through his pockets to see if he could find anything of use.

Loose change from the train buffet cart, around eight euros. A train ticket and a ripped Rizla packet. The other pocket was empty.

After several minutes a harassed-looking waiter came up to him and asked for his order.

"Orange juice and some tap water," said Hugo.

The waiter frowned at him, his eyes dropping down to the blood-stained rags on his arm.

Noticing the hesitation, Hugo fixed him with a level stare, aware the sweat was forming on his forehead. "Please."

"I think my friend needs a drink." The voice came from the girl opposite, also fixing the waiter with a stare, who then nodded and left.

Hugo nodded his thanks without a word and mopped his brow with his other arm.

"Are you OK?" she asked, genuine concern etched on her face.

"Having a bad day," Hugo grunted, his eyes fixed on the café entrance.

"I'm sorry to hear that. I'm Gianna." She held out a hand in a clenched fist and flashed Hugo a grin, who narrowed his eyes at her. After a pause, Hugo reluctantly bumped her fist.

"Right...Gianna. I'm Hugo," he replied evenly.

The waiter returned with the juice, a jug of iced water, and a large glass and disappeared as quickly as he had come. Hugo poured and then drained an entire glass of water before picking up the juice, the sugar a welcome relief to his tired body.

Gianna watched him with calm eyes and sipped at an espresso.

"I'm sorry you're having a bad day. Anything you wanna share?" Her voice was smooth like liquid. She sounded British—or was it Canadian?

Hugo drained another glass full of water and placed it back on the table.

"Share? Only that I can't stay here. Feds on my ass."

Yep, those goons were on his tail. It was only a matter of time before one of them came through the doors, and he'd be scrambling through the window in the bathroom.

Gianna's eyes narrowed now. "Feds? Why? What did you do?"

"Jack shit. I was on a train; a bomb went off. The next thing, I'm in hospital, and these feds, cops, whatever, are now hounding my ass."

Hugo's voice was filled with contempt. The anger swelled inside his gut at the situation he found himself in.

"You were on that train? Shit. That was like a total rerun of 2004. They did that before. False flag, no doubt." Gianna's eyes were widening.

"And the authorities are after you? You must have something they want."

Hugo said nothing, assessing the stranger in front of him, assessing whether to trust her. He pressed his hand over the bandaged wound and winced in pain.

"Better get that seen to. Take it you're not keen to go to any hospital?"

"Not after the last one," Hugo whispered.

"Let me help you. I have dressings, bandages, and all that stuff at mine. We'll get you set up."

Hugo jerked his head. "Who the fuck *are* you?"

Gianna frowned. "Like I said, I'm Gianna."

Hugo couldn't help smiling back and warming to her. Trust was a funny thing, an unseen, powerful force. Fuck it. His choices were seriously limited.

"OK. But mess with me, and I'll kill you."

Gianna nodded her agreement silently and placed a ten-euro

note on the table.

"My car's outside."

***

Juan Cerezo was sitting down on the ground on the edge of the car park, his head in his hands, the sun burning down, casting long shadows on the ground. The sounds around him of continuing chaos melted into insignificance. His baby was dead. Elsa dead? How could this be? Could he have prevented it?

He took out his mobile once again, but still, there was no signal. No doubt the networks were overloaded after the savage attack. Her mother would need to be told. Christ, he did not look forward to that.

"Señor Cerezo."

He looked up to see the female ambulance crew from earlier holding out a paper coffee cup for him.

Juan put his phone away, hauled himself to his feet, and dusted off his hands before taking the coffee.

"Thank you," he said quietly.

"They're taking your...daughter to the city morgue." She gestured to one of the numerous ambulances that were backed into the car park. There was a continuous stream of emergency vehicles arriving and leaving. All around them, a constant crescendo of sirens ebbed through the air.

"Are you going to be alright?" she asked as they headed over.

Juan caught the eye of a driver who was preparing to leave.

"Señor! Which morgue are you going to?"

"Right now, they're using the Ifema Convention Centre as a

temporary place."

"You might want to go home," the woman said. Juan shook his head.

"No, I must go with her."

He felt a vibration in his trouser pocket and immediately took out his mobile phone; the photo of his wife, Mia, flashed up on the screen as the ringtone beat out his favourite song, "Amor Inmortal."

Juan paused, staring at it, transfixed. For several moments, he found he could not physically slide the answer button and speak to her. He breathed out, answered, and held the phone to his ear, and without pausing, spoke evenly, without emotion.

"Anna. I'm sorry. Elsa is dead. She was on the train and didn't make it."

He felt the tears running down his face, the reality of the situation somehow becoming clearer now he had spoken the words.

He listened to the immediate silence, her questions, disbelief, and then tears, and as he did so, felt a rising anger at those who had taken their beautiful daughter away from them.

Chapter 17

Gianna drove her old Toyota through a quiet street where a canopy of trees kept the pavement in cool shadow. She turned into a side road and parked next to a line of garages that were covered in graffiti, and switched off the engine.

Hugo looked up from where he was lying flat on the back seat.

"OK, we're here," Gianna said. "We go in the back way because there's CCTV on my street. I spray over the lens, but they replace it pretty quickly."

Getting out of the car, Hugo followed Gianna up concrete steps that led to a wooden gate. Above them, the four-story building was covered with washing hanging from the balconies that peppered the exterior.

Gianna jolted open one of the wooden gates so they could slip inside and then closed it behind them before crossing a small courtyard.

They made their way through a back door that creaked loudly and into a gloomy hallway. A distant sound from somewhere upstairs of children laughing and rapid adult chitchat drifted down.

Gianna took out a bunch of keys and unlocked the third door they came to, and pushed her shoulder against it to get it fully open. Hugo glanced down the hallway and noted the front door was open slightly. A group of middle-aged women were milling around outside.

"Sorry. Excuse the mess."

Hugo stepped into the small flat, walking past a tiny bathroom and kitchen before entering a large room that was an Aladdin's cave of geekery.

There were old computer monitors stacked on top of boxes. Keyboards, cables, computer hard drives, and other hardware devices strewn everywhere. A large desk by the blinded windows had three monitors set up, and one of them was alive with a stream of data flowing vertically. A stack of boxed shelves rammed full of gadgets, small model toy cars, and comics on a desk finished out the look. The walls were plastered with vintage posters from cult films like *Pulp Fiction* and various comic characters. One of the comic drawings was of a woman in a skintight suit in a dynamic pose firing off a couple of rounds at something unseen. A stack of vinyl records lined the wall shelves, and large plastic boxes filled with tech junk were stacked up on the floor.

"What is all this old shit? 'You just never gotten round to trashing it or...'"

Gianna suppressed a snigger.

"Yeah, I collect it all. I like old things, real things. Things you can touch and feel, not just tap *like* on some app. As far as the tech goes, it's just a bit safer..."

"How d'ya mean?"

"Well. As computers, smartphones, and all the other stuff progressed, companies upped the number of ways to track and spy on you. The older tech isn't perfect, but it's less creepy. Do you remember there was a time when the *internet of everything* didn't exist and we could brush our teeth without our toothbrushes talking to our smartphones to monitor whether we're doing it right or taking a crap without our toilet roll levels being monitored on some app? I don't trust the modern gear."

Hugo laughed. "Believe me. I never trusted any of that smart tech shit either."

"Here, sit down," Gianna said, grabbing a closed laptop that was resting on the sofa and placing it out of the way.

Hugo slumped down wearily and breathed out heavily. He took out Batchman's iPad tucked inside his trousers and put it aside.

"I'll get the kit." Gianna disappeared into the bathroom.

"And water! Please!"

"Sure thing."

Hugo felt a wave of relief at being off the street. It was a much-needed reprieve from the snapping jaws of his pursuers. Gianna came back from the bathroom with a small green first aid bag, then disappeared again and came back with a large glass of water, which Hugo grabbed and glugged down in one swift motion. Gianna pulled out a roll of bandages as Hugo proceeded to take off the bloody rags of his shirt.

"Let's get you fixed up."

After swabbing the wound in alcohol and attempting to clean it as best as possible, Gianna dressed and rebandaged his arm, Hugo wincing slightly at the pain.

"You've done a better job than I could have," said Hugo admiring his arm. "Thanks."

"No problem."

Gianna cleared away the old, bloodied rags that Hugo had been using and threw them into a plastic bag and then the trash.

"Hey. Because you seem to know about computers and tech, maybe you should check this. I held on to this tab from the guy on the train," Hugo said.

He handed her the tablet in its green sleeve.

"I think it's important. It was to Nick, anyway." Hugo started up the device and sighed out loud. "Mierda. It's password protected."

"What did you expect? Give it here," she demanded and then began fishing around in a plastic crate filled with computer leads. She fished out a USB hub, connected it to the iPad, and then plugged a thumb drive into the hub.

"What're you doin'?" asked Hugo, rubbing his head lazily.

Gianna picked up her own laptop and then slumped down in a lounge chair opposite Hugo, the iPad resting on the arm of the chair.

"Looking for personal details on your friend. Names, birth-days, pets' names, anything that can give us a clue as to what that bloody password is," said Gianna.

She pressed the emergency medical ID app at the bottom of the screen and smiled.

"Well, he was a sensible chap," she continued. "He filled out his emergency details. I've got his full name, date of birth, blood type, and emergency contact, which is empty...so now I just have to try out any other information about him online—from his social media profiles, if there's any, and whatever else I can find. Then we take all that info and run the different scenarios through a programme. A clever little beast. Collates all the little personal details and then spits out a list of possible passwords."

She looked over at Hugo with a proud grin, but he had closed his eyes and fallen asleep.

***

When he awoke with a start, it was dark outside, but a small light in the corner gave the room a warm, homely glow. For a second, he felt happy, like he was at home and everything was alright with the world. And then the day's events all came back to him.

Gianna was still sitting opposite, still frowning at the tablet screen; the backlit hue reflected onto her delicate profile.

"Hey there," she said, noticing Hugo was awake.

"How long was I out?"

"A few hours."

Gianna put the tablet aside and pulled out a wooden box from a side table next to the sofa, and brought out cigarette papers.

"Maybe this will help the pain," she said with a smile on her face.

Hugo's eyes checked out the box with interest. He was dying for a smoke; it would surely help, but something told him he needed to stay alert and frosty.

"Hmm, much as I'd love to smoke that shit, I better not."

"Your loss," Gianna replied as she began to stick the papers together carefully.

"So, how'd you get on with the 'social engineering' or whatever?"

She showed him the tablet. A photograph of a serene lake, the sun setting in the background reflected in the surface of the lake like a polished mirror.

"I nailed it eventually," she said, flashing him a quick smile.

Hugo nodded, clearly impressed. "Nice work. So, what was it?"

Gianna sighed.

"It was the name of his mother's cat combined with his birth year."

He moved over to look at her screen. There was a maze of folders on the desktop, and Gianna began drilling through them with rapid taps until she came to a list of files.

Gianna opened various documents that made no sense to either of them—medical reports and other personal info.

She opened a text-heavy document named _press that contained a single article.

"Does that say Ljungborg? I think the doc on the train mentioned that name." Hugo pointed at the name under one of the photos that showed a balding man in his fifties looking across a valley.

"Yep, it sure does." Gianna scrolled to the top, and they both began reading an article.

The Alaskan Times
June 17, 1951

An expedition force of four men and one woman has made its way to the Brevig Mission in Alaska and dug up the remains of victims who had died there from the Spanish Flu in 1918. An estimated 50 million died from the virus that swept the world at the end of World War I.

Led by doctor-turned-virologist Klaus Ljungborg, whose family were victims of the virus, the group includes Peter Milton, Nicholas Batchman, and Beatrice Gray, the latter being the group's only female member.

"All in all, it took two days to reach the first body," said

Ljungborg. "*With help from the locals, we built a fire on the ground to thaw the permafrost and then shovelled off the melted soil and repeated the process.*"

Ljungborg's hope is that the lung samples taken from the bodies will provide some clue on how the infamous flu began and whether there could be a vaccine created to protect the human race against future outbreaks.

Only time and painstaking research will tell whether Ljung-borg's effort will ever be rewarded.

"Shit."

"What is it?" asked Hugo.

"There's a document here, and it's encrypted. Who was this guy again?"

Hugo shook his head. "I dunno. Some doctor. He said he was researching the Spanish flu from way back. It sounded nasty."

"Yeah, I read about that. It sure was."

Hugo rested his eyes while Gianna stared at the screen, muttering to herself.

"So, you can't hack it easily, then?"

Gianna sighed. "No. Encrypted data always has a key somewhere to decrypt it, which itself is password protected. There's some other files here outside of the encrypted folder, though. Someone's diary."

Gianna scanned it for a few moments.

"By a Doctor Ljungborg from around the First World War. Could be clues here. Want to listen to it? I can run it through the app and have it read out to us."

Hugo leaned back, closing his eyes, his face flinching in pain. "Sure, why not? I love a good story."

***

Diary of Doctor Klaus Ljungborg

Ypres, Belgium. October 19, 1917

The conditions are definitely getting worse. I have not slept for at least three days, although it's hard to tell anymore. The days and nights blur into one, broken up only by fresh waves of casualties that come into the makeshift hospital.

Today I had to walk over to the British Red Cross and beg for vital supplies of morphine. I think the nurses there were sympathetic because they thought I was American. My US medical corps khaki overcoat was doing the job.

On the way back, I walked through the brown sludge that was once a bustling main street in Ypres and now a forward base for the Allies. A sorry group of British infantrymen moved slowly as if a single mass, their green uniforms seemingly merging like a sloping caterpillar easing through the mud.

A white horse, legs completely blackened by the dirt, passed by, hauling a cart of supplies, probably to replenish the front lines. As it passed, I heard a crack as the wheel of the cart hit a small crater in the road, causing it to tip sideways. The horse panicked at the change, rearing up on its hind legs and fighting the shift in weight that was pulling it downwards.

The cart tipped over, pulling the horse onto its side and spilling boxes onto the road. It neighed wildly, thrashing its legs in the air, the terrified look of death on its face.

I stared into the horse's eyes, lost in its fear; a truly terrifying sight—and I saw a few things.

Naturally, I raced over to help the men surrounding the cart in what was a futile attempt to push it back up.

One of the soldiers nodded at me. "Don't worry, Doctor,

we'll take care of this. You get to your station."

I hesitated at first and then nodded back in agreement. I should be with my patients, and this was something six burly men should be able to handle easily enough.

At least the roads are not as bad as in the summer when the persistent rains came for the start of the Third Battle of Ypres. The heavy clay soil would not soak up the water, and the ground had been churned up many times over by consistent artillery bombardment.

Conditions were so terrible that men and horses literally sank without a trace into water-filled craters.

I walked on through the mud until I saw the familiar steeple of Saint Martin's church through the ruins of Ypres. The old church had fared well for its purpose since the German shelling had died down.

Although there have been whispers about an armistice, I choose not to get too hopeful. I don't think there is one person in this godforsaken world that has not heard since 1914 how the bloody war is supposed to be over by Christmas.

Now Christmas is around the corner again, but I have no stomach for it at all. Unless, of course, Beatrice wants to do something. Perhaps we could get an hour or so away from the dead and the sick. Anywhere there aren't open wounds and the crying of death.

Back at the church, I saw her comforting a soldier who was crying in despair. She is a classical beauty from Hastings in England. A beautiful smile. Neat blonde hair.

Like an actress, you might see in those moving films.

I sometimes wonder how she is attracted to an inexperienced, young doctor like myself. It is almost as if the suffering surrounding us exaggerates our intense purpose.

Beatrice and I have not managed to spend much time together, but the time we get is precious, and we make the most of every minute we have. There are some quiet fields well behind the front line that we sometimes escape to, although the distant guns are always thundering in the distance to remind us of the war.

Sometimes we make love; sometimes, we just talk about our country, our childhood. She knows about my family, which has been a source of tension between us. But it is soon forgotten. The thought of wasting our precious time together bickering or arguing is something neither of us wishes to sanction.

And then we have to return to work, to the "meatgrinder", as Beatrice calls it.

The green and pleasant fields of Europe had been ravaged with years of mud, blood, and tears.

There is an endless stream of wounded. Men with their limbs blown off. Complete trauma. There are head wounds that defy belief. I just do not know how much longer this hell can continue.

October 21st

This event occurred on the 21st, but I didn't write this entry up until weeks later, the reason for which will become obvious. I feel numb. I feel adrift at sea, unable to speak except for writing these words.

The stretcher bearers brought in another wounded soldier at around 5.30 in the morning. He was screaming in agony; the unfortunate fellow had his entire arm blown off. I directed them to an empty bed, which was actually a slab of wood with an old bloodied blanket strewn over it, and shouted for the closest nurse to get morphine.

She was already a step ahead of me and brought over the needle and bottle. We gave the platoon sergeant a shot, and I did my best to stem the flow of blood with a bundle of rags folded up into a square. We quickly dressed the stub that was left of the soldier's arm.

I remember the whistling sound growing louder. And I remember recognising that sound immediately as a 42-cm howitzer shell. Don't ask why I know these things; it frightens me that I do. I began to shout to anyone around me to take cover. A massive explosion caved in the far wall, launching bricks and debris in all directions. The ground shook, and I remember heavy, boiling dust rushing through the open space.

I slowly opened my eyes; my head was pounding, and my eyes did not work except for being able to make out blurry shapes. I became aware of a bright light that seemed to invade my consciousness. There was a voice, but the words formed no meaning. It sounded like a question repeating itself.

And then the pain that seemed to infect my entire body. My head felt like it would explode. I groaned, and then the words started to make sense.

Doctor Ljungborg?

My name. Yes, I was a doctor. The war. It began to creep back into my consciousness. My first thought was of Beatrice. I tried to speak, but the words made no sense. I fully opened my eyes and saw a kindly face looking down at me.

"Doctor. Good to see you are awake again. Can you under-stand me? Just blink once."

I did so. My eyes were sore, and throat was so dry it burned as I tried to swallow.

"What happened?" My voice sounded like a frog.

"You were caught in a loose shell blast at Saint Martin's. A

German plane bombed the hospital. One of the shells hit just outside, collapsing the church wall. It was hell, apparently. Three struck the billet where fifteen soldiers were sleeping. Two sergeants were killed, nine privates and one major were wounded, all receiving severe injuries."

The doctor leaned over, inspecting my leg.

"I think we'd better redress the wound."

I asked about Beatrice, but the doctor, Smith, I think he was called, just ignored me, instead summoning a nurse who began to carefully undo the bandages that I only just realised were on my head. For the first time, I became aware that I was in a large hospital tent filled with the moans of the wounded.

"Water, please," I croaked. The nurse looked at the doctor, some kind of grim expression on her face, and the doctor nodded.

He sat down and leaned closer to me. My alarm bells were going off because he had that look on his face—one I had put on myself for patients many times. I noted that his breath stank of bitter coffee and tobacco. Why I only remember that I really don't know.

"I'm afraid you've lost your lower left leg, Doctor Ljungborg and crushed under falling debris. There was not much left of your foot when they brought you in. There's no other way to say it. I'm sorry."

Simple and utter disbelief. I was lying flat, so I had to lift up my arms, and when my eyes fell on the bandaged stump, cut off just before the knee, I simply laughed.

"Doctor Ljungborg, please. I will make sure we get you the best prosthetic leg possible. You'll be walking around in no time." Smith's demeanour seemed a little jolly, but I couldn't focus. My mind spun like a fairground wheel, and I instantly vomited on the floor.

As a doctor, I knew that patients would often still feel their lost limbs sometime after amputation, and now there I was experiencing it myself, the dull ache of a foot that was no longer there.

I closed my eyes as if the nightmare might go away and I would somehow wake up from a dream.

But it was no dream, no trick of a morphine-addled mind. This was it now, and I was going to have to learn to live with it.

November 26th

For several weeks, the nurses washed my wound in carbonic solution, cutting away the tissue and wrapping the stub in gauze. I know this grim procedure too well; the practice of "debridement" to prevent infection. The doctors and nurses are the best I have met and thank god they are looking after me.

December 24th. Christmas Eve.

Doctor Smith came to see me in the morning, and I thanked him for everything he had done, knowing too well that the grim reaper had been knocking at my door.

"I have a Christmas present for you, Ljungborg." With a warm smile, he held up a prosthetic leg. "You're sick of that bed, I can tell. Once we're happy that there's no risk of infection, you'll be able to walk around again."

That sounded so good to my ears, so very good.

After a couple of painful fitting adjustments, one of the nurses spent a good few hours helping me get used to walking with the aid of some crutches. I still needed morphine on occasion for the pain, but taking steps had never felt so marvelous.

Later on that afternoon, after lunch, I was told I would be going home as soon as there was space on the ships.

I needed to find Beatrice. I checked myself out of the hospital as soon as I could and went back to the church. It was a terrible mess, bricks everywhere, the remnants of a perfectly good hospital blow to smithereens.

I shouted to a recognisable face walking by and showed them the only photograph of Beatrice, but he hadn't seen her.

I turned to another group of soldiers walking in the other direction and asked the same question, to which I received the same response. They were new recruits, just arrived. They'd love to meet her, though, they quipped.

After another hour of searching, I trudged back to my field unit; all hope of ever seeing her again had virtually vanished. As if to deliberately add to my misery, heavy rain began to fall, swelling the already flooded ditches and craters that pockmarked the town.

Considering the hell I had lived in for the past six months, I should be delighted to be heading home. My colleagues and friends have been slapping my back, giving me big congratulations, but inside I feel despair. Deep despair. All I can do is pray that she is somehow safe and in good hands.

January 15th, 1918. Fort Riley

A hellish trip back to America. All I can say is I thought more than once about jumping off the side of that rusty old trawler.

It felt like endless days at sea before we finally docked at Hoboken on the Hudson River in New York.

The others and I, the so-called c-category wounded that were able to walk without too much help, all trudged to a group of waiting buses that stood idling their engines.

I had been assigned a permanent sickness pass and sent home immediately. There is a chance I can continue working at Fort Riley as there is a shortage of doctors. Still, I am apprehensive about my return.

I'm not sure why I feel this way. Could I wallow in self-pity? Perhaps. But to continue to do my work, helping others is the only way I can see myself getting through this.

Before leaving for my ship across the Atlantic, I had searched every hospital and medical area in Ypres for Beatrice but had drawn a complete blank.

There was no record of where she had been taken; I surmised that she must have been wounded in the blast and, therefore should have been taken to a medical area. All I can do is pray that she is safe, alive, and well.

On the bus, I wondered if I'd ever see her again.

With that, thoughts turn to Ingrid and the boys. It will be good to see them again. How long has it been? Nearly a year, if my memory's correct.

The buses all began moving from the port, and a sea of shouts and hoots from the soldiers passing greeted us. They slapped their hands on the side of the bus windows as a show of support.

The driver gunned the engine, so it flew down the road, kicking up dust behind it as the gears ground, gaining speed. I stared out the window at the miles of cornfields as a sea of yellow blurred by. The lack of sleep was eating away at my brain again; it felt like it had been an age since I last had a great night's rest.

Perhaps I will get one soon when I get home.

January 17th

The buses pulled up at the huge gates of Camp Funston. An immaculately dressed soldier stepped out of a guardhouse and talked briefly to the driver.

He slowly walked down the bus aisle, checking the faces of the passengers. Apparently satisfied that no one on the bus was a potential saboteur, he departed the vehicle and waved it through.

Camp Funston, set within Fort Riley, sprawls over two thousand acres with around fourteen hundred buildings that the US military control. The camp was built last year due to the war and can accommodate some thirty-to-fifty-thousand men. It's quite staggering.

We passed what seemed like hundreds of long two-story wooden barracks. The vastness of this place is incredible, and I had forgotten how large it really was.

Their camp is quite advanced, with an underground system of waterworks, sewers, and conduits. It has its own refrigerating plants for making the ice needed to keep all meats and so forth cold. There is even a garbage collection and disposal system with incinerators for refuse and dead animals.

I made my way with the rest of the medical team to the living quarters for the mobile ambulance service that spanned a square mile in the east of the camp.

After reporting in, I was relieved from duty immediately, pending a review of my health and mental capability, hopefully for no longer than a week. I need to work more than ever.

One of the lieutenants kindly gave me a lift back to the house in the family quarter, and they must have heard I was coming.

Inga and the boys were outside, standing by the low wooden fence, watching the dusty track with expectant looks on their faces as we pulled up.

When the boys spotted me, they ran across and clambered all over me as I got out of the vehicle.

"Careful, boys, careful. Papa has an injury."

"Why, what happened, Papa? What happened?"

"Don't worry, Jonathan, I'm alive! That's the main thing."

I ruffled his hair, and we walked up to where my wife, Inga, was waiting. Thin-lipped and curt, nothing much has changed. She kissed me lightly on the cheek and then glanced down at my leg, a frown on her face.

"My dear, you're limping."

"Nothing to worry about," I said.

It was so good to see the boys again. Jonathan had changed the most, several inches taller with the smartest haircut in the camp, and Bertie—well, he's only five, making a mess and causing all sorts of chaos. I think Inga has been struggling to cope with him, judging by the way she snaps and scolds him.

"He is a boy with extraordinary energy," I told her. "Let him run himself out and be done with it."

The reaction to my "wound" was a shock, of course, but at the same time, there was an intrigued curiosity about the prosthetic leg. The boys will not stop asking me questions about it; they are simply fascinated.

Despite the way things have gone in the last few months, I feel happy to be home with the family. From the news coming out of Europe, it sounds like the war will be ended soon, and there will be no need for my sons or anyone else's sons to be sent into that hell on earth.

I pray they never have to experience it.

At night, sometimes, my thoughts drift to Beatrice and the few months we spent together.

Is she in good health?

Does she think of me?

I wonder if I should feel more guilt over my infidelity, yet it seems that in a place of such terror, she was the only thing that kept me grounded, the only thing that kept me sane.

January 20th

A doctor called Franklin Berg, who had studied with me in Sweden, waved from the rails outside the food mess. Berg was also a doctor at Funston. I smiled and walked over towards him.

"Klaus? So delighted to see you again. My god. Klaus!" He stared at my artificial leg, which had been exposed by the rolled-up trousers.

"Just a flesh wound from a shell explosion. They insisted on sending me back," I said, understating the damage.

"God, man. I'm so sorry to hear that."

"At least I'm alive," I said.

Berg lightly slapped me on the shoulder. "Yes, you are alive. So, is it hell over there? I hear it's terrible."

I paused and leaned on the rail. "It's like no other war, Klaus. Like no other war in history." I almost continued to tell him the whole truth of the matter, but I think I just smiled and invited him to catch up sometime over dinner.

I limped over to the main quartermaster barracks that housed the upper echelons of the 89th Division, overlooking the shooting range of the eastern part of the camp.

Apart from the distant crack of gunfire from the training facilities a mile away, the scrub could have been straight out of a perfect dream, as opposed to the nightmare of my recent hell in Europe. Fields that were green rather than churned up with mud, corpses and craters.

There is cause for hope.

I was shown to a waiting room by the army field clerk, who thankfully offered me coffee that was far superior to the mess, and then I was ushered into see the major.

The major was a short, burley type with cropped brown hair, fierce eyes, and a dominating aura about him.

"I heard you did great work for our boys over there. Helping soldiers to get back in the field is a great service to the United States Army."

There was something about his comment that made me feel uneasy. As if the idea of fixing and feeding men back into the mince grinder of war was something to be celebrated.

"Do you think you'll be fit for duty here at the fort anytime soon?"

I told him that I didn't have a problem with doing my job. I wanted to help the wounded men that needed my help. That was why I became a doctor.

"Good, good. Listen, Ljungborg, take a week's leave, and then we'll reassess your condition and see if we can get you back to looking after patients, eh?" he told me.

January 27th

It's been a relaxing week with the family. We borrowed a car and got out of the camp for short road trips for a couple of days. Unfortunately, the weather turned lousy, so we've been cooped up in the house, playing cards and keeping ourselves entertained.

Ingrid cooked a baked ham that I had taken from the kitchen. It was the best meal I had eaten for an age; the meat tasted jolly good.

Every night I have to redress my leg and remind myself how

lucky I am to be still alive and not dwell on the missing limb.

Tomorrow I will be assessed and, with luck, back at work. This war must end soon, and life will get better.

January 28th

The assessment went very well. They saw no reason why I shouldn't return to work if I were willing so that I could continue my duties at the camp hospital.

February 13th

I've been back working for a few days now. It is quiet, and there is not a lot to deal with. So different from the hell in Europe. It's almost as if I was never there, and then I catch a glance of my leg and remember everything. Still, it is good to be busy. For that, I am grateful.

March 1st

I strolled into the nearly empty hospital ward that had been set up in a small outbuilding near the dining quarters. It housed around twenty beds, and there was a stillness and calmness in the air, surreal compared to the hospital on the front, filled with the sounds and stench of death.

A soldier from the 89th Division who had been shot in the arm in training was sleeping in one bed. I checked his temperature and pulse, but the young private hardly stirred. He would be fit for duty again before long, ready for war.

An elderly man was mopping the floor, and at the far side, a station nurse was leaning over another patient. I strolled over and smiled at the nurse; Cathy, her name was. Barely eighteen and an intern from Nebraska.

"What have we got here, Nurse?" I asked, leaning over the

patient, and I have to say I was taken aback by his appearance. The man was pale, and dark purple shadows surrounded his milky irises.

"What's his name?" I asked, my tone taking on a sense of urgency.

"Gilton. Albert Gilton. One of the cook assistants. He has a very high temperature of 102 degrees, a sore throat, and aching limbs. Is that correct, Mr. Gilton?"

The cooking assistant nodded weakly and then had a coughing fit that was so violent I thought his chest would explode. After it calmed down, I held a scope to the patient's chest.

"He's struggling to breathe. Has he a history of any respiratory problems or childhood asthma?"

The nurse shook her head. "Nothing on his records at all, Doctor. This is the first time Gilton has been admitted for anything."

"When did he come in?"

"Just thirty minutes or so ago," the nurse replied. I nodded. It seemed to me to be a case of influenza or possible pneumonia.

I took the young nurse aside. "Go and get yourself a facemask immediately, and bring me one. This could be contagious, so best to take precautions. Then call all staff to be on alert."

The young nurse nodded and dashed to the staff quarters in the next block.

"Private Gilton. Are you able to answer some questions? Just nod if you cannot speak."

"Go ahead," he croaked.

"When did you start to feel unwell?"

The patient had to take his time answering between coughing fits and difficulty breathing. I ran through the possibilities in my head and ruled out dyspnea and haemoptysis.

I hated pushing him, but I had the distinct feeling it was important to know as much as possible.

He ignored me at first, saying how much he did not want to die. He had asked for a transfer to Europe to be close to the war, having never been anywhere away from his hometown in Louisiana.

He asked for his wife, and after much conjuring from myself, he finally answered my questions.

"Halfway through the evening dinner shift...I took a break out of the back. Had a smoke. Some fella offered me one. By the time I went back, I was feeling unwell. I didn't make it to the end of that shift, Doc."

After that, Gilton became worse and was struggling to get air to his lungs. He was rapidly deteriorating in front of my eyes. A bile of blood-tinged foam flowed from the corners of his mouth and nose.

The nurse reappeared with the face masks and gloves, and we pulled a curtain around the patient and went to work to try to drain his lungs.

Just then, the doors opened, and two soldiers brought in a third man who was struggling to stand, his face deathly pale. Before even checking, I instantly knew he had the same illness as Gilton.

My worst fears were beginning to manifest themselves.

***

Hugo nudged Gianna's arm and stared at her, looking half-alarmed and excited. She quickly told the app to pause, and the audio reading of the diary stopped.

"This is about the start of the Spanish flu outbreak!" he said.

She looked at him with a similar realisation and nodded slowly. "The flu that killed fifty million," she said.

"Batchman said that his mentor, Ljungborg, had been on the front line of it, and this must be his personal story..."

"I could do with a drink and a bite. You want anything?" asked Gianna. She stood up and stretched her long arms high above her, and padded into the kitchen.

Hugo winched at the throbbing pain in his arm, pulling him back to current events.

"Say, if you have any painkillers in there...?"

There was the sound of clattering and the slow boil of a kettle.

"Oh yes, of course. I'll get something for you!" she shouted back. There was a popping sound followed by the smell of burned toast and swearing.

"I'm cool with burned toast," he said, loud enough for her to hear.

"No! No! It's cacogenic."

Hugo snorted with derision and glanced along the stacked wall shelves full of vinyl. Hidden behind an old monitor was a stack of books. Some fiction but mostly those monster computer books Hugo had seen on a rare library visit once. He wanted to get up and look at the records, but it hurt to move around.

"Where'd you hear that?"

Gianna came back out and handed Hugo a mug of coffee, along with a packet of capsules.

"Sorry, all I have...It just is, trust me. Never eat burnt toast.

I'm doing a fresh batch."

She returned to the kitchen as the toaster popped again and, after a few minutes, returned with buttered toast on a large plate.

"Keep us going," she said, smiling at him.

"So, how long have you lived here?"

"A few years. I worked doing an IT repair service, just freelance, but it's tapered off a bit now. Before that, I grew up with my adopted parents in London and then travelled a lot, moving around, just keeping my head down, y'know." She gave him a knowing smile. "Like yourself? Travelling around?"

Hugo took a bite of toast.

"Yeah, something like that. I was in LA and decided to move on, see some people over this side..." He drifted off, and there was silence as they both became lost in their own thoughts.

"Well, I'm interested to see how that story pans out," she said, breaking the silence.

"Yeah, hit that play button. Maybe there's some clues to this whole mess I'm in."

***

March 1st continued...

"Very ill man here, Doctor!" shouted one of the soldiers. I came over and pointed to a bed near Albert Gilton. "Put him near the other one. Looks like similar symptoms."

A mere ten minutes later, two men with the mystery virus were brought in, quickly followed by three more. I suddenly felt overwhelmed; a few weeks of only minor problems had made me complacent. Still, it was nothing compared to the front.

I marched to the nurse station, a desk near the door and picked up the phone receiver and gave the dial a quick rotation.

"Doctor Feldmann. We need all available staff to report to Block C. There's a contagion that appears to be spreading."

There was an acknowledgement at the other end of the line, and I went back to the patients. Colleagues of one of the ill soldiers were still hanging around.

"Are they going to be all right?" he asked.

"I don't know. You'll need to leave, Private."

"But what about my friend? What's wrong with him? Is it contagious?"

"Private, please could you leave now? We all have jobs to do."

I stood closer to him, eyeing him threateningly. I could see the fear in the soldier's eyes, not of me but of the mystery disease that had erupted in the camp. The soldier said nothing more and glanced back at his friend on the bed, who was looking even worse than before and backed out of the door.

Then two nurses came in, ready for duty. Nurse Helda and Nurse Frances; were two experienced nurses that I knew, and I inwardly breathed a sigh of relief at getting help.

"Nurse Helda. We need to make this block a sealed-off area. There are"—the doctor paused to look behind him and then turned back to the nurse—"six men with suspected acute influenza."

She nodded and then gestured to the soldier with the broken arm, who was still sleeping through the whole commotion.

"What about him?"

"Get him into another block as quickly as possible."

"But if there is a contagion situation, should we not keep him here?"

I paused for a moment. It was true. The soldier may already have the virus, and there was a risk of further spread. If he didn't have the virus, then he probably would have it soon enough if they just left him in the block.

"He should be isolated. We don't know if he has it or not. Have we got an empty block?"

Nurse Francis, a woman in her mid-forties with grey hair, gestured outside. "Block E is empty, I believe, Doctor."

I nodded. "OK. Get him in there as quick as you can."

"And make sure you all wear protective masks and gloves," I added, remembering to tie mine on at last.

The influx grew over the afternoon until we had to commandeer other blocks to house the sick. By midday, there were over a hundred cases. The staff were overwhelmed, and a few fell sick themselves. I wasn't sure what had hit them, but I was increasingly feeling like a fish out of water.

I decided it was time to take this up the chain and dialled the internal line to speak to Major General McNara.

McNara had insisted on coming to the block to see for himself the viral havoc that had been unleashed. He donned a facemask at my recommendation and stepped into the door frame of the block that had become a den of plague.

"My god," he uttered.

What confronted him was perhaps something that he, in his experience of peace or war, had never seen. A groaning, heaving mass of sick, pale bodies, convulsing and vomiting, choking and gasping for air as the handful of masked nurses rushed from patient to patient.

"What is this exactly?" asked McNara, struggling to rein in

his shock.

"We're not entirely sure. Some kind of virus that is spreading fast. I have never seen anything like it."

"Neither have I," muttered McNara. "Influenza based?"

"Yes, but as I said, I haven't seen anything like this. It's like flu but much, much worse. It's not looking good for most of them."

McNara nodded and moved back through the door, ripping off his facemask when safely outside.

"Keep me informed. I'll let my superiors know."

"I'll need more medical supplies and help—a trained virologist. I don't know what we're dealing with here. We should also try and contain it by stopping all training and have the troops confined to barracks!" I shouted after him.

He assured me he would do his best but was already walking away as if to put as much distance between himself and the hospital block as possible.

March 12th

My first entry in almost two weeks.

We have been overwhelmed with what can only be described as some kind of plague. There were over five hundred sick after the first week, and I have stopped counting now. Hundreds are dying.

Most of the patients have symptoms typical of a flu virus: headaches, body aches, muscle and joint pain, sore throats, and very bad coughs. Harsh breathing is also common.

As if some kind of harbinger of death facing us all, the sky turned black a few days ago. You could not see the sun, and the worst dust storm ripped through the entire area.

As if things weren't bad enough.

I have only been to see the major general once again about the situation.

We are, simply put, completely swamped, and each time he nods his understanding and promises help, but then nothing happens at all.

The general consensus is that it is a virus as opposed to a bacterial strain, and I have heard that there are outbreaks at some other military camps here in the US.

But can we just go ahead on hearsay and rumour? No, of course not.

All I'm asking is for some kind of research into this illness so that we have a strategy to try to combat it.

Another insanity that the major general will not discuss (because it is confidential) is the rumour that the 89th and 10th Divisions are to set sail for France anytime now.

This is ridiculous!

Some of those troops, even if they are showing no symptoms, could be carriers of the disease.

March 14th

Today I was walking past the major's office, and I saw an official government car with Washington number plates drawn up.

A small man wearing a tailored suit—in his twenties, I would say, with black curly hair—greeted by the MG himself, no less!

Doctor Berg told me he was there for several hours, and as the old devil is romantically involved with the MG's reception-ist, I have asked him to let me know if he hears of anything. All he could tell me was the man's name was Wes Helms, and to swear on my life to keep this information to myself.

I agreed, of course, and kept that name to memory.

I am pouring myself a strong drink and am going to write a letter to one of the leading pathologists, Doctor Granger, based in Boston, with a detailed description of the symptoms. I feel the need to take action on my own as my requests seem to fall on deaf ears.

God knows why when you look at the state of the camp.

March 22nd

My wife, Inga, has been taken ill and caught this cursed flu. She is almost purple in the face and is suffering terribly, choking and retching. I have managed to get her isolated from the other patients and am doing everything I can for her, but she only gets worse.

One of the nurses is kindly looking after the children when she is not working, and I am desperately trying to make arrangements to get them away from the camp.

Every night, my dreams are becoming darker and more suffocating. An albatross drags me under a black sea, and I sink deeper with no control over my body. As my lungs flood with that black liquid, I wake up shouting out, covered in sweat, as if the pneumonia is clawing at my skin, wanting to infect me.

And then I remember my beautiful wife suffering in her sick bed, and I rush to her. My guilt over Beatrice is rearing its head. Was this some kind of reckoning? Some kind of judgement?

My small office is now plastered with notes and drawn diagrams regarding the virus, and I managed to get hold of some laboratory equipment through a friend of Berg.

When I am not tending to the sick, including Inga, I am conducting my own research. There are plenty of dead to take samples from, and over five hundred cases and growing.

I sectioned off part of the morgue to carry out my own tests on one of the bodies. They have taken to doing mass funerals with very little notice for families, which is a sign of the desperate times.

One body belonging to the unfortunate Harold Fairbrother, who has no immediate family to protest my research, had experienced massive pulmonary haemorrhages.

His lungs were swollen, and the spleen was oversized. I am making extensive notes in a separate journal and trying to make some sense of this, as no one else seems to be!

April 2nd

Two days ago, my beloved wife and mother to Jonathan and Bert lost her battle with the vile sickness and passed from this world.

I am distraught and completely beside myself with sadness, anger, and rage.

I don't know what to say or how I feel, except that this despair and hollowness are eating me alive.

My mind keeps wandering back to our courtship in Sweden and those carefree days when we first met and fell in love.

All I see now is the deep, dark abyss of emptiness stretching down below me, vast and unconquerable. I was hardly getting any sleep when the outbreak hit, but now I can't imagine ever sleeping again.

One thing I know for sure is that I must stay strong for the boys.

They have been sent away to stay with the family of Doctor Berg, who kindly agreed to take them in. The camp is no place for them, and there is a distinct squalid air about the place.

Inga's was a very quick funeral, as there are so many others.

Only fifteen minutes were allowed! It seems so inhuman and undignified. I was angry at first, but then we lived in dark and extraordinary times.

April 5th

The pain of Inga's death lingers in my consciousness; there are still no words to describe my feeling, so I will not even try. I work through my shift, tending the streams of the sick and the dying with a newfound numbness that penetrates my entire soul.

I find some solace in the bottle. A sympathetic sergeant gave me an Irish whiskey I secured from supplies, and its fiery texture burns and brings a small amount of comfort.

Still unable to sleep, and it adds to my numbness, my madness. Inga was a fine woman and mother to my fine young boys. This mountain will be hard to climb. Yet for their sake, I shall try.

My research continues, and focusing on it seems to help.

April 9th

After my last diary entry, I received an urgent telegram from Franklin's mother, who is looking after the boys. The message itself hit the pit of my stomach and almost made me physically retch...

Chapter 18

4.05 AM, Present Day
CNI Madrid

Over the city, the sky was like a dark blue blanket beginning to transform into the orange glow of dawn. A dark SUV snaked through the back roads behind the CNI buildings, pulling up at the security block before being waved into the agency grounds.

Jamall, along with the two agents that had accompanied him to the city hospital, got out and moved towards the entrance in silence.

The man he had tracked to the hospital had somehow escaped, with injuries from the bomb as well as the bullet that had only winged him.

How had he managed to disappear after that?

Pure luck, Jamall surmised.

The game was interesting now; there was no doubt about it.

But Jamall didn't like losing. The mission had to be completed.

He needed to get more intel on this guy, some wannabe gangbanger by the look of him. Anyway, he had the professor's tablet and needed to be taken down ASAP.

Back in the control room, Ortez was nowhere to be seen,

which meant Jamall could get on with finding his target without the big moustache wagging in his ear.

The TV news continued to show drone footage of the accident scene, rerunning the same reports over and over again.

An operative nodded as he demanded data feeds from all CCTV, ATM cams, and in-store cameras around the hospital that fed into the central surveillance grid.

Then Jamall strolled to the front and faced the room, clapping his hands sharply three times. All eyes turned on the American agent as he transformed from an aloof figure to an animated showman.

"Everyone. Great work so far, but much more to do. We've all the feeds for a ten-block radius of the hospital. Our suspect was last seen at the southeast entrance at approximately 1400. Let's track him down and see where the rat has run to. I need not stress how time-sensitive this matter is.

"Update the timeline on the main screen with any sightings you get, and we'll tighten the noose. Your people are under siege and need you to make them proud more than ever!"

He paused and looked around the room in silence for a moment and then said more softly.

"Thank you for your time."

Jamall paced back to the alcove where Zara was skimming through footage from around the hospital.

Briefly, he inwardly thanked the executive surveillance orders that had been passed since 2001 that made his task so much easier. With each new "terrorist" scare or incident, the laws covertly expanded in the Western democracies, increasing in their octopus-like reach.

Jamall smiled. What did he care? They were mere cattle in the bigger scheme of things; clueless animals.

Once he had identity details on a subject, they would be able to plug into that person's entire online history, accessing phone records, email, GPS tracking data from cell phones, and whatever else he wanted.

Jamall sat down next to her and looked at the screen.

"What have we got?"

She double-tapped the file with her forefinger, and the CCTV began to run, showing the hospital entrance from that morning.

"Take us to 1402, and can we see the footage from the rear car park?" he said. Then he added, "Have we got a different angle?"

"No, that's as best we have."

There was a movement on the footage, and straightaway he knew the man on screen was the one he had chased. The bulldog-like head, the short, stocky frame. A tough son of a bitch, there was no doubt. A shirt rag covered his arm; it must have been the bullet that grazed him.

"Looks like he had some assistance," Zara said. With him was an athletic-looking young black woman with tied-back dreads.

Interesting. Another player on the field.

"Suspect with accomplice spotted near Avenue de Andalucia, heading west through the crowds," said the operator.

"Get enhancement on both of them and then run it through face rec quickly."

On the screen, the two figures got into a vehicle.

The built-in technology immediately identified the number plate, displaying it as clear as day.

Jamall cracked his knuckles.

"You know what to do," he clipped.

For him, the game was just beginning. His targets were so close he could almost smell them.

Chapter 19

The early morning sun had not yet risen above the Sierra Nevada foothills that served as a kind of wall on the northern side of the Andalusian farmland.

Starlings chirped as they flew overhead towards an old group of whitewashed houses that were tucked in amongst olive groves at the crest of a hill, beyond which the snowy caps of the Sierra Nevada mountains could be clearly seen.

Joe Bowen made his way down the hillside track alongside the stream that brought fresh water down from the ancient system of the Acequias channels that had either been built by the Romans or the Moors. No one was sure which.

The estate agent representing the sale of the land hadn't been sure, but either way, it was pure genius.

It had indeed been the Stone Age system of bringing the snowmelt from the Alpujarras into vast aquifers feeding the rivers and springs and controlled by partidors, a crude but effective system of bricks and mortar to distribute the water flow to different regions. The potential of that water source, ideal for a community stronghold in Southern Europe, made the location perfect.

Joe stopped, brushed a hand through his trimmed beard, and looked through the binoculars that hung around his neck, peering at the flat valley below that was like a laid-out patchwork quilt of fields.

Farther down the hill, Hanna stopped walking and glanced back up towards him expectedly and then waved when she realised he had her in his sights.

Beyond her, another two men, Marcus and Javier, both wearing short-sleeve shirts and slacks, continued their stumbled walk down towards the riverbed that lined the bottom of the slope.

Joe was dressed in stark contrast to them in knee-length shorts, a military-green T-shirt, and sandals. His black curly hair and beard gave him an unkempt appearance.

Those that didn't know him would never have guessed he was ex-military.

He continued walking while Hanna waited for him, flashing a smile, her dreadlocks tied up into a bun, the contours of her body showing through the tight, patterned dress. In direct contrast, she wore military-style boots that drew attention to her calves. Meeting her had definitely been a lucky strike, Joe surmised.

She was the intelligent and smart woman he had always wanted to be with. They met when a nearby travelling convoy had camped farther down the river at an impromptu party.

Bonfires had been lit, music drifted through the night, and a cocktail of drink and drugs had fuelled the revelry. She had been chatting to a few of the travellers, but her gaze always returned to him.

Joe had never been approached by a woman as he had always been the chaser, the one who made the selection and decided who he wanted in his life, not the other way around.

Maybe that was why he had been slightly star-struck by her.

Her confidence and allure made a big impression on him.

"It's beautiful," she said.

Joe gestured to the patchwork of fields below them.

"And if we can get this farmland or make a deal with the farmers, there's a good food source. Definitely enough for a large community."

They crossed the clay riverbed and passed through a line of orange trees to a neat arrangement of fields. The hoses were gushing out water into the freshly dug earth. Joe knelt down and scooped up a mound of soil in his large, burly hands, feeling it between his fingers.

He looked around, nodding slowly to himself, and then stood back up.

Marcus, the elderly black man, grinned and slapped Joe on the shoulder.

"See I told you, my man. What did I tell you?"

Just then, the satellite phone on Joe's belt began vibrating, and he glanced at the number before answering.

"Si, Sphinx."

"Nightowl. I hope all is well in paradise?"

"It's all good, all good. How can I help?" he asked quickly.

He was concerned about authorities being able to listen in despite the encryption precautions they had taken and wanted to spend as little time as possible on the phone.

He nodded and listened for twenty seconds or so.

"OK, leave it with me. There may be someone that can help. I'll get back to you." He cut the call short and looked around at his companions.

"I have to do something. Shall we head back to the house?"

Fifteen minutes later, Hanna, Marcus, and Javier were in the courtyard of the house, sheltering from the rising midmorning heat under a canopy that was supported by steel cables attached to the north-facing wall and the gated wall that surrounded the property.

The house itself was beautiful, although it had seen better days. Nestled into the hillside, it gave a commanding view of the surrounding landscape. It was the gem that Joe had been looking for, and now it had been bought and paid for. His work here could really start.

Under them, they could hear the stream gushing down to the fields as they sipped lemon water and talked through their day so far.

Joe went out of the gates to the stony track that led up to the mountain road and poked around in his van for a laptop that looked like it had been through war—which, in fact, it had.

It was an ex-military intelligence kit. Something Joe loved to collect and a few of his ex-army friends had helped supply.

Grabbing another small metal box, he took the gear back into the cool house that was a labyrinth of rooms and hallways. Walking through a series of arched doorways, Joe headed down some wooden steps, the increase in humidity hanging heavy in the air. He arrived at a secluded alcove where the flashing green and blue lights from a bank of monitors winked in the darkness.

Joe placed his machine on one of the tables, opened up the chunky metal lid, and fired it up.

Going via a proxy server using the encrypted Tor browser, Joe logged on to the Icarus chat room. Tor-enabled anonymous communication that concealed a user's location from the preying eyes of network surveillance.

Icarus, an encrypted app for secure communications, had been developed by Troy Rhodes.

Troy, the only son of John Rhodes, who founded Liberatus, had led the digital expansion of the group's projects, including the online presence of Liberatus News and WikiTruth, the platform to upload sensitive information, as well as Icarus.

He began typing on the screen.

"Calling Sirus. Nightowl requests your presence and favour. Are you in right now?"

He leaned back in the leather recliner and watched the cursor flash on the screen.

After several minutes, he still had no response. Where the hell was she? He checked his watch: 11.37 am central Euro time, so it was 6.37 pm in Tehran.

Quite possibly, she was offline. He rose from his seat when a beep indicated Sirus was typing.

Text appeared on the screen:

"Good to hear from you, Nightowl. What news? How's little Z?"

Joe sat back down and rapped fingers onto the keyboard.

"All good, all good. And progress couldn't be better. Got a little challenge for you."

"Really? I love your challenges :)"

Joe smiled to himself. If anyone could hack it, she could. He proceeded to outline the situation. Sirus didn't ask what was on it. If she was being asked, it must be important.

He passed on the IP address and coordinated so Sirus could communicate directly with Gianna—and if needed, she could go in remotely from her station.

A message appeared on the screen: "Leave it with me."

Joe cut the connection and went back up the steps, intending to join the others. His mobile chirped, and a message told him to get back to Icarus urgently. He raced down the steps and logged back on to read a message from Sirus:

"There's a big problem. Your friends are about to be raided."

Chapter 20

5.13 AM
Madrid

Gianna saw the phone buzz on the coffee table and grabbed it, knowing it was Joe.

"You sure do move fast," she said, impressed.

"Forget that for now. You need to get out of there. We picked up the chatter, and you're about to get an unfriendly visit."

"What?"

"Your local agency picked you up; they have your details." Joe paused. "I'm sorry, but they seem to know everything."

"Fuck!"

She couldn't believe it. Over the years, she had been so bloody careful. She'd modified old equipment to stay away from the big-tech surveillance and been extra careful when using comms, and now all of that had gone to shit.

"Listen carefully," the voice at the other end spoke low and evenly. "Head to the first place in España where we ran into each other again, you remember?"

"Yep, I sure do," she said under her breath.

"Move your ass. Get out of there...and don't forget to bring your new friend."

The line disconnected, and Gianna looked at Hugo, who was staring at her with a puzzled look on his face.

"Shit! Shit! Shit! They tracked us down; we have to bounce," said Gianna, eyes wide.

"Already?"

Gianna pointed to a cupboard door next to the kitchen.

"There's a backpack hanging up in there. It's already got stuff in, ready to go. Grab it, and there's another spare empty one for yourself. I need to wipe some hard drives. We have to get out of here fast!" Her voice was tense with an undertone of fear.

Hugo went to grab the bags as Gianna tapped a screen to wake up one of the computers resting on the main table and immediately began tapping on the command prompt window.

Hugo came back with the bags and put Batchman's tablet into the empty one.

"OK, there you go. What have you gotta do?"

"Running a script called 'scorched earth' to fry my entire network and drives. I don't want them to find anything!" She hit return, and on her screen, a series of progress bars became active.

She ran to her bedroom, swearing out loud. The sound of crashing drawers hitting the floor punctured the whole apartment as Gianna frantically looked for something.

"Do me a favour!" she shouted. "As soon as that program completes, unplug everything in sight."

"Hey, I'm not being funny, but this is no time to pack your favourite clothes." A silence told him Gianna had decided to ignore him, and sighing, he walked to the screen to check her programme—only 5 percent.

"This is slow as shit. We're gonna be here all day."

"I need to find one thing. I can't leave without it!"

Hugo moved over to the window, peeking through the blind. The prospect of being arrested or shot by some police snatch squad made him anxious.

"Even if that means getting busted? Let's fucking go already!"

Gianna started throwing open a series of small drawers, quickly rifling through one before moving on to the next.

Then, more calmly. "Look, go and wait in the car if you want. I'll be right there."

She rifled around in her jeans pocket and threw him the keys, which Hugo caught and then stared at in his palm, hesitating.

The thought of Ponytail busting through the door and shooting him again made him want to run. However, there was something about this crazy girl, some sort of security that he felt from being with her.

He sighed.

"I'll wait."

Moments later, she rushed back into the living room as Hugo turned from the screen. He noticed she was clutching some kind of chain in her hand.

***

5.45 AM

Jamall crouched in the hallway, holding an MP-9 subma-chine gun with a couple of extra magazines, each holding thirty rounds deep in his inside coat pockets.

Lined up along the wall ahead of him, heavily armed black-clad masked men of the CNI military wing waited for the word through their earpieces.

He was in that forest again, a boy running through the woodland.

Aim, fire, manoeuvre.

The barking orders snapping at his heels, the drizzling rain hitting his face, one of many random memories that seemed to increase with each day.

Why now? Why were they coming back?

The black mass of uniforms suddenly sprang into motion and began moving down the hallway.

Two men took position outside the door.

With a quick hand signal, the enforcer stepped up, a large monster of a man who began pounding the battering ram against the door.

Jamall waited. His eyes focused on the dark shadows methodically pummeling away, the sounds reverberating throughout the house.

The door must have been reinforced because it felt like he was waiting there for an age.

Eventually, there was a crack, and the door frame gave into the force; another violent swing and the door crumbled in, a fountain of wooden splinters showering the ground.

Figures rushed inside; only the sound of their rustling fatigues could be heard.

No shouts or grunts, just pure determined professionalism. Jamall was quietly impressed as he followed them in.

It wasn't a big apartment, and within fifteen seconds, they had established the terrorist suspects were not there.

Jamall pushed past several armed men towards the window and looked out of the blind onto the courtyard below and a dusty back street. Several black vans he knew to be undercover CNI were parked, out of which a small crew of military police had assembled to cover the back. They had escaped, for now.

Jamall cocked his head slightly, studying an old chunky computer monitor in its yellowing plastic casing resting on a large desk. His eyes diverted to a movement on the windowsill, visible through the bottom of the blind.

The patterned orange and black wings of a butterfly fluttered slightly as it settled on the ledge. He almost stopped breathing, watching its serene composure, and moved suddenly along-side the desk towards the window, knocking it slightly.

A glass tipped and smashed on the floor, but Jamall ignored it, eyes fixed on the beautiful wings as they fluttered into life, disturbed by the vibration.

With fluent grace, the insect drifted into the air and then disappeared from view.

Jamall turned around to see some of the policemen glancing at him and then quickly looked away.

There was a shout as the commander ordered his men out of the cramped apartment and walked over to Jamall, who was staring down at the shards of glass on the wooden floor.

"No suspects here. What do you want us to do?"

Jamall didn't look at him, his focus still on the floor. He brushed it aside with his shoe.

"Search the entire building," he replied.

"That's a police matter. We're just here to..."

Jamall turned to face him, his dark eyes suddenly calm yet menacing.

"Search the house, Commander. These are dangerous people, and I wouldn't want the responsibility for their escape to fall on your...head."

The commander went to say something but thought better of it and nodded before heading towards the door.

Jamall fished out his mobile and spoke a single word—"Zimmer"—that auto dialled a number, and Zara answered.

"They're not here. Are you in front of a console?"

"Yes."

"Look at what kind of vehicle she has. Call me back when you have it, and email me the suspect's files."

"OK...are you going to..."

Jamall cut the connection, placed the mobile back inside his jacket pocket, and started pulling out drawers from the desk onto the floor.

A pile of batteries, old mobile phones, screwdrivers, and other stuff scattered across the wooden floorboards. He picked one of the mobiles, an old Nokia that must have been twenty years old, pre-smart technology. His thumb pressed the power button, but it was dead.

He glanced at a pile of plastic boxes that were filled with tech equipment and opened the lid. Pulling old leads and remote controls onto the floor, eventually, he found what he was looking for an old Nokia charger.

Plugging it into the wall, the phone gave a little beep as power started to flow into it. Satisfied, he continued fishing through the boxes for possible clues.

A senior police officer appeared at the doorway of the living room.

"Who's in charge here?"

Jamall ignored him as he studied the content on an e-reader—a list of e-books about conspiracies, avoiding surveillance, survivalism and general anti-establishment propaganda.

This girl must have been flagged up somewhere before now. Anyone sharing this kind of stuff with their readers were generally put on a list of persons of interest and had been for decades.

"I'm Mr Salazar, a special agent working with Director Ortez from CNI. You can have control of the scene when I'm finished," barked Jamal, his eyes never leaving the device.

The officer snorted, and Jamall heard him speak into his earpiece. "Connect me with headquarters. Some joker here fucking up my crime scene."

Jamall still hadn't looked at the policeman as he checked the Nokia spluttering into life. He scrolled to the contacts list, which had been wiped, and then to messages where it was the same story.

The analysis lab back in the motherland might be able to fish something out of it, but he didn't know what expertise they had here.

No time anyway.

He picked up another one of the mobiles and began to go through the same process, charging it to check for any clues.

The officer in charge stepped up to him, and Jamall noted the voice pattern had changed—more respectful although struggling to be apologetic.

"My superiors have confirmed you are who you say you are. Anything I can do?"

Jamall completely ignored him, his face a mask of indifference bordering on contempt for everyone around him as he focused on the old phone.

Inside his jacket, his own phone chirped. It was Zara calling, and he swiped to take the call.

"Anything?"

"You hung up on me. No one ever teach you manners?"

When there was no response, she continued.

"Gianna Madaki owns a Toyota Camry, white. It's an antique, so no onboard tracking. It shouldn't be hard to find. I've already put out an apprehension order on it."

"Good. We need to hunt them down quickly."

Chapter 21

6.55 AM

Gianna slammed her hand on the steering wheel. "Shit!"

"I'm sorry. I'm the reason you're deep in it, is that right?" Hugo said from behind her.

Gianna shook her head. "No, no. If it wasn't this, it would've been something else, y'know? I'm in all kinds of business, and I wasn't careful enough. Simple as."

Gianna had run this scenario through her head so many times, replaying what she would do when the knock at the door came. Now that it was finally happening, she was almost relieved.

Hugo was lying in the back seat again, watching a blur of whitewashed buildings and trees rush by.

"If they got your address, they'd know this car, won't they?" Hugo said, concern in his voice.

"You got that right. Which is why we have to dump it ASAP."

"What are we waiting for then?"

Gianna was glancing around, slowing the vehicle. "Need a quieter street without cameras." She spotted a bus and pulled the car over into a space.

"Think we need to jump on that bus," she said, nodding in

the direction of the vehicle.

They left the car and ran along the side of the road, Gianna taking the lead, the backpack that she had hastily packed bopping up and down on her shoulder.

She managed to get the driver's attention just before it pulled off, and the two of them got on, clambering into a seat. Hugo adjusted the cuffs on the long-sleeve shirt Gianna had given him, his muscles tight against the material as it was several sizes too small.

They had both donned baseball caps, the peaks pulled low over their foreheads to at least attempt to hide their faces. Both knew that modern facial recognition software could probably still flag them, but it should keep any member of the public from recognising them.

"A fucking bus; is this a good idea?" Hugo asked. "If they have the same setup as back in LA, we'll be stars on some fed camera feed by now."

"Look, Hugo, whatever we do, we're going to be seen. We just have to move faster than they are. This'll take us to central station. From there, we'll get out of the city. There is a plan."

Hugo shook his head. They wouldn't last ten minutes; he was sure of it.

"When were you gonna tell me this plan?"

"We haven't exactly had time to discuss it."

"And who were you talking to on the phone?" he asked.

Gianna looked offended. "A friend. Someone we can trust. Am I not helping you out here? I'm now running, too, remember?"

Hugo waved a hand in dismissal. "Hey, don't get me wrong. I appreciate all you've done for me, Gianna. I really do. I just wanna know what I'm running into next."

Gianna stared out at the passing Madrid streets.

Crowds of young Arab men hung around a plaza. These were some of the endless streams of Middle Eastern war refugees who had been appearing in countless European cities over the previous ten years.

A few hundred metres farther down the street, they passed a stationary van full of *policia*. Next to it were two armoured personnel carriers. A group of men stood around idly chatting, dressed in full black military fatigues, some of them wearing masked balaclavas.

A scene that had become an everyday sight in most European cities.

"Trust me. We're running to safety, Hugo. My friends are connected in these matters. If anyone can help us, it's them. The people we want to be running away from are the authorities. Running as fast as possible."

Hugo nodded, understanding.

A look of resignation fell across his face, a face drained with exhaustion. The reality of the situation seemed to stare back at him in the reflection of those police visors.

He felt it in the pit of his stomach, and now that he was being hunted, he would have to use every skill from the streets in LA to evade the wolves.

Chapter 22

7.12 AM

Jamall sat upright in the back of the CNI van that was equipped with the latest European state surveillance technology.

He had another one of Gianna's old phones in his hand, clicking through the contacts. It was the same as the others, wiped of anything useful apart from a few games.

The radio had a clear, crisp tone of local Madrid police comms. The description of the white Toyota was being passed around so patrol cars could keep an eye out for it.

Being such an old vehicle, it would hopefully stand out and perhaps not be too long until it was found.

He turned off the old phone and took out his own mobile, pulling up the files Zara had sent to his encrypted email.

Hugo's file appeared first, showing a mugshot of the bulldog-like face, closely cropped hair.

A gangbanger.

Interesting.

Ran with the Florence 13 crew, arrested once. Disappeared several months ago from the US and had obviously now popped up in Spain.

Jamall continued reading and then pulled up Gianna's file.

Born in Kenya and adopted by British foster parents then raised in London.

A few arrests for activism in her late teens.

Her passport trail showed worldwide travel for a couple of years before settling in Madrid, working as a tech consultant.

Recently added to an activist list by the Spanish authorities.

A fast-speaking voice from a patrol car came over the radio. They had found the Toyota in one of the calles of the Centro district. Instructions were passed on to the driver, and the vehicle turned and picked up speed.

They were there within five minutes, and the van screeched to a halt.

Jamall jumped out first and nodded to the officer who had found it and was now proudly standing guard.

He peered inside the rusty car. A sea of wrappers, empty soda cans, and other rubbish littered the floor.

The doors weren't locked, although it would've taken Jamall less than ten seconds to break in. He slipped into the passenger seat and looked around. Sometimes, valuable clues would be left behind.

The car had the same distinct smell of the apartment, almost like he'd walked into an old museum. He flipped down the window visor to let in air and opened the glovebox, where there were a stack of receipts and a few loose coins.

A few metres ahead of the car, he spotted the Metrobus shelter.

He reached underneath the steering window and found the button to the trunk, depressing it before stepping back out of the vehicle.

The boot just had a spare wheel and an old newspaper spread across the bottom; news from a few weeks ago.

A police car crawled up the road, and a couple of officers got out, blocking the road. Jamall gestured at them. "Seal off this street, and get a tow for the car. If anything turns up, let me know." Jamall was walking away as he spoke towards the bus stop.

His phone rang. Zara.

"I have footage from the cameras opposite where you are. They jumped on a bus."

"Did you see the number?"

"No. Impossible. It was obscured by a shop sign."

Jamall had reached the stop and scanned the timetable, looking at the routes. Most of the buses headed to the central station or past it. There were a few other buses that didn't, though.

He would have to play the numbers.

"What time does it show on your camera?"

"07:14."

"So long as the buses are running on time, there's a few possibilities; C1, N12, N15...Call the bus company, and get onto the drivers of those buses. They are only twenty minutes ahead of us, so there is a chance they are still on one of them. My money says they're bolting for the train station."

Jamall hung up the phone and paced back towards the white Toyota. They knew he was on their tail and were most likely attempting to get out of the city and away from all the cameras.

The train station was the obvious location, but did they really think they could slip out undetected? The vibration of his phone brought him back from his thoughts.

"Yes?"

"They were on the C1; the driver thinks he dropped them off at central station eleven minutes ago."

***

Jamall headed back to the van, clicking his fingers rapidly. It was only a matter of time before he'd catch up with them.

"Get over to the main train station, pronto," he demanded to the driver through the window before sliding into the back and slamming the door.

The vehicle dovetailed into the traffic, joining the main Ronda de Valencia road towards Central Station.

Jamall strolled a finger through his phone, tapping up maps, checking train lines and their times for the next hour. Zara's name appeared on the screen, along with the familiar low ringtone.

"Yes?"

"You were right. We have footage of them at the station, buying train tickets."

"Run a card check on that girl's name for a transaction."

"Already done. They bought tickets for the 12.15 to Barcelona."

Jamall quickly checked his watch. Ten minutes time, they weren't going to make it.

"We need a team waiting at the next station. We've got to stop it. Can you check the next stop it makes?"

There was a pause while Zara did as he asked." 'It's Guadalajara."

"Right. Get a team over there. No one gets off, and keep the train at the station until I arrive. Fail me in this, and there will be consequences."

"It's not going anywhere," Zara replied, and the phone went dead.

Chapter 23

"Can you hotwire a car?" Gianna looked over his shoulder at Hugo.

They were both crouched low in the train station car park, between cars, attempting to stay out of sight from the CCTV cams. After purchasing the tickets to Barcelona, they had doubled back out of the station via the quietest exit.

Hugo laughed a little too loudly, considering they were trying to lie low.

"You been watching old black-and-white movies or something? Most cars have immobilisers and have done for years. They're all rigged into the smart grid anyway. Unless it's a real banger from way back, then that would be a piece of cake."

"I know they're all on the *traffic hub*. Why do you think I had an old car? Anyway, whatever. We need some wheels. I just wondered if you knew how to steal one."

"So, you want to start breaking the law now? Stealing cars. What next, huh, G?"

Gianna turned to look at Hugo, ready to argue and noticed the wry smile on his face. A few rows down, they heard the slam of a door.

Hugo stepped up and slapped Gianna on the shoulder, pulling his cap lower. "Watch this."

He started casually walking back across towards the station entrance.

A few metres away from him a young man in a suit had just locked his SEAT Toledo, pocketed the fob, and then began to walk in the same direction towards the station.

Hugo was a few steps ahead and began to search his jean pockets as if he had lost something.

He turned suddenly and bumped into the guy. The city slicker began to gabble in Spanish as Hugo held up one hand apologising, walking back towards the car park.

He looked over at Gianna, grinning, but wasn't heading towards her—instead making a beeline to the car. He glanced behind and then held out a key fob. The Toledo bleeped to life, and Hugo opened the driver's door.

He looked over at Gianna, who was staring back, suppressing a smile.

"What are you doing crawling around on the ground? Looking for spare change? Let's go."

Hugo started the engine and threw his baseball cap onto the back seat. Ten minutes later, they were on the A-5 Autovía heading south, the cityscape of Madrid in the rear mirror.

"Whichever route we take, we want to end up in Seville."

"And we cannot keep this car. As the owner was heading to the station, I'm guessing we have a bit of time?" Hugo was picking up speed to adjust to the new limit on the motorway.

Gianna found the pay and display ticket on the dashboard and glanced at it. "He's got a six-hour ticket. So, I guess that's our limit before he calls it in."

An endless sprawl of industrial warehouses gave way to the expanse of the sandy-coloured Spanish landscape punctured by electric pylons that dotted off into the distance. A crisp, blue infinite sky opened up overhead.

"We're coming up to tolls pretty soon."

"Do they take cash? I might still have coins."

Gianna snorted with laughter.

"Who takes cash? "

"You got a way of paying for this toll then?"

She nodded. "No problem. Luckily, I have a prepaid card in a different identity. I think every liberal aware citizen should carry one."

She pulled out a transparent card with a bank logo imprinted on the top and held it between her two fingers, flashing Hugo a cheeky grin.

They approached the toll booths, traffic forming orderly queues. Hugo aimed for one in the middle.

"Shit! Over there," Hugo said. Gianna followed his eyes and spotted the familiar black-and-white police vehicle parked on the far side, facing the incoming traffic.

"Hopefully, they're not looking too hard."

An uneasy silence pervaded the car as they edged towards their booth. Hugo lowered his driver-side window and took Gianna's card to swipe. After a few minutes, they were on their way again, collectively sighing with relief.

"So, what do you think is in that encrypted folder?" Gianna asked, glancing at Hugo. She was rifling through her backpack for water.

"I'm damned if I know. Not sure I wanna know, to lay the truth on you, Gianna."

Gianna looked unimpressed. "Yeah, but assuming you need to know..."

Hugo let out a long sigh.

"That vato, Nicky Batchman, was in deep with the flu virus.

I mean, he and the virus were really good friends, from what he was saying. We saw some of that diary, right? And all those notes to do with his research. Whatever he's encrypted has to be the same shit...but more secret."

"Yeah, judging by the fact that guy was trying to kill you. Any idea who *he* is?"

"The ponytail? No idea, but he's an expert in everything he does...he's good, I know that much."

"Probably one of the government agencies...MI6, Mossad, or CIA. Did you hear him speak or anything? Any clue about his accent?"

Hugo shook his head. "But your friend knows someone who is. So, who is your friend Joe? This guy I can 'trust' with my life, who I've never met. You know how well that sits with me?"

"I think we already had this conversation," said Gianna, staring out across the dry landscape.'

"Tell me, Gianna. If the shoe was on the other foot, what would you be thinking?"

Gianna was silent so long Hugo thought she hadn't heard him. Only the purring engine and the hiss of the AC filled the space.

Gianna sighed quietly.

"Put it this way. He saved my life...I'm pretty sure he did. I'm sure I was going to get killed that day."

"How do you mean?"

"I was at a civil rights march in Boston. There were a few hundred. An old homeless man beaten to death by a group of cops. I couldn't stand by and not do anything. I believe if you're on the fence about these things, then you are allowing it to happen.

"The march was peaceful enough for most of it, making its way through the town's main streets against a backdrop of the demands from a megaphone to stir the rhythm of chants.

"Alongside the marchers, set back on the sidewalk, masked police pointed face recognition cameras. I knew what the tech did: scanning, linking to their central database, and pulling out known activists in real time. That's why I was masked.

"There was a main street that led to the federal courthouse.

"This was the same court where those murderers got acquitted. I looked down the side streets, and all of 'em were blocked by riot police with shields, looking like bloody robocops. I had a bad feeling straightaway. You know, when your heart sinks 'cos there's defo gonna be trouble ahead?"

Hugo nodded, remembering incidents from the Firestone days. "Yeah, I've been there too many times. Sounds like it was about to explode."

"Hmmm, a true description. The tension was electric. Straight ahead, our way to the court was blocked by another row of police. There were surveillance drones hovering overhead.

"I moved to the outside of the crowd, suddenly wary about getting crushed. There were a few men in the crowd: masked, dressed in black fatigues, military boots.

"They were undercover, I'm sure of it. I read about them pulling that kind of shit but still couldn't believe it when I saw it with my own eyes. They hurled glass bottles towards the front line, and then all hell broke loose.

"Someone let off a flare or something, and smoke hovered over the crowd.

"At the next side street, I nearly ran into a line of police; they had closed in bloody fast. Two of them began dragging stragglers away from the outside of the march so they could give them a kicking. Those nearby started screaming at them to stop, and more debris and bottles rained down on them.

"One of them turned their attention to me as I tried to back away.

"A wall of people behind hemmed me in. There was nowhere to go. I saw a baton, hard and fast. Then felt the electric shock of intense pain. All I could do was curl up into a ball, cover my head."

"Shit, sometimes that's all you can do," said Hugo. "Fucking bastards."

"So, that's when Joe must have come out of the coffee shop.

"I remember clearly getting a glimpse of him drop-kicking the copper, who shouted in pain. Next thing I know, I'm been dragged back.

"Apparently, the cop tried to come after us, but others moved in and blocked him. By that time, store windows were getting filled in. He carried me back into the coffee bar and demanded they let us out the back. That's what Joe told me later, although I was totally out of it."

"That sounds like a rough ride, G. And a close call."

Hugo glanced at the fuel gauge.

"Shit, we're low on gas, by the way."

"No drama; there's a station just there." Gianna gestured to it with a wave of her thin arm.

"We'd better get our baseball caps back on then in case of *dem cams*," he replied.

Chapter 24

Juan watched the numbers spin through their sequence on the petrol dial, barely taking in their meaning. Normally, he'd watch them like a hawk, making sure that he didn't go one cent over a rounded amount. There was nothing worse than having to break a nice rounded figure and end up paying a stupid amount like fifty euros and twenty-two cents.

But now he didn't give a flying shit and was struggling to hold in his emotions.

Was that body really her?

His daughter?

Of course, it was. He had seen her with his own eyes. She was dead, and he would never be able to speak to her again, never listen to her excited stories of university escapades, friends, and worries.

Never again would she be at the family table on her frequent visits home. Juan shook his head, knowing the tears were forming in his eyes. He couldn't shake the memory of her looking at him with *that look*.

"Are you taking me to the station, Papa?"

It seemed to echo in his head in a loop. If only he had! Just took her to the station, but then...maybe they would have missed the train. It was possible. If they had stopped for a drink...

Juan tried to snap out of it. He wasn't doing himself any favours, reliving some kind of alternative scenario that never happened.

The previous evening had been a whirlwind of fighting bureaucracy: signing papers and trying to make arrangements to get his daughter's body back to Zafra. Everyone in charge was completely overwhelmed, and that was the only thing that stopped Juan from breaking someone's neck in frustration.

Yes, he knew the situation; many had died, and the city's facilities were at breaking point, but he just wanted to get Elsa home—even if he had to drive her corpse back himself.

Eventually, one of the doctors signed off so she could be transported back and persuaded him to go home. After an hour of persistent persuasion, Juan finally agreed that everything was now in motion. He had tried to sleep on a row of seats in the stadium but, after an hour, had given up and headed to his car.

***

Juan sighed again, steadying his emotions, looking up at the rusting roof of the petrol station. The buzz of traffic drifted over from the main road, a constant hum of people going about their daily lives. Lucky for them. Would they ever feel remorse? The empty pit of loss?

A black car pulled into the forecourt in Juan's peripheral vision; his tank was full. He slotted the nozzle back into the pump and queued up inside the store to pay, eyes scanning the newspapers on the side stand, the train explosion dominating the front pages. There were still frames from the news drone footage showing the burning train and a scene of confusion from above. It had been confirmed as a terrorist attack.

Juan swallowed hard and looked away, his eyes drifting out to the forecourt at a young bullish guy filling up his vehicle. Something flickered in his memory.

A young black woman with tied-back dreads got out and opened the boot for something before sliding back into the passenger seat.

At the makeshift morgue, he had spent some time flipping through the online police hub that fed through encrypted updates to any verified police employees.

Naturally, there had been a lot of chatter about the train attack, and then CNI released photos and identities of several suspects. Juan got out his mobile and checked again. From what he could see, one of the images matched the man in the forecourt.

He read through the information on them.

The bulldog was called Hugo Reese, a criminal from the States and a total scumbag, no doubt. The black girl was from Madrid, Gianna Madaki, some activist.

It was them.

Although it had not yet been made public, they had been named as the main culprits in Spain's worst terrorist atrocity since the eerily identical attack in 2004.

Juan looked up at the man and woman on the forecourt again, the pain of his loss slowly draining away, replaced by darkening hatred.

Chapter 25

The surrounding road and small car park at Guarajuara train station looked like a scene from a Hollywood movie.

Around ten police cars with flashing lights were clogging up every inch of the road. Alongside were military vehicles, where a team of soldiers waited for orders.

A stream of tape cordoned off the entrances, and everyone in the station had been evacuated. They stood around farther down the road, arguing with a few equally confused police officers.

Jamall shouted at the driver to stop immediately as he slid open the rear door to the van and jumped out. He marched through the crowd, flashing badges at anyone who stopped him. Once past the scrum of police, it was surreally quiet inside; he continued through to the platform.

There was a welcome cool breeze coming down the line as he stepped up to the edge and peered up the tracks.

He opened his jacket and let the air circulate inside.

"What took you so long?"

Zara's voice behind him. Jamall didn't turn, his gaze locked on a glint of an approaching train in the distance.

"I don't know. How did you beat me here?"

"I commandeered a motorcycle. Remember? It's the only

reliable way to get around a big city, especially after a terrorist attack."

Jamall spat onto the rail line and turned around.

"Let's get some guns aimed at that train. We need to get these guys, even if it means killing everyone on board."

"We'll get them. If they try to run, they won't get far."

A line of armed police came through onto the platform. The commander, whom Jamall had met at Gianna's flat, spoke into a walkie-talkie, giving orders as the train pulled in.

Once the train had stopped, a row of faces looked out in shock as they saw a stream of armed police begin to board the train at either end, along with demands for identity papers from the passengers.

Jamall stepped onto the train, strolling down the corridor, his eyes flicking across to each face as they stared back up at him in a mixture of fear and curiosity.

He took in each face, every detail, recording it to his memory. Eyes glancing ahead, he spotted a male with shaved head facing away from him.

He fitted the suspect's description.

Jamall grabbed the man's shoulder, his hand on the handle of his Glock inside his jacket, ready to press it against the man's head in a flash.

The man turned, frowning with a look of indignation that quickly turned to surprise as he saw the dark eyes of Jamall staring down at him.

It wasn't Hugo Reese.

There was a pause, and Jamall said nothing before moving on up the train.

Walking only three carriages, Jamall soon reached the end of the short train quickly. No sign of them. He walked back to the toilet he had passed and slammed the side of his fist on the bathroom button.

Empty.

He walked more slowly back down the carriages, scanning the passengers more carefully this time, but he was now certain they weren't on the train.

Jumping back out onto the platform, Jamall spat on the dusty ground.

What have you missed? You are the hunter. Then hunt!

His mobile vibrated in his inside jacket pocket, and he fished out the phone, hesitating for a moment as he saw the word Red displayed on the screen.

"Agent Haydes," Jamall said, answering with his call sign.

There was a moment's silence and then a click. Jamall knew that encrypted calls were necessary for any communications.

"What is the status of White Horse?"

"Two suspects are close to being apprehended, but we need more time. They were supposed to be on the train..."

"Look, Jamall. You had best take control of the situation. The main asset we're interested in is the device that has White Horse. Do you understand?" The voice was low and menacing.

Jamall stared at Zara; she was walking up the platform along the train, looking through the windows.

"I understand." The line clicked and died.

Zara reached him and stopped, her hand on her hips, looking at Jamall questioningly.

Jamall shook his head at her unasked question.

"No fucking dice. Must have never gotten on the train. And that was Doctor Red expressing his concern."

Chapter 26

Hugo drove as Gianna played with the tablet, swiping and cursing out loud as she continued to try to hack the encrypted document herself.

Eventually, she gave up and placed it back into his rucksack. They continued down the A-5 that traversed westward; their plan was to head south towards Seville.

Hugo switched on the radio and ran the tuner. A tinny pop tune belted out. The next station was local: a discussion on whether there was still enough being done to combat terrorism despite the escalating laws that had been brought in since 9/11.

"Won't hear any good news from that thing. State-sponsored propaganda and brain-dead manufactured pop for the masses."

Hugo sighed and switched it off. "What?"

"The main news stations are all controlled by the state. Whether you're here, in England, or in the States. We're only going to hear one thing from them: how we are the terrorists that need to be hunted down and how they need to declare martial law or some shit to find us."

"I hear you, but I just wanted to find out what they were saying. It might help us."

"Won't help at all, Hugo."

Gianna nodded to the next exit.

"We need to get off the motorway ASAP. Let's take this one."

Hugo weaved the car into the exit lane, keeping his speed steady.

"Of course, *Lib News* tried to stay on track with some real truths. Got targeted by the authorities real hard, though," Gianna continued.

Hugo nodded. He had remembered something on his radar about Liberatus News, an online TV channel that had itself been in the news lately, the UK and US governments pushing to have it closed down.

Something like that.

"What was that about?" he asked.

"They tried to say Lib News was an activist channel helping incite anti-government sentiment across the West. What they were really afraid of was they were exposing some grim truths of what has been going on."

"What kind of 'grim truths' are you talking about, G?"

"Where do I start? Just the *Matrix* we're living under. Controlled and moulded from the shadows. The education system, the military, monetary policy, and Big Pharma: all controlled," Gianna almost spat with contempt.

"Conspiracies?"

"Yeah, conspiracies. Did you know conspiracy theory was originally a term made up by the CIA to discredit those who questioned the Warren Report? The label of conspiracy the-orist is used to this day to attack anyone who challenges the 'official' narrative."

"Hmm. Heavy shit. So, err, what's the Warren Report?"

Gianna sighed. "A whitewashed report about the JFK assas-sination."

"Right. So, they made up the term?"

"Look it up if you want. Anyone that questions anything is labelled a tin foil hat-wearing nutter, so they can just keep rolling on with their agenda without giving a solitary shit. Look at all this surveillance we have now. Our phones, TVs, cars, everything is spying on us. That was a conspiracy theory until Snowden blew it wide open."

"Snowden?"

"Wow, have you been living in a cave? He was a legendary whistleblower that had leaked NSA info about the mass surveillance going on. And about fourteen years before that, in the 1990s, Liberatus News broke the story from the GCHQ whistleblower, Sarah Edwards, about their entire plan. Joe's father, Frank, was mixed up in all that. Soon after, WikiTruth was set up by Troy Rhodes, a portal for anonymous information to be uploaded and released. That opened the gates for more whistleblowers to come forward."

"This is the same Joe we're supposed to be hooking up with?" asked Hugo.

"The very same." Gianna pointed to a road sign.

"Let's turn off for Talavera de la Reina. We want to keep heading South, but maybe we should ditch the car there?"

"Yeah. Sounds like a good idea," replied Hugo. "I'm feeling extra paranoid after your conspiracy theories chatter." He gave Gianna a lopsided grin.

Gianna switched on the radio.

"I thought you didn't like the radio, G?"

"Yeah, well, I just need to try and find info on the trains. Sometimes it can be useful."

There was a voice of a man running through the events. The train explosion was believed to be terrorists, and a man was being sought. A source from the Madrid police department claimed that roadblocks had been set up as the suspects are believed to be in a vehicle.

They exchanged a glance.

The man on the radio continued to mention that most trains were re-running again—but with delays as security had been raised at Madrid train stations.

"That might be good for us. More crowds, easier to keep low," said Gianna.

"Or bad for us. More security. More chance of getting caught," Hugo responded.

"Let's take a look."

They drove the black SEAT Toledo into Talavera de la Reina and reached a roundabout.

"Turn right here. We can ditch it somewhere quiet," said Gianna.

After a few turns, they found a quiet street and parked the car, put on their baseball caps, grabbed their bags, and headed in the direction of a nearby hospital through the quiet suburban *calles*.

After a few minutes, they reached a busier street, where a row of shops stood, striped canopies offering shade to a couple of elderly locals who sat in fold-out chairs outside, watching the early morning commuters and gossiping.

Gianna spoke quietly.

"There's a clothes shop. I'll go in and get us some gear."

"OK, I'll stay low over there." He pointed to a bench on a strip of grass shaded by overhanging trees, looking forward to chilling for five.

Gianna wandered into the store and looked around. She grabbed a couple of zip-up trainer tops, roughly guessing

Hugo to be a medium, and picked a couple of new shirts from a round rack.

Placing them on the counter, she took out a large euro note, avoiding the gaze of the middle-aged shop assistant.

She felt her eyes on her for a moment, panic slowly rising at the thought she may have been recognised.

Had they implicated her in the attacks?

Was her face now being blasted out on all the different media channels?

As soon as the assistant had de-tagged them, Gianna hastily grabbed the bag of clothes and left the note on the counter, hurrying out the shop and calling over her shoulder to keep the change.

Back on the street, Gianna steadied herself, took a deep breath, and headed for where Hugo was sitting.

"It's all in your head; stay calm," she said. Hugo looked up at her, weariness evident across his face.

I've got us a few things. Let's find somewhere to change and freshen up."

Hugo nodded and slowly pushed himself to his feet. They walked for a few minutes and entered the first bar they came to. Gianna handed Hugo the bag and nodded in the direction of the toilets.

"You get changed, and I'll get us some tapas. Anything you don't like?"

"Right now, I could eat anything, G. Grab me a cafe solo as well. I might fall asleep if I don't get some caffeine in my system."

After ordering an array of *patatas bravas*, chorizo, and tortilla slices, Gianna sat down and brought out Batchman's tablet, using it to check the news.

A quick search revealed what info had been released about the events earlier in the day. Hugo sat down, looking slightly more alive after freshening up.

"Bad news, I'm afraid," Gianna said, turning the screen so he could see.

The grainy image was clearly Hugo, with 'Main suspect in Terror attacks' in bold above it.

Hugo stared hard at the screen for a second, his eyes widening. He glanced around and slowly pulled his cap down lower over his head.

"Shit! This is a nightmare. What the hell is happening? They have anything on your involvement?"

"No, the article just says 'may be working with accomplices.' We shouldn't linger. Get some of this food inside you, and let's get moving again."

Soon they were on the go again, keeping as much to the back streets as possible. At the end of a narrow road, they came to a small roundabout outside the train station—a tall red brick building with arch windows—a line of cars parked in front of it.

There was another road that ran parallel to the station and a rail line and merged with the roundabout.

They loitered halfway down the road in a doorway, pretending to check out their phones.

There were people coming and going, and although it looked fairly busy, there didn't seem to be the heightened security they expected.

"What do you think?" Hugo asked.

"It looks quiet enough. I'd say the police around here aren't on the ball with the media frenzy," Gianna said.

Hugo nodded. "I say we go in separately and buy our tickets.

Keep our heads down and meet on the platform."

"Si, except maybe it's a good idea not to communicate on the platform. Wait until we're on board the train."

"OK. Let's do it. Who's going first?"

"That'll be you, amigo."

Hugo gave Gianna a look and then shrugged and set off towards the station entrance, casually strolling and swinging his arms as if taking a Sunday stroll.

Then his mood changed quickly.

"Mierda!"

A police car rolled up along the road by the rail tracks and pulled up outside the station entrance just as Hugo reached the doors.

He cursed under his breath and walked up to the ticket booth, and asked for a single Huelva.

Casually turning, he eyed the police car outside, beyond which he could spot Gianna, with her head down, following his route.

The policemen didn't get out and seemed to be casually talking to each other as if discussing football.

Hugo turned back around, paid for his ticket, and then walked on towards the platform. He was hoping to grab another coffee but wanted to put as much distance between himself and the cops as possible.

Glancing over his shoulder, he saw Gianna at the window getting her ticket, and behind her could see a bald guy leaning over, saying something to the police.

That's right, ese, you keep them busy.

For a second, he thought the man glanced in his direction. Was he looking at him?

Stay frosty, Bruh. Just paranoia kicking in.

Or was it his street sense?

Hugo stepped onto the quiet platform, his instinct taking him to the far end where he could spot anyone coming and had an easy escape route. Sitting down on a bench, he closed his eyes, the trail of the day's events spinning in through his mind.

What a truly fucked-up end to a holiday, huh?

Looking up, he could see more people coming onto the station and milling around.

Where was Gianna?

She should have been here by now. Was something wrong?

The thought of her in danger had his senses on full alert: his mouth felt dry, and he could feel the perspiration on his palms.

That cop car. Had that bald guy warned the police? Were they questioning her downstairs now? Hugo kept his eyes firmly fixed on the entrance.

Would they walk through now, guns drawn? Ready to take him down, shoot first and ask questions later?

Hugo weighed up his options. He could bolt now, get ahead of any shit that might be going down.

It could all be in his head, though, so maybe he should just go and see.

That could lead him straight into their hands. As more people walked onto the platform, Hugo eyed them all cautiously, looking for any tell-tale signs of them being official.

It's all in your head!

Reaching into his backpack, he grabbed a bottle of water and drank deeply. Placing the bottle back, he realised the tablet was not there. Gianna still had it. Now, if the cops had her, they had it as well!

Was he now a hunted man for nothing?

The info on the device was obviously really important and might be the only thing that he could negotiate with.

Was Gianna a plant?

Stringing him along to get the device?

So, she turns up out of the blue and offers to help him. Her mysterious friend calls and says they're about to get raided, and they've been on the run since.

Did he have any real evidence? He's just taken her word on all accounts.

Hugo shook his head. No, the girl was the real deal. Something must have happened to her.

A train was approaching—the one they needed to catch.

Standing up, Hugo began walking towards the entrance. His heart picked up the pace and hammered in his chest. Can he do much against two armed police? Different scenarios kept running through his mind as he neared the corner.

Then Gianna appeared, casually walking onto the platform with a coffee in her hand.

All the fear drained away almost as quickly as it had arrived. Glancing up, Gianna gave him the briefest of smiles before walking away from him.

More people drifted into the station as the train pulled in. Hugo shook his head, the relief evident, equally frustrated at his own paranoia.

Shit's fucking with your head, Bruh. Gotta keep calm if you're gonna get through this.

The doors slid open, and after a few people got off, he stepped on. The older-model train was dated and showing signs of wear. Making his way up the aisle, Hugo slipped into a table seat.

Let's hope this journey is less eventful than the last.

Chapter 27

Juan checked his phone, scrolling through the online police files, once again checking the photographs of the latest terrorist suspects.

Glancing down the train aisle, he could see the backs of their heads: Hugo Reese and Gianna Madaki—the people responsible for his daughter's death?

The things he'd like to do to them. His thoughts turned to how much pain he could bring to their lives.

His daughter would still be alive, still be part of his life, if it wasn't for those two.

If it was them?

He couldn't be 100 percent certain. Somehow, he would need to make a positive identification.

Once he had spotted them at the service station hours before, Juan had to really use every ounce of self-restraint not to pull out his police-issue Glock and blow them both away right in the middle of the forecourt.

The air con of the store had brought calm, and he made the decision to stay out of sight and track them every inch of the way. Juan had then returned to his car, careful not to be seen by the two suspects as he called them in on his radio to the central police network.

He had identified himself as the police chief of Zafra and gave them the situation, reporting that he had sighted the possible train-bombing suspects heading towards Talavera de la Reina, along with their vehicle car licence plate number.

The black woman had paid for their gas and returned to the car carrying a bag of groceries. She tossed it into the back seat and got into the passenger side, slamming the door closed before their vehicle moved silently out of the forecourt.

Juan had then followed them at a distance, drumming his fingers on the steering wheel impatiently.

"Nothing on that vehicle, I'm afraid, sir. It has not been registered as stolen, but we can keep an eye on it. Registered to a Mr Pedro Gonzolez. Pulling up details on him may take a while."

"It's important. I repeat I have sighted the suspects."

"Do you have a positive identification? Is it the suspects named on file, sir? We have had hundreds of these sightings."

Juan paused, gritting his teeth in frustration. He knew why they were asking. The standard fucking routine. Continuous cutbacks to frontline police enforcement had made getting back up when it was needed harder and more bureaucratic. Meanwhile, the military and intelligence agencies enjoyed the kind of blue sky budgets Juan could only dream of.

"No, not yet," he said reluctantly. "But I'm working on it. Over and Out."

He slammed the handset back in its place and swore out loud.

Just stick with the suspects, Juan. Do not let them out of your sight.

He tracked them until they reached Talavera de la Reina, where they parked in a residential street, and then followed them to the train station, ready to arrest the suspects at any point but intrigued as to their plan.

Then a police car randomly turned up, nearly blowing Juan's plan. Discreetly flashing his police identity badge at the two policemen in the car, he leaned close to the driver.

"I'm tracking the Madrid bomb suspects. Seen any around here?"

"They're here?" the officer asked. Juan glanced at his name badge.

"One just fucking walked past you. The other is heading this way. Do not apprehend them. Let them through."

He walked up to the ticket booth, identified himself, and asked the attendant what their destination was. They were going down south, past his hometown.

Where his power base was. Where he called the shots.

If he arrested them immediately, it officially meant they would be sent back to Madrid straightaway.

Now he watched them, sitting on the train, unaware of his presence, and knew that forty minutes down the track, they would be in his lair, if only for a short time.

Chapter 28

Gianna took out the tab, swiping through to the welcome screen. Hugo went to the bathroom to check and redress his wound. It had to be cleaned thoroughly because there was pus forming, a clear sign it was becoming infected.

He felt a wave of weakness for a moment, as if the continuous running was overwhelming him.

Rest and food are what he needs.

After wrapping a clean bandage that Gianna had thoughtfully grabbed in the store, he made his way back to the table seats and slumped back into his foam chair.

The train gathered up speed; the early evening was closing in, and the aqua sky had turned to indigo, the buildings reflecting a pinkish hue in the light.

Hugo rummaged around in his backpack and ripped the foil packaging off a takeaway burrito. Despite it being cold, the shredded, salty beef, peppers, and salsa tasted as good as any he'd had in LA.

"We'd better see if there are any more clues in this Ljungborg story while we have the time," Gianna said.

Hugo nodded, his mouth full. "Run it through the app."

Gianna hooked up the old pair of headphones, and they shared an ear each as the audio began.

***

Diary of Doctor Klaus Ljungborg

April 9th

The telegram from Franklin's mother hit at my deepest fears, and I had to steady myself as I read the words.

The boys were sick with the fever, and could I come there as quickly as humanly possible? I immediately left a message with my superiors and, without waiting for a reply, quickly packed a small suitcase as well as some medicines.

Berg drove me in pouring rain, and we arrived several hours later.

Their initial appearance was not good.

Bert isn't as bad as Jonathan, but in all, they are both bedridden and showing all the symptoms.

All we can do is what I have been doing with all the other patients, but they need to be in a hospital. However, moving them with this contagious disease to a civilian hospital is definitely not a good idea.

I have arranged to get them back to Camp Funston where they can at least be properly treated. There are no decent facilities here except for the fact it is a loving home.

Then as soon as that thought appears, I think that they are best placed where they are. Perhaps a virus-ridden camp is the last place to be. I pray every chance I get that we will rid them of the flu.

April 27th

Ten days ago, Jonathan lost his battle with the illness. I never thought I would feel such pain. A father should never have to bury his own child; how I can empathise with that sentiment now.

I wanted to throw myself under a train and end this miserable life. Last week, Bert, as if surrendering to the fate and sorrow of losing his mother and brother, was lost as well.

I have nothing left to live for, nothing...

It seems I will catch that train after all. Tomorrow is Bert's funeral. I will say goodbye, and then I will join my family through death as I am sick to the gullet of this world that is clouded with nothing but suffering and despair.

April 28th

Amongst the cloud of my misery, a letter arrived that is hard to define my feelings about. There is a numbed joy, and there is heartache because of the guilt it brings.

A letter from Beatrice.

Yes, she is alive and well, thanks to god.

At least there is some silver lining. Some hope at possible happiness, however slim.

Then as soon as these thoughts occur, I am disgusted with myself, and the dark thoughts return on how to end this wretched life.

Apparently, she had been transferred to Poperinghe, twelve or so kilometres from Ypres and had a long, drawn-out coma. Her memory had been affected, and it was only through sheer luck that a friend of mine—Rupert—visiting a soldier in the hospital recognised her.

It is a ray of hope, but with it, there is guilt that I cannot shake off. I don't see myself being able to reply.

Not yet.

May 1st

It has been confirmed that the 89th Division is shipping out to France.

God knows how many of those soldiers are harbouring the virus.

It is pure insanity, and I have outlined my disgust and anger to the MG in an internal memo.

After three days, I have had no reply.

May 2nd

I went to the MG's office and refused to leave until he saw me. After five hours of keeping me waiting, he agreed. I suspect because he knew that to leave the office, he would need to walk past me.

He stood glaring at me and made no effort to offer refreshments or even a seat.

"What is it, Ljungborg?"

What is it? Am I going insane?

"There is a contagious epidemic in the camp, as you well know, sir. We need help, and every soldier needs to be confined to barracks. We cannot afford for this to spread. The implications are just too great. Too horrifying to contemplate."

"I understand your concerns, Ljungborg, but there are other priorities that need urgent attention, such as the war! The government and the whole of the US Armed Forces have been mobilised to help push our Allies to victory. That is what matters now, not the idle complaints of the men."

I could not believe the words of this man.

"You have seen it yourself. Men are ill and dying. My family is dead! Dead!"

"I am sorry for your loss, Ljungborg. I truly am. But this is above your station, well above. We have orders to deploy divisions, and that's that!"

With that, he dismissed me, but I carried on as if nothing else mattered.

I was shouting at one stage and threatened to expose what was happening to other powers or even the press.

As it turned out, my temper got the better of me, and with that, he called the military police. They arrived almost immediately and dragged me out to their truck, where I was driven to be confined to the detention barracks.

I was able to get Berg to sneak me this diary so I could at least write. God only knows how long they are going to keep me cooped up in this.

The conditions are fit for animals, not men. Speaking of which, I am locked up with a group of around twenty-five prisoners. They are a rugged bunch of soldiers incarcerated for one reason or another: fighting, refusal to follow orders, or some other minor indiscretion.

The nights are long and freezing cold, and at 5 am, the yard sergeant drags us out every morning for exercise and then a cold shower, which irritates me no end due to the fact I know they have hot water in the rest of the camp.

Lieutenant Harris gives us cigarettes. I don't smoke, but they make good currency in here. You have to barter for any kind of luxury in this hole.

I don't know how long they intend to keep me here, but I'm certain it's illegal. If I can find a lawyer, I will write to them. I will ask Franklin next time he comes.

May 5th

After a lunch of the worst stew I have ever tasted, I was approached by Lieutenant Harris, who strolled along towards me with a grin and informed me that I was to be released immediately. Thank god. I threw my tin dish aside and collected my things. Franklin waited outside the fence, but his face was ashen white.

"What is it?" I asked.

"Your office. Your papers and research. A fire, apparently, caused by an electrical fault, ripped through about three of the huts. I'm sorry, Klaus."

I am incensed, shaking with rage. This is all too convenient. A bloody fire while I was locked away.

Franklin drove me there so I could see for myself. Sure enough, the hut I used as my office was a burn-out carcass, blackened wood pillars jut upwards where, as far as I could see, nothing remained.

There was a military police officer standing guard, who shook his head at my questions.

Eventually, he allowed me past to look, and I was right. Only black ash and scorched floorboards. The fire must have burned for hours. Why was it not put out?

Franklin was correct insofar as all my papers and research materials were completely gone. The huts alongside were also damaged but not half as badly. This fire must have been fanned by some devilish hand.

"The samples in the morgue?" I asked Franklin, but he shook his head.

"You can check, but I heard they cleared out your section and incinerated everything."

May 7th

So, my family is gone, and the army is about to ship thousands of troops over to Europe. God knows how many have the virus.

Darkness pervades my soul. I feel completely numb, as if I have been saturated by morphine, and every breath I take feels completely detached from my body.

The world spins by, but I feel no part of its fabric and yearn to be rid of it.

Chapter 29

Gianna lazily pulled out her earpiece with the cord attached to the tablet and let her head rest; eyes focused on the passing dusty plains for a moment before packing it away in her rucksack.

"That's some story," Hugo muttered.

"So, what does it tell us?"

"The guy I met on the train, the prof, from what he told me, had picked up the research into the virus from where this Ljungborg left off. And they discovered something big. Some major conspiracy...and we're right in the middle of it."

Hugo lugged a bottle of water.

Gianna nodded. "It has to be in that encrypted folder. Something in there they badly want."

"For sure...it's in there, whatever it is."

Just then, the train tannoy crackled, and a low male voice told them that they would soon be arriving in Zafra. Gianna zipped up her small backpack and placed it on the seat next to her.

Hugo turned his head to glance back down the carriage for no other reason than to see if there was a view of Zafra in the distance.

A shaven-headed man was walking briskly down the aisle;

his white shirt rolled up at the sleeves, a dark jacket over his arm.

Something flickered in Hugo's memory: the man at Talavera de la Reina station who had been talking to the cops in the car.

It was the same guy.

Their eyes locked, and Hugo instantly knew he was coming for them.

He went for his gun, tucked into his belt behind his back, where it would have been if he was back in LA, but of course, there wasn't one there.

Idiot. You don't have a weapon, Bruh.

The man was now standing next to their seat, a pistol barrel clearly visible behind the jacket pointing right at them. On the other hand, they saw a flash of a police badge.

He looked down at them with a glare of contempt.

"Now, listen to me, you pieces of shit. You're going to do exactly as I say, or I will not hesitate to splatter your brains over the window. You understand?"

Hugo and Gianna both stared back at him, Hugo with disdain—he was used to threats—just a sick feeling of regret that they had not covered their backs properly.

Gianna looked scared. The pistol aimed at their heads, and the dark menace of the determined-looking cop left her in no doubt they were out of options.

"Do you understand?" the cop hissed again. He waved the pistol slightly under the jacket for emphasis.

They nodded.

"Now stand up, and keep your hands away from any pockets."

Gianna and Hugo did as they were told, rising from the seats slowly. Hugo reassured Gianna in a low whisper, his eyes darting around the carriage.

It had thinned out, and the passengers left were not inter-ested or had not seen what was happening.

"Pick up your bags, and move down the aisle towards the doors. Any sudden movement and I will shoot you."

They moved to the doors, Gianna leading the way, the Policeman close behind them.

"Raise your hands up...higher," the cop demanded suddenly as if just remembering the process.

They did so slowly.

The train was gearing down its speed as it approached a bridge.

Hugo's eyes drifted up to the red handle of the emergency brake just within reach of his hand. He made a mental note of its position and risked a slow half-turn back towards the cop, who glared back at him.

The bright Spanish sun was momentarily gone as the train hammered through the dark shadow cast by the bridge.

Momentary confusion.

Now, Bruh!

Without looking, he grabbed and yanked the emergency brake handle with his right hand.

A screech echoed through the carriages, and a lurching movement caused the cop to stumble, losing his balance.

Hugo was expecting it, and he rode the momentum like a surfer catching a wave, holding himself upright on the handle.

The sudden surge had left the cop off balance, and in one darting movement, he sprang forward, punching the cop on the jaw with a left hook, using all his momentum and force.

The cop was thrown back, his head smacking against the carriage floor, his gun clattering on the ground. Hugo grabbed it and glanced at the cop, who was clearly dazed.

It gave them a head start, if nothing else.

Hugo turned to see Gianna picking herself up from the floor, a surprised look on her face at the turn of events.

"We're getting off!" Hugo shouted as he forced open the train door. The train was still slowing down quickly, but looking at the passing ground still seemed pretty fast to Hugo.

No time for hesitation. You gotta do this, Bruh.

"C'mon, Gianna! Let's go!" he shouted again, and she came up to the door.

He checked down the track in the direction they were heading and grimaced at the dusty, hard ground. The station was looming metres away.

"Just stay loose and jump!" he added.

Gianna grabbed the side of the door, gritted her teeth, and flew off the train, her long legs and arms waving around in a circular motion before curling up in a ball as she hit the ground in a flurry of dust, then rolled like a pro.

Good girl.

Hugo quickly checked the safety of the cop's pistol and slipped it into his backpack before hauling it onto his back.

He took a sharp intake of breath and then jumped himself, his eyes fixed on the ground, forcing himself to relax the muscles in his legs.

He soon felt the force of the ground rush through the core of his body like a hard punch in the gut.

Rolling his body over several times, he finally came to a stop, letting out a loud groan.

To top it off, the wound on his arm was throbbing like a bitch; it must have been caught in the impact.

The sound of the train melted away, and the warm sun

beating down on his skin intensified his pain. He opened his eyes and saw the stretching blue sky, cloudless except for a series of contrails high overhead.

Padding feet, drawing closer, he watched as Gianna leaned over him, grinning.

"Nice trick. But we still have to keep moving, old man."

Hugo groaned again and heaved himself off the ground, every fibre of his body wanting to stay horizontal for just a few minutes.

"The tablet!"

"It's fine. In my backpack."

"OK. We might want to think about hiding it somewhere. Once the local police have it, it'll disappear back to that CIA guy."

A few metres away was a road and some kind of industrial complex with six large steel cylinders reflecting in the sunlight.

Across the narrow road, Hugo could see gates to a school. It seemed quiet.

"Let's get over there. We need to keep moving. Let's see if we can get another car or something."

"We're gonna need supplies, too. It might be a long road ahead."

They took off at a gentle pace, skirting a fence that ran alongside the industrial area, and crouched, waiting for a gap in the traffic before running across and through the gates into a small car park.

Crouching down by a wall, they caught the sound of sirens in the air, growing closer.

"That guy must have alerted his pals...they'll be heading this way," said Hugo.

"Then we need to put as much distance from them as possible. We can't outrun them...we need to be sneaky."

Hugo nodded in agreement and pointed to a gap in the buildings. Beyond was a field. The place was empty. Obviously, the school had long finished.

They jogged to the side of the building and moved along the wall towards the field, jumping over a small fence and then following a dirt track along the side, leading them back to a road running behind the school.

Crouching again by a low wall, Hugo waited, the sirens echoing in the distance.

Cruising towards them now, just visible behind the lemon trees that lined the road, was a police car. Hugo tensed and held his hand out to warn Gianna.

The car reached the mouth of the track and slowed, pale faces looking hard down towards their position.

"Stay really fucking still," whispered Hugo.

Time seemed to slow down as the car took an age to cruise by. Eventually, it disappeared from sight and carried on up the road.

"You got any water?" Hugo asked, wiping his brow with a bandaged arm.

Gianna rummaged around in her backpack and pulled out a half-litre plastic bottle that was running low, and offered it to Hugo.

Hugo waved it off. "You have a go. I just wanted to see what we had. We ain't exactly prepared for this."

Gianna took a long swig and offered it to Hugo again.

"Drink some water, for god's sake. We'll get some more soon. It's not like we're in the Sahara or anything. We're close to the town, but we just have to keep low."

She jerked her head, gesturing to the exposed dry field ahead of them.

"We either head over the field, which is a long run and risk being seen—there's a hut over there we can head to—or go to the other side of the road over there. I can't see much cover, though."

Hugo took a gulp and handed back the bottle.

"Let's keep moving then...over the field," he said, grunting, and they moved off again, across another fence and onto the wide open plain.

Hugo felt way too exposed.

Any vehicle on the road could easily see them. Their objective was a small white hut that sat stoically near the far edge, a rest point if nothing else, beyond which was a pack of parked caravans, vans, and houses. Gianna set a steady pace, keeping an eye on the road, her athleticism exposing Hugo's lack of fitness as he lagged behind.

"Car!"

They both hit the ground instantly. Hugo felt the impact reverberate through his entire body. Months of sitting around his aunty's eating tortillas and drinking beers hadn't helped, and he was feeling old and unfit.

Another police car drove up to where the caravans were and stopped. A large man in a yellow shirt appeared and began speaking to them. He walked off, and the car moved out of sight.

They reached the hut; an electricity generator hummed inside, and they crouched down next to it, out of sight from the road.

Leaning his hand on the hut, Hugo steadied himself and took in several deep breaths. The sweat was freely running down his forehead, the hot Spanish afternoon taking its toll. After a few seconds, they continued across the field, and reaching the end they came alongside a large truck. Skirting alongside it to the cabin, they stopped again. They were close now to another small road, and on the far side was a row of white houses, the start of a residential area lining the edge of the field.

There were a few more caravans and trucks in front of them before they got to the road, leaping over a low fence that cut through the land. Gianna tripped and rolled in the dry grass.

"Shit!"

"You OK?"

She was up and on her feet again within seconds.

"Yep. All good."

They kept running towards the houses. Suddenly, a sharp barking came from behind them. Hugo glanced around and saw a black dog in front of a caravan making a noise. A man stepped out of the caravan. Yellow shirt. The one who had been talking to the cops.

He looked up at Hugo, waving a fist and began shouting at them in rapid Spanish. A woman and a boy appeared, looking at them curiously.

"Keep moving!" shouted Gianna, who was way ahead now. They left the commotion behind them and raced onward towards the houses. The sound of sirens again.

***

The residential area was a mix of different houses; all white-washed with shutters on the windows. They paced down a few streets, putting distance between them and the family with the dog.

The suburbs were quiet, devoid of people, just the sound of their footfalls echoing off the buildings. Running down an alleyway with washing hanging overhead, they came out into a large square, the grass in the centre having long turned yellow, and headed to a street on the far side.

As they reached the road, there was a screech of tyres behind them. Hugo chanced a look and saw it was another police car arriving on the square.

"Move it!" yelled Hugo as they both picked up the pace, digging deeper into their depleted energy reserves.

"Did they see us?"

"I don't think so, but let's not hang around to find out."

They busted left and then a right down a series of alleyways that came out onto a dusty hill road. A church stood, set in shadow like a monolith against the crisp blue sky.

Hugo gestured to it without a word, and they began to run up the hill, splitting up on either side of the road as they approached the old building.

As they got near it, Hugo realised it was derelict; a crumbling old wall jutted out from the side facing them. They reached the church entrance archway on the far side and went through a gate set in a railing that surrounded the building. With graffiti sprayed over the old stones, it was apparent that what once had once been a tourist attraction now lay in ruins.

Forgotten and low priority in a crumbling economy.

Inside, the cool, sheltered building was a welcome relief from the searing heat that they had been running around in for almost an hour. Panting from the effort, Gianna took out her bottle of water and took a long glug, then handed it over to Hugo.

"What the hell are we going to do now?" she asked.

Hugo finished the last of the water, wiped his mouth, and stared at the empty bottle.

"Guess we're out of water...better try and get some as soon as we can."

"Think we have more pressing problems. Hugo, I'm not sure what our chances are."

Hugo shook his head. "I dodged the cops a million times. Stay with me."

"It's one thing losing cops on the streets of LA, but in rural Spain? I'm not so sure. You've also been named the number-one suspect in a terrorist attack. Every cop is going to be out here, and I bet they move faster than the donut-scoffing ones you are used to back home," Gianna said, raising an eyebrow.

Unstrapping her backpack and opening it, Gianna took out the tablet in its leather pouch.

"Even so, I think it might be a good idea to stash this...can't afford for them to get hold of it. Perhaps, it's our only ticket to staying alive."

Hugo stared at her for a moment, then looked around, his eyes settling on the stone steps that headed up into the tower lodged against the outside wall.

Finally, he nodded, seeing sense in her suggestion, and gestured for her to give him the tablet. "OK, keep an eye out. I'll take a look up there."

He moved up the steps quickly, glancing out of the small slotted window that looked out across a dusty plain and the residential clumps of white houses baking in the dry heat. His hand brushed across the old stone bricks, searching for any loose ones or somewhere that could act as a hiding place, but there was nothing.

Eventually, the steps disappeared into a wooden ceiling, and his head popped up at the bell tower at the very top of the building.

The bells themselves had long gone, and the small space was exposed from the arched windows on each side. The floorboards were mostly intact, but a few were obviously loose or missing. He crouched on the floor and found a suitable place. Not ideal, but it would do. He pushed the tablet inside and replaced the board.

Satisfied, nothing looked out of place in the small tower. He glanced out a small window. A police car had turned onto the road and was coming towards the church, rolling slowly, clearly keeping an eye out.

Chapter 30

The police car stopped several hundred metres away, and an officer got out.

He jogged alongside the slowly moving car, peering over walls and fences, steadily getting closer to the church.

Hugo tried to swallow, his dry mouth not making the job easy.

What to do?

Gianna wouldn't see them as the front faced the opposite direction.

Hugo hopped through the narrow gap and descended the steps as fast as he could.

"Gianna!" he rasped, trying to get her attention without being heard outside.

No response.

He stumbled on a loose step and lost his footing for a moment, nearly plunging down the narrow stairwell, but he grabbed the windowsill of the porthole window in the nick of time and corrected his balance.

At the bottom, Gianna sat just inside the archway, staring into space, the day's excursion clearly catching up on her.

"Cops! Walking up the road behind us!"

Gianna shot to her feet, her face fully alert.

"What should we do? Can we hide upstairs?"

"I'm not so sure," said Hugo shaking his head. "They're combing the area, and it's a likely place to look and with only one way in or out. It's game over if we get seen."

"More running," Gianna sighed.

"'Fraid so, G. If we head out that way, the church will offer us cover for a while, but we're gonna have to make a dash for that next set of buildings."

They set out at a light jog, straight ahead along a raised walkway that led to the church. After a few metres, they ran out of cover.

Hugo gestured to a row of apartments set in angular blocks across from a park.

"You ready for this, G?"

Gianna looked up at him and smiled.

"Just imagine we're doing a hundred metres in the Olympics or..."

Before Hugo could finish, she was off, running hard and fast through the trees towards their goal. Hugo swore out loud and then started running after her.

An indistinguishable shout echoed far behind them, and then a shot rang out, the bullet whistling past Hugo before hitting a wall, dislodging a chunk of stone.

"Puta!" shouted Hugo.

Another shout.

A clear demand to stop.

They reached the buildings and quickly turned into one of the alleyways between the apartments, ducking out of the line of fire.

As they came out the far side, a police car pulled right into their path, seemingly from nowhere.

Gianna, using her momentum, jumped across the bonnet and slid over the other side of the car, hitting the ground at speed, and kept running. Hugo came to a sudden halt, the bonnet taking the impact.

Glancing up, he caught a brief look of surprise on the driver's face.

His colleague went to open the passenger door.

Hugo, turning in one smooth movement, booted the door shut and darted up behind the vehicle in the direction it had come.

Turning left again, he raced through another alleyway heading back the way he had come.

At the end of the alley, there was an expanse of wasteland. A row of houses on the other side looked like they offered a few hiding places, the derelict church just visible to his left.

Hugo pushed on, his legs burning, sucking in large lungfuls of the warm afternoon air, clearing the buildings as he made for the wasteland.

A flash of black uniform.

A cop!

His face turned to surprise. With no time to think, Hugo used all his weight to shoulder-barge him.

Taking the full brunt of the force, the cop fell onto the ground with a grunt and a slew of swear words.

Hugo staggered and just managed to keep his balance and kept running across the dry ground. His feet kicked up a cloud of dust as he paced across the open space. Reaching the closest building, Hugo ducked out of sight again.

No time to rest.

Hugo pushed on, dripping with sweat, eyes darting around for options, knowing the cops were not far behind.

Reaching a cubist building, he spotted a potential nook, a small bolt hole out of sight behind a fence and under a walkway. Hugo raced in, diving for the cover before anyone got a bead on him, slumping in the shadow, hidden from sight, his chest heaving from the final sprint.

Waiting. Listening.

It sounded like chaos out there; sirens blared, angry shouts and footsteps pounded past.

Safe for now, maybe.

Hidden, except possibly from people in the offices themselves.

As it was a Sunday, Hugo summarised the town's population was out to lunch as it had resembled a ghost town so far.

He needed water badly, but there was little chance of that. Covered in sweat, it seemed like every muscle in his body was aching badly.

Had to focus on resting; otherwise, he'd be good for nothing.

His mind reeled, and he swore under his breath at the situation but mostly for losing Gianna.

They hadn't really made any kind of plan if they separated. Turning on his phone and texting or any other communication on a mobile would probably be picked up in a matter of seconds and would literally put them on a map for the authorities.

Speeding police cars screeched past at full speed. They were gone as quickly as they had come, and the street fell quiet again.

Time to move.

Getting to his feet was a challenge, and his muscles screamed in protest as he shook out his legs, trying to get some life back into them.

Avoiding the street from where he had come, he moved on,

heading through the building complex to find a way through the other side.

He was on the grounds of some kind of institute, with large dark windows in stark contrast to the whitewashed walls that cast back his reflection. Hugo studied himself for a moment: ragged, dirty shirt, the bandage on his arm was half falling off, and his clothes were caked with orange dust.

The haunted look of the hunted man in front of him fuelled an anger deep in his core.

How had it come to this?

Running around, being shot at. Exactly the life he had been running away from. This was supposed to be his new beginning, to start again after that dark day.

Not again. Got to get back in charge of this shit

He moved off with a new resolve. After a few minutes of stumbling aimlessly around the complex, Hugo found a low wall that looked down onto a stretch of pavement.

In front of him was a fenced square of grassland, and on the other side of that, a similar set of empty, quiet buildings.

Checking both ways, he jumped down and moved quickly along the pavement until he reached the corner and a narrow road and more open ground. Looking up and down, Hugo saw no signs of the police. But for how long?

The buildings on the far side looked promising. A lot of ground to clear, though.

Ain't got much choice. I'm exposed like a naked hooker on this corner.

Hugo headed out, moving from one bit of cover to the next.

As he reached the end of the obstacles big enough to hide behind, he sprinted, making for the row of white residential buildings.

A man walking a small dog glanced in his direction but looked away, perhaps sensing danger.

Jogging at a gentle pace, Hugo followed the buildings, constantly scanning for the feds.

He soon came to a white metal gate that led onto a series of courtyards. Ducking inside, he was glad to be out of sight from the road again and moved through the houses, keeping his steady pace. Soon he heard the familiar buzz of traffic from a main road.

Cutting through a gap in the houses, he saw a large intersection and busier streets. Turn back? It was tempting just to go find a crawlspace somewhere and hide it out till dark, but he was starting to feel dizzy from the dehydration.

Too much fuckin' exertion for such a hot day.

They'd also start tearing the place up looking for him shortly, and if they brought in dogs, he wouldn't last long. Best to try to get some more distance behind him.

Getting transport would be good; steal an old motorbike or scooter?

He'd seen plenty of them around, and they were much easier to start. Then he'd be able to make some good time, but what about Gianna?

Should he risk trying to contact her on the phone? Where would she go if she'd managed to get away? Would she head back to the church? It would be crazy to head there now. Best stay clear of ground zero.

Through the open gate, he could see cars drifting by; on the far side of the road, a woman struggling with her bags and several hundred metres up ahead on a corner, two elderly men talking, gesturing with their arms.

Quiet as it was ever gonna get.

Walking casually so as not to draw attention, Hugo headed for a small supermarket with its cool air-conditioned space. He grabbed a basket and filled it with several bottles of water, opening one and glugging down the cool liquid that felt like silk on his dry throat.

He added a ready-made baguette and looked around the aisles. There was no sign of what he really needed: a spare T-shirt, some sunglasses, or anything else that might help him change his appearance, so he paid for what he had and left.

A wave of heat hit as the automatic doors slid open, and Hugo cautiously stepped out, checking the street for any signs of the authorities.

As he started heading up the road, a low humming caused him to look behind, and he spotted a surveillance drone, about twenty-five metres high, flying over the street. Too far away to spot him, hopefully.

You need to change your threads, Bruh. Gonna stand out way too much like this.

He passed two teenage boys, who both looked at him. The buzzing from the air was getting closer. Drone is closing in. Up ahead were a few more stores. Somewhere to duck inside, hopefully.

Then he saw it, just ahead: a flash of familiar white, a police van moving slowly down the street towards him.

Fuck!

Hugo wanted to turn back and run but forced himself just to keep walking casually. Any sudden movement would draw their eyes—limited options. There was nowhere to turn yet, except maybe a small side street up ahead.

The buzzing was directly above him now, as if the drone was

coming in closer.

Hugo reached the corner and cut left into a long narrow calle with residential white blocks on either side. Keeping his speed even, he could almost feel the eyes watching him.

Had he managed to slip past? Each footstep seemed to last an age, each one bringing him a tiny piece of hope.

A screech behind him, and he knew he had been spotted.

Fuck, Bruh! Do you want to stay free?

Hugo leapt into a sprint, his feet pounding the pavement hard and fast. Apart from a few sunken doorways, there was no turning in sight. Reaching the end of the street, he moved around a row of parked cars and kept on running. Chancing a look behind, he spotted the police van as it pulled to a stop, figures in black balaclavas pooling out of it. He weaved around a line of cars, hunching low. Shouts echoed along the walls. He broke from his cover and headed for the closest street, half expecting a volley of gunfire to erupt behind him.

More shouting in Spanish and another screech of tyres.

His feet hit cobbles on a narrow road as the shouts echoed from behind, but they only seemed to strengthen his resolve. Drawing in some deep breaths, he flew around a quick succession of turning, legs burning with the effort. Every road looked the same, bumping past the occasional person—no time to stop.

The footsteps of his pursuers were gradually falling behind, a comforting thought, and he kept moving, blocking out the complaints of an exhausted body. Each road seemed to lead to another maze, so he focused on heading away from the noise of the sirens, too disoriented to know where the hell he was.

Only a few metres now.

Another turning meant another chance at freedom. The

cobbles under his feet changed to the tarmac as he left the old part of the city, and then Hugo stumbled momentarily, falling against a large rubbish bin, just keeping his balance as he came to the end of the street. He rounded the corner, coming face to face with a cop. They both looked at each other in surprise, the cop immediately going for his sidearm. Hugo didn't hesitate and, with a few large steps, closed the gap. His right fist connected cleanly with the cop's jaw, landing the blow with all his weight behind it, and he fell to the ground in a heap. Hugo hopped over the prone body and bounded on, so exhausted he barely noticed the police van swerving onto the pavement in front of him. The side doors slid open, and out spilt a sea of black bodies, weapons drawn, anger etched over their faces.

"Hold it there. Put your hands in the air. Slowly." A commanding shout from one of the officers rang out.

Hugo's eyes darted around, looking for an escape route that wasn't there. Like a wild animal finally coming to terms with its imprisonment, Hugo gave in, collapsing to his knees and raising his hands.

"Take off your backpack very slowly, and place it on the ground, and then slowly raise your arms again. Do it now!"

Lowering his arms, Hugo slipped the straps of the rucksack off and dropped the bag beside him.

No sooner had he raised his hands again than he was bundled onto the ground with what felt like a rugby tackle.

A rain of kicks and punches pummeled his head and body.

He tried to curl up but was quickly flattened out onto his stomach, arms roughly forced behind his back to be handcuffed.

A crowd had gathered, some of them filming the commotion

on their phones, staring in awe at Hugo, who didn't even dare to think about what lay ahead.

Hugo's mind rewound in double quick time: being chased by the police, meeting Gianna, his former life in LA, and the boy he shot.

Was he paying his dues?

He wondered who his mother was and what she was doing at that moment just as a boot swung into his ribs once again.

Chapter 31

Juan Cerezo paced his office, coming to a stop by the window and stared down at the courtyard where a few police officers milled around, smoking and chatting.

What a day. However, anyone looking at him would only see a calm police chief in total control. Just below the surface, however, was a boiling sea of emotion. After losing the suspects on the train, Juan had been organising the manhunt, closely following the radio chatter as his men hunted and then chased down his suspects.

Now they were being brought back to his station; his mind was split. The policeman in him wanted the full weight of the law to hold these two accountable; the father in him just wanted to gut the bastards and let them rot.

A determined footfall from the corridor grew louder, coming to a sudden stop outside his door, followed by a rapid knocking.

"Adelante!"

It was Enríquez, a young bullish man with thick eyebrows and steely eyes that Juan had worked with for only a few years, but he had quickly gained his respect.

"They have the suspects. Cells 20 and 33."

Juan immediately headed for the door.

"You're going down there, sir?"

Juan didn't answer as he swept past Enríquez, who quickly followed him back out of the office into the corridor.

"Where did you pick them up?" shouted Juan over his shoulder.

Enríquez gave him the details as he struggled to keep up with Juan's quickening pace. They arrived at the ground floor, and Juan jerked his head at the junior officer, who was sitting at a desk that acted as a guard for the cells area.

Juan snapped his fingers. "Give me the access key."

Enríquez hesitantly pulled out the credit card–style access card.

"But there are procedures."

Juan was already through the door with the card snapped from his subordinate's hand, striding down the bleak white corridor. He stopped at one of the cell doors and opened a small slot to peer inside.

The terrorist scumbag lay on a bed in an almost arrogant way. Did he not give a solitary shit about his actions? Surely, any normal person would be pacing the room at this point, especially if they were innocent, as this one claimed.

But no, he lay there relaxing, almost as if he had come to terms with the fact that his penance for his crimes had caught up with him.

As Juan scanned the passcard to open the door, his hand was shaking as he struggled to keep control of his rage.

Stepping inside the sparse cell, Juan looked down at Hugo with contempt. Their eyes met, and Hugo stared back, slowly lifting himself into a sitting position, sensing danger from Juan.

"I want a lawyer," Hugo grunted.

Juan stared back, a small smile spreading across his face at the sheer cheek.

"You think you still have rights?" Juan said, taking a small step into the room.

"What about the rights of the thirty-five people whose lives you took yesterday?"

"Look, vato..."

Juan leapt forward with lightning speed, his hands grabbing Hugo's shoulders and slamming him against the wall.

"You killed my daughter, you son of a bitch!"

Before Hugo had time to respond, Juan drove a vicious knee into his stomach, doubling him over in pain.

Enríquez stood by the door, shifting from foot to foot, watching his boss unleash explosive violence on the prisoner. Hugo gasped for breath in between blows. The noise and sudden thuds drew shouts and whistles from other prisoners along the cell block.

Holding up his arms, Hugo attempted to shield himself from the onslaught, but Juan continued to rain blows down on his face. Hugo shot out a kick at his shin, but with no shoes on his feet, it hardly broke the police chief's stride.

Finally, another officer came to the cell and immediately pushed past Enríquez and hauled Juan back.

"Sir! That is enough. We need to question him and the girl. Plus, if he's hurt in custody, he could walk."

As soon as Juan was pulled away, Hugo collapsed on the floor, spitting out a mouthful of blood and looking up at the chief. Eyes flashing with defiance as he smiled, revealing a mouth full of blood-stained teeth.

Juan shrugged off the officer and spat at Hugo before storming out of the cell.

He continued his stride as if he had never broken it and

marched towards the girl's cell. His thirst for revenge was not yet quenched.

Juan Cerezo stood in the doorway of the cell, looking down at his second suspect, the female. He breathed so heavily that it was the only sound in the room.

The devil's whore.

What possessed them to carry out this attack, Juan had no idea. The terrorism alert had been steadily rising across Europe and the US for what seemed like decades.

Almost half his adult life, in fact.

The suspects and those thrown onto international wanted lists no longer strictly came from Arab descent. They were all races. The rise of activism and terrorism had no religious or racial boundaries when it came to ethnic breakdown.

So, they were likely to have been recruited by UIS or a similar group. This girl probably got signed up in Nigeria, where the ravages of terror were pretty much out of control.

Juan wanted to hurt her so badly. She was responsible for taking so many lives, causing so much pain. But the beating he had lashed out on the other one had eased his hate, albeit a small amount, and now he had a different route in mind.

"What's your organisation? UIS?"

The girl looked up at him with dark brown eyes. He could sense the fear there, something to work with.

"I don't know what you're talking about. We didn't do anything. And he certainly didn't blow up any train."

The voice was defiant and confident.

"You're both currently the main suspects in the whole operation. Your friend was on that train, and you're his accomplice. The whole of the CNI and Spanish authorities are hunting for him right now. They want to throw him to the lions. Did he rope you into it? Where did he recruit you?"

The girl shook her head.

"I was just helping a friend," she said. "I already said this in the interrogation."

"Helping a terrorist, you mean."

"You're going to spend the rest of your life in a maximum-security prison. It's not going to be fun. For him? You want to throw your life away?"

Gianna shifted uneasily on the uncomfortable excuse for a bed.

"You've both been caught on the run. How do you think that makes you both look? Heading straight to Morocco, no doubt. Look, the sooner you talk, the more helpful you are, the better a deal I can get you."

Gianna remained silent. Juan moved into the cell but kept his distance. He wasn't sure what she was capable of or what kind of training she had been given by her group. She avoided his eye contact, choosing to look at the floor instead.

"Give me something. There's still time. Not much, but some. You could still get a minimal sentence. Maybe with good behaviour, you'll be back walking the streets within five or so years. An innocent party, sucked into the web by your controllers, huh?"

Gianna fired a defiant look of contempt his way, and Juan felt his temper rising, taking a deep breath to try to keep it in check.

"Keeping silent only confirms your guilt. Innocent people have nothing to fear by telling the truth. So, tell me, how did you get caught up in all this?"

All his questioning met with stony silence, and the final thread holding him together broke.

Juan stepped forward and threw an almighty slap, the crack echoing off the walls of the small cell.

Gianna fell to the floor, curling into a protective ball.

Drawing his hand back for a second blow, Juan approached her.

As he unleashed his anger, his hand was caught. He looked back in surprise and saw Enríquez, a concerned look in his eyes.

"Come on, Jefe, we can say the puta in the other cell resisted arrest, but we slap this one around, too. They gonna ask questions."

Juan steeled himself. Enríquez was right. He looked down in disgust at the woman on the floor before turning on his heels and heading out.

***

8.50 PM
CNI Headquarters, Madrid

Jamall leaned back in his chair, the leather squeaking as he shifted his frame. Such a peculiar day: The game had dragged on, and it was definitely not his best performance. Still, the result was what counted; the time frame or methods were inconsequential.

"Zafra police have apprehended the terror suspects, sir." A female voice came out of nowhere.

It was the helpful Dana Amador, who hadn't taken her eyes off Jamall since he arrived. She was not someone Jamall was remotely interested in, but he played along by occasionally catching her eye. Since then, the information flowed freely from her lips to his ear.

"Are you certain about this, Dana?"

She beamed. "Si, the Zafra police headquarters reported it just now. There had been a fair amount of noise on their radio networks about it as well."

Jamall smiled back. At last, he had them.

***

11.50 PM

Hugo lay awake staring at the artificial light from the courtyard that streaked across his cell ceiling.

A small part of him was relieved. He'd been running for so long.

Not just here but back at home. Even before the last shootout, where he'd killed that child, a part of him had been trying to get away. It felt like a weight had been lifted, and he was ready to take the heat. Only then could he really begin again?

Still, there was much uncertainty ahead. Could they really pin the bombing on him? There would be a long sentence if they did.

What evidence did they really have?

It all had something to do with the Mexican.

Whatever was on that tablet must be really important to these putas. They must have friends in high places to pull this kind of move. Something didn't add up.

Well, the tablet was hidden, and it would take a lot for Hugo to give up where it was. He wasn't so sure about Gianna, though.

Still, here in the legal system, they would be safe, right?

Shifting his weight on the foam mattress, he winced in pain. That fucking cop had dished out quite a beating.

He moved again and groaned as his ribs seared in intense pain. He wasn't sure if they were cracked or what. It certainly felt like it. Punches had smashed into his ribs and stomach mostly. Obviously, the cop hadn't wanted to damage his face too much. All the other bruises could be put down to his jumping from a moving train and leading the cops on a chase through the city.

What about Gianna now; how would this play out for her?

Their meeting had genuinely been by chance; how could they possibly link her as a co-conspirator?

No fucking way, unless that ponytail motherfucker fabricates some kind of proof.

Judging by the manhunt launched in their honour, maybe he already had—then they were definitely heading to a maximum security prison, no doubt.

Thrown to the motherfucking lions for some bullshit that had nothing—absolutely nothing—to do with them.

Shit, it was worse for her. She had reached out and helped him when the shit was real and in return? Well, now she was finding out.

They did have one card to play: the tablet. But without being able to talk to Gianna, he couldn't really tell her his plan. Shit was messy.

Dammit, Bruh. What have you done?

The patterns of the light moved on the ceiling. There was a low hum of a vehicle entering the station. Hugo forced himself off the bed and slowly shuffled over to his cell window that was half-underground, set in the basement of the building. Bars and thick frosted glass hindered his view, but there was a section that was clear, and if he pressed his face against the bars, Hugo could just see the courtyard.

A police vehicle had come to a stop in the central courtyard. A small welcoming committee stood ready to greet the visitor. Then he saw a familiar figure jump out; a dark suit.

Shit!

Hugo paced the confined cell. The pain from the beating was quickly forgotten.

Damn, ese. That is not good news.

Chapter 32

Juan stood looking down onto the courtyard at the black police van and the figure of the driver moving into the building. It was inevitable the Madrid authorities would want the terrorists as soon as possible. Understandable that the public would want quick results.

He walked back to his desk, slumped down in his leather chair, and took a shot of the harsh Scotch whisky that he always kept in his desk drawer. The liquid calmed him a little. The previous forty-eight hours had been extremely stressful, but running across those shitheads in the gas station had been a gift from god.

At least he had managed to give the cocky son of a bitch a nice beating. The satisfaction wouldn't touch the feeling of the loss of his little girl, but it scratched an itch—just a little.

There was a rapid knock at the door that Juan was expecting.

"Si!"

It was the young officer Enríquez who entered and nodded.

"Chief Cerezo. A Mr Jamall Salazar, working with the CNI in Madrid, is here wanting to collect the prisoners. Do you want me to process the release? I think he's an American."

Juan nodded and waved his hand.

"Si, si. Let them have the scum. I wish they'd throw them to some very angry lions. A dose of Roman-style justice is what we need, Enríquez."

The officer smiled and left with a salute.

Juan poured another shot. The firewater just wasn't hitting the mark tonight.

He hoped he would get the deserved credit for apprehending the purveyors of this atrocity. Most of all, he wanted justice for his daughter.

Did Enríquez say he was American?

The police chief was leaning back in his chair, looking across at the map of his town spread out on the wall. Despite technological advances, nothing beats an old-style map. Something real, something you could touch.

A map of his Zafra. His town.

Those fucks had strayed, or rather he had let them stray, onto his turf.

Big mistake.

Juan almost smiled at the thought of his triumph, but then the memory of his daughter loomed, and the smile faded.

An American?

He poured another and rubbed a hand over the stubble forming on his chin, and logged into the Interpol system.

It at least gave him access to certain information, including personnel from other European and American agencies. After ten minutes of searching, Juan was unable to find any reference to this Salazar character.

He picked up the phone and, after a couple of minutes, was speaking to the Secretary State Director of the Centro Nacional de Inteligencia, Rafael Ortez.

The man grunted a brusque greeting at the other end, and Juan introduced himself and quickly outlined the story of how he had apprehended the main bombing suspects.

"I congratulate you, Chief Cerezo. We need more proactive figures in the fight against terrorism." The tone was matter-of-fact—standard response.

Juan nodded and continued, ignoring the compliment.

"The prisoners are being collected by one of your agents. An American called Jamall Salazar?"

"That sounds correct. I'm not involved in those processes, but yes..." The director trailed off, obviously distracted and possibly unsure of the police chief's point.

"Director. I simply wanted to verify..."

There was a moment of interference on the line, which quickly fixed itself.

"Are you there, Director?"

"Yes, I'm here, Chief Cerezo. Please continue."

"May I ask why the Americans are involved in Spanish affairs?"

There was a sigh at the other end.

"I'll be candid with you. I don't like it either. But we are working with agencies across the world in the fight against terrorism. The end objective is the same, whichever country it is."

Juan laughed. "You make it all sound so simple, Director."

Ortez's voice warmed.

"Sometimes, it's the only way to get through the days."

"Thanks for your time. I appreciate it."

The call ended, and Enríquez was already back in the office, standing in front of Juan with the release paperwork, looking at him with mild anticipation.

***

Ten minutes slowly ticked by before the cell door swished open, and a posse of officers rushed in, grabbing Hugo by the arms.

"Get off me you hijos de puta! My lawyer's gonna track you all down and make you fucking pay for this!" Hugo hissed pure venom. He was livid, and the adrenalin rush quickly masked his pain.

The three men struggled to contain Hugo, even in his weakened state, handcuffing his hands behind his back before eventually dragging him into the corridor. Hugo turned and saw Gianna was getting the same treatment. They caught each other's eye for just a second.

"Be careful with them. I don't want bruised fruit."

Hugo turned to see the direction of the voice. A figure stood at the end of the harshly lit corridor, staring down towards them.

The Mexican?

Hugo couldn't get a long enough look.

The figure quickly disappeared through a side entrance, and the officers continued bundling Hugo forward through a series of thick steel doors until he was at the police reception area.

Gianna was pushed next to him, and they both stood in front of the on-duty cop, who pushed a tray with plastic bags of their belongings and their backpacks across the desk.

"Sign for their stuff. You'll be taking them back to Madrid," said the cop.

They were both escorted out into the cool night air and found themselves being dragged to the back of a police van. Hugo struggled to get away from the strong arms holding him like a calf being led to the slaughter that had realised its fate.

"Be careful."

That voice again.

Inside the caged interior, Hugo looked up to see Gianna directly opposite him. The rear doors slammed shut, leaving them in darkness apart from the little light the barred windows let in. Hugo hung his head. How had it come to this? The heat inside was stifling, and he could just hear a murmur of voices between the officers and their nemesis, the Mexican.

Then the engine started up, and they swayed into motion, the cool breeze from the AC now bringing them slight relief. Hugo could feel the vehicle turn, speed up, and then turn again. It was impossible to know where they were going.

He glanced at Gianna. "I'm sorry, G. I didn't wanna mix you up in this. I shouldn't—"

"Forget it. I'm the one who felt sorry for your ass."

Was there a hint of annoyance in her voice?

She must regret meeting me all right, he thought.

And how could he blame her? But all that meant nothing.

Now they were in the hands of that lunatic. He was way above the local police or authorities. Hugo knew that much. And it seemed pretty likely the guy might just take them into a field and put bullets into their heads.

"What's gonna happen to us?" Gianna asked, fear evident in her voice.

"I guess we'll find out," Hugo heard himself say, but he couldn't stop thinking about some deserted field, their unmarked graves already dug.

After several minutes the vehicle slowed down, and they both felt it stop. The engine switched off. A slam of the driver's door. Footsteps made their way to the rear.

What the fuck? Not only was the guy going to get rid of them, he wasn't even going to wait until they got out of town!

The rear lock clicked, and the doors swung open. The figure

standing before them was cloaked in shadow.

Gianna and Hugo froze.

"Joe? Is that you?" Gianna stared hard at the figure as Hugo glanced at her curiously.

"It certainly is, Gianna. Good to see you again."

Gianna let out a rush of sound that Hugo realised was a laugh—a laugh of pure relief.

"What the fuck is going on?" he demanded. More questions were coming into his head at that moment than could possibly be answered in a lifetime.

"It's Joe!" said Gianna again. "The friend I told you we were going to see in Seville. Remember?"

Hugo looked again at the figure who stood smiling back at him and immediately realised it wasn't the Mexican. It wasn't the guy who had chased him through the hospital at all.

"What?" he just spat out. A mix of relief and disbelief swirled around his head. Hugo didn't know what to think.

Joe spoke again. "Listen. It's not over. We need to get out of here. We're still on the outskirts of town, so keep the noise down. Understood?"

Hugo and Gianna both nodded. Whatever this guy suggested, they were going to do.

Joe unlocked their handcuffs and led them to a nearby car. They were joined by a white woman with blonde dreadlocks and dark clothing, who nodded a silent greeting in their direction.

"This is Hanna," said Joe.

Hugo nodded at her but said nothing.

"Hi, Hanna. Good to see you," said Gianna.

"Hugo. I know you don't know me from Adam, but I need to ask you a question," said Joe.

Hugo glanced at Gianna, who was sitting in the rear of the car with Hanna next to her. "You can trust him completely," she said to reassure him.

Hugo looked back at Joe. "What do you want to ask, Bruh?"

"The tablet. Where is it?"

Chapter 33

2.10 PM, ten hours earlier
Seville, Spain

Joe moved through to the kitchen, placed his used dinner plate in the sink, and started the coffee machine. He switched on the radio as was his habit and flipped through a tablet on the counter, intending to spend twenty minutes checking his encrypted mail, the Liberatus News headlines, and the general geopolitical situation as he sipped his coffee.

It didn't seem any different to the usual: the UIS, a radical Islamic group spawned out of ISIS, were getting active on the Iranian border. Calls from particular politicians for increased militarisation of the police. The transatlantic tunnel is near completion, apparently.

An urgent message alert popped up on his screen from the Icarus chat room. Joe immediately opened the message. It was from Sirus.

"This concerns your friends...It looks like they were arrested in Zafra."

There was a link to an online news feed that featured a grainy image recorded on a cell phone: a stocky man with his hands on his shaved head, on his knees as a group of police surrounded him at gunpoint. Joe recognised them as the Grupo Especial de Operaciones; the Spanish anti-terrorism special forces.

The headline read, "Terrorist suspects seized in Zafra."

He closed his eyes for a second. This was not good at all. And Gianna? Was she OK? He scanned the text. A woman of African descent had also been arrested, it said.

There was a video inserted into the article, and he tapped through the play button. The footage showed the same scene, Hugo Reese on his knees, hands on head, but from a different angle, from someone closer. As they seized him, it was obvious to all that some of the kicks and punches were wholly unnecessary.

Joe wondered what might have happened to the tablet they were carrying. The information on it must be gold if they were going to this amount of effort to recover it.

He had to get hold of that device, get Sirus to unlock it, and find what the hell was hidden there. Whatever was going on, the stakes were high; that much was clear. They had already blown up a train to cover their tracks, and somehow Gianna and her friend were right in the vortex of it.

And the risks for himself were huge if he was actually going to carry out the audacious plan that was forming inside his head. A long stretch doing jail time would be one possible outcome. This was bigger than anything he had ever attempted before. But if it was going to work, he would need to work fast and put his military thinking cap on.

He pinged a message through Icarus to a contact of his across town and then auto-dialled his girlfriend, Hanna Friedmann.

"Hey," the voice was quiet.

"Hi, hon. Something's come up that's important. I might

need your help."

After speaking for several minutes, Joe cut the connection and drained his coffee.

Sirus had indicated there was CIA activity in Madrid and had promised to look into it. According to the last update from Gianna via Icarus, while en route to Seville, Hugo had been pursued by a Mexican-looking man with a ponytail in a dark suit with the full intent of killing him.

If he could get more information on this character, it might give him an edge, however small.

Joe grabbed his keys and locked the door to the flat. Descending the faux marble stairs, his footfalls echoed through the old tenement building. He glanced out on the sun-baked street, looking both ways before heading across to his old Ford.

He'd specifically chosen to avoid having the traffic monitoring system that was a requirement on all modern vehicles. This gave the authorities instant access to the details of the car's location, speed, and a host of other information that Joe wasn't willing to give.

He drove through the San Bernardo district and past the university. Apart from a few people enjoying their afternoon tapas, sitting beneath parasols that baked in the sun, the streets were quiet.

Crossing the Puente de San Telmo bridge, one of several that connected the city, Joe headed east. After twenty minutes' drive, Joe pulled up outside one of the many high-walled properties in a quiet street lined by palms.

The white gates parted with a low whining noise, and a bulky man in his mid-forties, dressed in short-sleeve shirt, slacks, and flip-flops, stood waiting behind them.

"Andreas! Long time no see, bud," said Joe. They shook

hands.

"Damn right, Joe. How come we haven't hooked up for so long?"

Joe shook his head. "I know, it's my fault. You know how it rolls. I've been away with a project."

"How's that girlfriend of yours?"

"Keeping me on my toes; that's all I'll say," Joe quipped. Both men shared a smile and stepped inside the driveway. Andreas clicked a button on a device in his hand, and the gates closed again.

Andreas had been a staff sergeant in Joe's army days when he was stationed in Basra. The two men had struck up a friendship long after their army careers were both behind them.

"So, how can I help you, Joe?"

"You have a family member in the vehicle trade, right?"

Andreas nodded, narrowing his eyes.

"I'm looking for a van that looks the part. Like it is a CNI or police vehicle."

Andreas raised his eyebrows. "I won't bother asking what kind of gig this is."

"A dark or black vehicle will do; it needs to have a cage in the back for authenticity. And I'll need another car with plenty of horsepower under the hood."

"Right. Tricky but not impossible."

"I need it in a couple of hours."

Andreas laughed out loud, almost involuntarily. "Impossible!"

Joe wasn't smiling.

"Oh, you're perfectly serious then?"

"Yeah, 'fraid so. It's no easy task, but I'm willing to add an extra 20 percent on top of the usual."

Andreas shook his head disparately. "Joe, it's not about the money...the turnaround, it's..."

"Tighter than a gnat's ass. I know."

Joe stared at Andreas with his piercing blue eyes that had attracted many women throughout his life. Now they were demanding, menacing even.

Andreas knew that look well and fished out his mobile from his trouser pocket.

"OK, OK. Let me make some calls."

***

While Andreas was sorting out the van, Joe had received word that Hanna could meet her contact for creating the ID. Joe headed to Hanna's apartment that overlooked the Guadalquivir River to pick her up before driving towards the south of the city and Bellavista.

'Think this idea of yours is going to work, Joe?' she said after ten minutes of silence.

Her accent had a trace of her German background still, but her command of English occasionally seemed better than Joe's. They had been in a relationship for eighteen months or so now, having met at an anarchist travellers gathering in Seville.

Not that Joe considered himself an anarchist, but he liked to keep ties with the traveller groups around Andalucia. As far as he was concerned, it made sense to know as much about what made any communities or groups tick as possible.

Could they be part of his planned Liberatus community in the future? Probably not.

They had their own ways of doing things and seemed more intent on getting wasted than building a foundation for anything good. Plus, there were continuous conflicts within the groups, with fights being a regular occurrence.

It made sense to keep channels open with them—for trading goods or making deals. After all, no one knew what the future held.

Hanna seemed intelligent, a step apart from the people in that world. And yet there she was, standing amongst them, shouting in anger at another government crackdown. She was classically beautiful with bright green eyes and delicate features, but she didn't advertise the fact if anything playing it down with her naturally grown dreadlocks and grungy clothes. But Joe noticed her straight away.

"It'll work," he mumbled, following her direction through the narrow streets and turning left along a row of double-storey houses.

Hanna pointed to a block of flats at the end. "That's the building. We should stop somewhere here."

They pulled over onto the pavement, and Joe switched off the engine. They sat looking over at the main doorway, the exterior lamp above the entrance attracting a swarm of insects.

The street was deserted. The blur of a car passed the junction up ahead, and a door slammed in one of the apartments, breaking the otherwise quiet night.

Hanna typed into her phone and then placed it on her lap. She took Joe's hand and rubbed it with her fingers.

"What are we doing?" he asked, slightly irritated.

"Just waiting for the go-ahead," Hanna replied mockingly. Her phone chirruped, and after glancing at it, she nodded her head. "That's her."

They got out of the car and strolled across the road towards the flats. Hanna pressed one of the bells and spoke briefly into the intercom. They were buzzed in and made their way up a flight of stone steps.

A middle-aged woman in a dressing gown, nursing a mug of coffee, opened the door and glared out at them. She nodded towards Joe as she spoke to Hanna.

"What is he doing here?"

"He wanted to check the merchandise himself."

She swore in Spanish under her breath and allowed them in nevertheless. Inside, the apartment was cramped with too much furniture for the size of a flat, and they squeezed past a row of chairs in the hallway and walked into a small living room.

She made her way to a drawer and pulled out a large envelope, and handed it to Hanna.

"Best I could at such short notice," she said. Hanna immediately handed it over to Joe, who took out the ID card and studied it closely. It had the CIA insignia, an employee number, and the photograph of Joe that he had handed over for the job.

"Are you sure this is accurate?" Joe asked, suspicion lining his voice.

"Do you know what a CIA identification badge looks like?"

"No, but..."

"So, do you really expect a small-town police office to know either? Look, as long as you believe you are who you claim to be and have the confidence and bullshit to carry it off"—she cast her eye up and down Joe's frame and gave him a smile—"and I'll bet you do, then you should have no worries."

Joe shook his head, unconvinced.

"I need better assurances than that."

"Give me a week, and you can have bells and whistles. With mere hours? This is the best I can do. It'll do the job; trust me.”

Joe knew she was right. Besides, they couldn't wait around any longer and had to head to Zafra as soon as possible if he was going to pull this off.

Chapter 34

Juan picked up the coffee jug, pouring the hot liquid into his mug. He drank down the caffeine to try to sober up before the drive home and then headed back towards his office.

The station had quietened down, leaving a skeleton crew until the next shift. His section of the building had not been renovated for years, although it was scheduled, and the mustard-coloured paint flaked from the walls like sunburnt skin.

Enríquez walked past him and nodded.

"Goodnight, Enríquez. Thanks for your help earlier," said Juan gruffly.

The young cop nodded. "Thanks, sir...and once again, my condolences for your—"

"Don't mention it," Juan replied without breaking stride. "Have a good night."

Juan reentered his office, slumped back down behind his desk, and gathered up his papers. Elsa's funeral was looming, and there were a million other details to sort out. Some time off was badly needed, and now that the terrorists had been caught, he could just focus on the rest of his family and the period of mourning.

The ring of the internal line shook Juan out of his thoughts just as he was preparing to call it a night.

"Si?"

"Chief?"

It was Officer Acosta at the front desk. That new female recruit that Juan had taken a shine to.

"There is a Jamall Salazar acting on behalf of the CNI in Madrid here to see you."

Juan frowned, hesitating as he reached for his mobile phone on the desk.

"The American? He's come back?"

There was a brief silence on the other end of the line, and the police chief realised that Acosta had just come on duty, so he wouldn't know if it was the same person anyway.

"His credentials check out," came the voice at the other end.

"Send him up," Juan said quietly before dropping the phone onto the receiver, his alertness spiking.

A few minutes later, a figure appeared in his doorway and then entered his office, looking around with mild curiosity until his black eyes fell upon Juan.

"What are you doing? Salazar was here already. Who are you?"

The man loomed over the desk and dropped his identification in front of the chief.

"I have not been here already, Chief Cerezo. I am here for the terrorist suspects, and I don't like the sound of this already."

For the first time in years, Juan felt threatened and uneasy. He didn't like this guy one bit but picked up the ID, glancing back at him quizzically as he did so.

As he had suspected, American intelligence, although he wasn't too knowledgeable about the SSEUR connection.

Juan tried to regain his composure, yet he could feel the

sweat forming on his brow.

"There seems to be some confusion here. Jamall Salazar came and collected the prisoners twenty minutes ago."

"Well, as you can see from my ID, Juan", Jamall said, looking down his nose, "I am Jamall Salazar."

Jamall's face remained flat, expressionless. "Now, my question to you would be: Where are my prisoners?"

Juan stood up suddenly, tossing back the ID across the desk.

"You come into my station, you cocky Yank puta..." He stopped dead, eyes falling to the pistol that had a silencer attached, aimed casually at his chest.

"I don't have time for your bullshit. So, let's start from the beginning. Firstly, sit back down."

Juan did so slowly.

"Someone claiming to be me came and collected the prisoners. Is that correct?"

Juan was frowning deeply now, his mind racing, attempting to fathom what was going on. Firstly, he had been duped, and now he was being held at gunpoint!

"Yes. I saw a standard black police vehicle in the courtyard. Now will you..."

"Tell me, Juan. Do you mind if I call you Juan? I'm aware that you followed them on the train from Talavera de la Reina. Where did they depart exactly?"

"They jumped off at the outskirts of Zafra as we were getting close to the station."

"And then they were caught? Which particular area in Zafra?"

Juan thought for a moment. "Well, the male was captured near Plaza de España, and we picked up the woman on the N432 near the gas station. Listen, Mr Salazar, can you put the gun away, please?"

The dark eyes seem to process the information quickly, flicking to the side as if mapping the route.

"Listen, Mr Salazar..."

"Did they have a tablet? In a green leather zipper? You must have seen the prisoners' personal effects manifest, so just answer the question, please."

The voice was low, calm, yet menacing. The pistol raised to a level with Juan's forehead.

Juan began to put up his hands, instinctively knowing he was dealing with someone with no fear of consequence.

"Please...my daughter was..."

"Answer the question."

"No...no, there was no such device. Now can we—"

Jamall fired the weapon, sending a spray of red across the wall and the painting behind him. Juan slumped across the desk, his face hitting the pile of paperwork and then slowly sliding down until his body collapsed onto the ground.

"Thank you," he said quietly, checking his weapon.

Jamall moved to the door, checking the corridor before walking out, closing it behind him.

His mind was already calculating the next step like a computer mechanically playing chess. How pathetically incompetent they were, letting the suspects be taken like that. Whoever was helping them was clever, very clever. Perhaps it was something he needed to tell Doctor Red?

Need to move fast now. They can't be that far away.

He strolled nonchalantly out of the police station without any problems. Staff were thin on the ground at that time, and it was probably a few hours before another shift clocked in.

Zara waited patiently in the Audi provided by the police

station to transport them from the helicopter. She started the engine as soon as she saw him stroll out onto the street.

"Well?"

"They're gone. Someone impersonating me took them away. Well, that idiot police chief won't make the same mistake again. It's just us now. I've got a vehicle description and a rough idea of where they stashed the tablet; we might be lucky," Jamall said with a shrug.

***

Hugo hauled himself out of the car, struggling to keep up with Joe, who sprinted ahead to the church entrance.

Joe glanced at Hugo and waved him back. "I'll go. Just tell me where."

He could only spit out instructions.

"The boards in the bell tower; it's under one of them..."

Joe switched on his flashlight and illuminated the dark interior of the ruined church. Hugo could hear him making his way up the steps. Across the small wasteland where Hugo and Gianna had run out of cover from the pursuing police officers only five hours earlier came a buzzing sound. They are too prominent to be drones. This was the low whooping of helicopter blades. Had Joe's little trick been discovered already, and the search for them begun again? Outrunning a helicopter was no easy feat. Still, they'd changed vehicles, so they had the upper hand.

Hugo hobbled over to the car to let the girls know about the chopper, but they had already heard it. After a few minutes, Joe reappeared from the church, tablet in hand, and got back into the vehicle. He handed it to Hugo.

"Just confirm to me it's the same one."

Hugo glanced at Joe and shrugged before opening up the pouch.

"Yeah, vato. It's Batchman's," he said before securing it inside one of the backpacks Joe had brought.

"Happy days. Now, keep it close, and let's get the hell out of here."

As they headed North on a quiet road away from Zafra, there was a distant sound of chopping blades catching the wind and disappearing as quickly as it had appeared. The rolling countryside was divided up into fields, a patchwork of greys in the moonlight. Up ahead were the outbuildings of some derelict farm, its working days having long since passed.

"You think that helicopter is getting closer?" said Hugo

"Hard to say," said Joe. "I'd guess it's pretty high up and trying to get a bead on us. Problem with it being so late is there ain't going to be too many cars on the road."

Hugo, Gianna, and Hanna peered upwards fruitlessly into the darkness. Despite the near-full moon, there was no sign of it.

"If they have infrared sensory tracking on it, there's not much we can do," said Joe.

"Hanna, in the bag...there's some NVs."

Hanna fished around and pulled out a pair of night vision goggles, and handed them to Joe.

"Thanks. Probably futile, but let's not make it easy for them."

Joe slipped on the NVs, flipped off the headlights, and concentrated on the road ahead.

The sound came back again, louder this time, growing steadily as it moved, unseen in the night above them. Gianna kept peering out of the rear window, desperately scanning the sky.

"I think I see it," she said, almost shouting. "Almost up above."

"Can you outrun the fucker?" asked Hugo, more out of hope than anything else.

The rattling of the car windows answered his question. Suddenly dropping from the dark sky like a condor, the beast in the night appeared several hundred metres ahead of them, hovering above the road before it finally touched down on the tarmac.

"Shit! Hold on!" Joe slammed on the brakes and pulled the handbrake up, sending the vehicle careering across both sides of the road in a dust bowl of burning rubber.

The car finally came to a standstill, and the occupants all looked ahead at the characters in the cockpit staring back at them. They could see each other clearly. For a second, time froze as Joe locked eyes with the assassin, the man he knew was Jamall. In the milliseconds that followed, he studied the emotionless face and realised for the first time what kind of sociopath Hugo and Gianna had been dealing with. Joe had no idea who the woman with him was, but she looked equally eager to start killing for fun.

A spotlight switched on from the helicopter suddenly broke the spell, blinding them all for a few moments.

"Heads down!"

Joe swiftly pulled off his NVs and slammed the gearstick into reverse. He let the handbrake down and drove the car backwards. Jerking the handbrake up once more, he spun the steering wheel into a sharp right, spinning the car to face the direction they had just come. Behind, the figures jumped out of the cockpit onto the road, their suit jackets flapping as they both aimed weapons at the car.

Joe expected a crescendo of bullets to hit the back window, but instead, they began pounding the road and their tyres, blowing out one of them instantly. The car pulled sharply to the right. Holding tightly to the wheel, Joe kept the vehicle as straight as he could, putting as much distance between themselves and their pursuers as possible.

"Get ready to bail and split up. Make for those buildings!" He jerked a head at the farm. Suddenly, he lost control of the steering.

Another tyre hit!

The vehicle veered off the road and almost tipped onto its side. Joe wrestled with the steering wheel and managed to regain some control, but the bullets had already done the damage. The car was going nowhere.

"Bail!" Joe shouted, opening the door. Gianna went with him, running across the road towards the buildings as Hugo and Hanna went the opposite way, slipping into the darkness across a grass verge towards a cattle shed on the far side.

Joe and Gianna ran hard and fast, reaching a low stone wall, and they ducked around the edge of it as a round of bullets smashed the stones to smithereens. They moved again, and Joe caught a glance of their pursuer in the moonlight; it was the woman purposefully striding in their direction and reloading her weapon.

"Keep moving," Joe urged Gianna. "Gotta get out of sight."

They followed the crumbling wall that led to a stone building and bolted inside. The little house had clearly been abandoned for some time; the door was long gone, and the interior was empty, showing only signs of being used as a hangout for local kids. A hole in the roof let in just enough light to make out the walls, and Joe wondered how much longer before the rest of the roof gave up. They pushed forward into the dark, and Gianna tripped, falling over something in the dark and staggered into the back of Joe, her hands grasping at him for support.

"Shit!"

"You OK?" Joe whispered

"Yeah. Just can't see Jack—"

"Shh, keep it down."

Joe took her hand in the darkness, but she let it go immediately. "I'm good," she said.

"Suit yourself." They crept through the small room towards the rear of the house. In the open doorway leading back outside, they could see another building, and jogging across to it they slipped inside. This house was similar to the first, dust and damp filling their nostrils as they navigated through the dark, reaching a long room at the end. The doorway was blocked by a metal door that had rusted tightly shut. Joe tried it, but it would have taken too much effort to get open quickly. On either side, there were windows that had long lost their glass and frames.

They both waited for a few seconds, listening. There was the distinct sound of footsteps a few rooms away. Joe nodded at one of the windows, and they crept towards it, Gianna carefully lifting herself up and through it to the outside as Joe kept watch on the doorway behind them, straining his ears to catch any clue of their pursuers whereabouts.

Joe followed suit and hauled himself through the window, catching himself on a nail that made him wince with pain. Gianna crouched against the wall, waiting for him, and gestured towards another building across a yard. On their right was a wall with the old thin metal skeleton frames of greenhouses that stuck out in the moonlight like some jagged puzzle against a sky that was now turning from black to dark blue. The hint of dawn nudged at night behind the distant hills.

The moon, casting an eerie light over the whole derelict site, made hiding out in the open difficult. Should they sit and wait where they were? Or make a break for one of the other buildings and risk making a noise and giving away their position? There was no sound coming from their pursuer. Not yet, anyway. But Joe was convinced she wasn't far away, waiting for them to make a noise.

Joe searched around with his hand on the ground and found a fairly heavy stone. He flicked his arm away from his body, sending it across the yard to the greenhouse area on his right. It clanked against a stone wall—hopefully, enough of a distraction. Joe caught Gianna's eye and jabbed a finger across the yard. Creeping quickly but silently towards the next building ahead of them, when he reached the outside wall, he crouched in the shadow of it and waited for Gianna as she made her way across.

Gianna made her move across the open space. A single shot whistled through the air, and she collapsed to the ground, hands clutching at her left leg.

Shit!

She moaned in pain, clearly fighting hard not to scream out, blood pooling around her fingers as she held tightly to the wound.

Joe looked around towards the greenhouses, and anywhere else the shooter could be. There was no sign, and he hadn't caught sight of any muzzle flashes.

He needed to think, but time wasn't a commodity he had.

There was no sign of her, but he knew the shot had come from his left-hand side. The woman was waiting for Gianna to give away his position or for Joe to reveal himself. Had she circled around the second building while they were inside?

Or was she in the building they had just come through?

Joe moved to his right, still crouching in the shadow. He caught Gianna's eye and put a finger across his lips before crawling on his hands and knees away from her to try to loop behind where he thought the shooter was.

Standing in a half crouch, Joe moved around the building to his right, along the side of it, until he arrived at a window to a small room that was clearly empty. He slipped through it as silently as possible and stood still inside, frozen as if a static part of it. Stepping slowly to the door, he waited again and drew his pistol from the holster around his chest. Then he heard it; a very quiet sound of something, like a foot slowly lifting off rubble. It was enough to tell him where she was, the next room at the far wall.

Had she heard him, his element of surprise gone?

Joe slowly slid off the safety on his firearm and moved into the corridor, his eyes fixed on the doorway to that room.

Moving silently, he began "slicing the pie," placing himself against the wall as closely as possible, making sure he was an arm's length away from the door frame so as not to expose his hand.

He scanned inside the doorway vertically, checking each segment of space before stepping forward and repeating the process until he was sure it was clear. Moving into the room, one slow footstep after another, he spied a small square of moonlight reflected on the dusty floor—the far corner was clear. The only place the pursuer could be hiding was in the corner to his right, standing back in the shadows looking out the window to where Gianna was.

Joe fired off a couple of shots into the corner, the muzzle flash revealing the woman just a foot to the right of his shot. Quickly adjusting his aim, he let off another two rounds.

The target was moving, rapidly backing away from his arc of fire, and he heard her shout with pain. Another flash suddenly lit up the darkness.

Flying brick fragments and a plume of plaster dust hit his face and eyes.

Fuck! Blinded.

Joe immediately wiped his hand over his eyes, trying to get back some vision, ignoring the searing pain in his eye sockets.

He caught sight of a shadow moving swiftly towards him, her right arm hanging limp at her side.

Sensing an attack, he held up his arms, shielding his head.

The force of the following blow rocked him, his arms taking the impact. Joe swayed but managed to stay on his feet.

With his head ringing and eyes watering, he could just make out a shadow moving in front of him. Jumping forward, she threw another vicious roundhouse kick, this one aimed at his lower leg.

Joe barely had time to react, the pain shooting through his body and bringing him to his knees.

Grabbing the back of his head, she drove a knee into his face, and Joe's world was plunged into darkness. He fell backwards, head spinning and fighting to stay conscious. A hand grabbed his ankle and dragged him into the centre of the room, towards the sliver of moonlight on the floor.

Drawing in several deep breaths, Joe tried to regain his composure, the metallic taste of blood in his mouth. The woman let go, slowly walking around her prey.

He adjusted his body, moving on his back to try to keep his legs between them.

Still struggling to see anything, Joe squinted at the vague shadows that penetrated his vision. He wiped his eyes, which were still watering, with one hand as the woman laughed with contempt.

She moved at him suddenly, and Joe kicked out, but she anticipated and sidestepped out of the way.

She laughed again, but he could make out she was holding her right arm. At least he had hit something. Some pain had been inflicted on her, not that she seemed to notice—definitely grade-A psycho material.

"Hope the arm isn't too painful for you," he said.

"Hope your eyes aren't too painful. I can take them out if you like."

She moved again, and Joe instinctively kicked out.

Zara feinted to her left, sidestepping his outstretched leg, and swung another hard kick, landing a boot against his face.

Joe's head fell back, cracking against the floor, his senses in free fall, spinning mixed with extreme pain.

He barely registered the knee on his chest as a rain of punches battered his face, his arms struggling to defend himself.

She threw a hooking punch to avoid his defensive arms, and Joe, grabbing her more out of desperation than any kind of skill, used all his strength to pull her down.

Struggling to get away from his clinging hands, the woman pushed back, trying to put space between them, but Joe continued to use all his force to pull her down.

In an instant, he let go, and she stumbled backwards, falling onto her rump.

Scrambling back, Joe tried to regain some kind of advantage, but she was too good, moving straight back at him.

Joe's back hit the wall. He was trapped, and he suddenly realised that he was going to die in that room. Just as the thought flashed through his brain, his fingers brushed a cold metallic object on the ground—his gun.

Without thinking, his training kicked in. Grabbing the weapon, Joe unloaded a volley of shots at the centre of the mass coming at him.

The bullets hit but had little effect, and she kept advancing towards him.

She would not fall. Was she wearing armour?

This was it then, his final moment.

As soon as she was in range, she threw out a thrust kick. His arms shielded his head from the blow, but the force smashed him back into the wall.

A series of vicious roundhouse kicks followed, raining down on him. Joe curled up to try to protect his head—a futile move.

As the barrage continued, Joe felt his body giving up, the dark abyss of unconsciousness pulling him inside.

All his plans, his dreams, ended here, lying on the dusty floor of a derelict farm.

Then he noticed something. The kicks were becoming weaker. Glancing through his fingers, he noticed the moon-light reflecting off the pool of blood forming at her feet.

A groan and the figure stumbled back, falling to her knees, her breathing heavy and laboured.

She cried out again.

"You bas—"

Slumping forward, she curled up, clutching her stomach.

A series of whimpers and moans were the only sound in the deserted building.

Joe focused on breathing and kept wiping his eyes if only to confirm that she was indeed down and out. He struggled to his feet and limped over to the woman, grabbing her hair and pulling her face upwards.

Eyes stared out blankly. Face frozen in pain.

"Adios, honey," Joe muttered and let her head hit the floor before shuffling off through the shadows to find Gianna.

***

Hugo pushed through the pain from his bruises, half limping towards the black shape of a large disused shed. His speed was way off his usual pace. What a great time to be getting chased when he could hardly run.

Joe's girlfriend, Hanna, was just ahead of him.

He stole a quick glance over his shoulder. Didn't look like anyone was behind them.

Then a sudden movement caught his eye in the moonlight. A figure half crouched and jogged away, disappearing behind a small tree.

Hugo couldn't tell if they'd been seen by their pursuer, so he kept low. The moonlight cast a long shadow from the building that at least kept them hidden for the time being.

They both reached the structure and paused, allowing their eyes to adjust to the low light.

The entrance had corrugated iron sheeting bolted over it, but half of it was loose, so he tugged at it to create enough space to get through. A low, creaking sound made them both flinch with every second. It felt like a glowing red beacon was placed above their heads.

"Ssshhhh," whispered Hanna.

Hugo winced and then carried on, aware that their pursuer was closing in fast. But the grinding sound was just as bad, if not worse. After another few painful seconds, he finally had it opened up wide enough.

"Go for it," he whispered to Hanna, who quickly eased herself inside. Hugo then pushed himself through and slowly pulled the iron sheet back into place, the creaking sound returning.

"Fuck," Hugo mouthed to himself. If their pursuer had not heard, it would be a miracle.

They quickly moved across the concrete floor, the dappled moonlight just giving them enough light to see.

The musty barn smelt of decay, and they moved past a rusty old tractor, old jerrycans, and a stack of feeding troughs out of which a rat scurried across their path. Metal pens were fixed along the rear wall, but any smell or evidence of livestock had long gone.

On the other side of the building, another door.

They stepped back outside, the moonlight revealing eerie, white ethereal forms floating in the breeze, attached to a cluster of metal frames. For a moment, Hugo couldn't figure out what he was actually looking at and then realised it was ripped netting attached to a series of long metal frames that stretched back for around one hundred metres, forming tunnels that faded into darkness.

On their left a couple of concrete storage sheds.

Some kind of abandoned fruit farm?

Hugo caught Hanna's eye in the low light and gestured with his head towards one of the tunnels.

They moved silently under the frames, the moonlight casting spindly shadows across spilt plant pots, dry grass, and leaves that lay scattered on the ground. Rows of dead cane stick jutted upwards from the earth, reminding Hugo of a mass of war graves.

Holding up his hand, Hugo gestured to stop, and they both froze.

Just the sound of the light breeze, a creaking of unsteady metal frames and chirping crickets.

A brief whisper, and they moved again, zigzagging through overgrown weeds and clusters of dead bushes, occasionally pausing to listen before moving on towards the far side of the old nets.

As they reached the end, they saw a dirt track in front of a large field of dead sunflowers and a group of trees in the distance beyond the field.

To their left, the path led to the dark shapes of what looked like a dying olive grove and a gate.

To their right, the track looked like it curved away back to the main road.

Hugo looked across the field and frowned.

"Looks way too exposed across there," he whispered. "The moonlight will flush us out like a couple of cockroaches."

"Too loud as well," said Hanna. "All those sunflowers left to dry are going to make some serious noise."

Then a loud crack in the distance from the far side of the farm.

Hugo and Hanna both caught each other's eye.

"That was a gunshot...from where Joe and Gianna headed," whispered Hanna, her voice almost faltering.

Joe and Gianna were being hunted just like they were, and

there was nothing they could do about it at that moment.

They had to save themselves.

"They'll be OK," Hugo replied. He wasn't sure if he believed that. Had to say something.

Cat and mouse is no fun when you're the goddamned mouse, is it, Bruh?

This was bullshit, thought Hugo.

He was used to being the lion of the streets, and ever since the train bomb, he had been reduced to the status of a timid deer caught in headlights.

Every fibre of his being wanted to attack.

Take some kind of action.

Deep down, the odds were stacked against them...or him. He had no idea if Hanna had any fire in her belly, although something told him she held a few more cards than she let on.

They headed left towards the beginning of the olive grove, Hugo glancing back towards the supply sheds that were ten metres or so away.

Hugo pointed towards them. "Listen, hide over there. I'm gonna try and lead him off. I'll come back and find you in a minute."

"What're you going to do?"

"Just go 'n' hide! Quick!"

Hanna didn't wait for a second prompt and disappeared into the dark shadows.

Moving as quietly as he could, Hugo headed a few metres up the track towards the olive grove.

If only he could get the guy off guard, surprise him and give him a taste of LA brute force.

Hugo took his phone out of his pocket, a rush of pain shooting up his arm. He shook his head slightly as he approached the gate and began to look around.

You can barely run, let alone fight.

***

The moonlight hue made a bunch of thick plant leaves appear plastic and laminated. Barking dogs protested far off in the distance, and the crickets seemed close.

Jamall, clutching the pistol tightly, aimed directly ahead, moving slowly through the nets, every careful step barely audible even to his own ears. A gust of wind created movement somewhere through the nets, and he focused on the shift in light and shadow.

Just loose netting.

An indent of a shoe caught in the light. He crouched down and brushed his fingers over a footprint in the hard ground.

They had come this way. And he would finish this business soon.

The nets seemed to stretch on forever, around the size of several football fields from what he could see.

A distant gunshot from behind him.

Jamall stopped, listening out for more, and on hearing nothing carried on.

One down, from Zara's hand, with luck.

Eventually, he came to the end of the derelict greenhouses to a track that ran across his path. He looked around, quietly listening.

Across the field, a sea of wilting dead sunflowers seemed to stretch out for miles.

The crisp dead stalks would make too much noise if they were in there, and he couldn't see any movement.

He slowly turned his head up towards the olive grove, split

in two with a gate at the end of the middle track.

Tuning out the other sounds, he focused on breathing lightly and listening.

Then he heard it.

A crunch.

Distant but unmistakable—soft as if a foot had stepped on dry leaves.

Jamall froze and narrowed his eyes.

Target located.

It had come from the cluster of olive groves up ahead. Crouching slightly, he focused on the direction of the sound. It came again, a similar softer rustling but definitely nearer the gate.

With slow, measured steps, Jamall moved to the edge of the track and then slipped along a row of trees, carefully staying in the shadows away from the light until he reached the end of the grove.

When he was in position, he crouched and waited, staring across the path to the clump of olive trees on the far side.

A cluster of shrubs next to the gate was the only place they could be.

No sign of movement, but the sound had come from there.

Must be close. I sense their fear.

Some deep part of Jamall felt the sensation of joy, a rare segment of his soul.

You are the hunter, the assassin.

A rush forward into the gap. Weapon aimed high.

Empty. There was no one.

All clear.

Behind the shrub, there was a dip in the ground leading to another few acres of olive grove but no sign of the targets.

Scanning the area through the trees, Jamall began to step forward, and then something caught his eye on the ground.

A faint hue of blue light.

He crouched down to look closer and soon realised it was a phone hidden partly under leaves on the dry soil, the screen brightening as he touched it. On the screen was an audio app in play mode that appeared to be on a loop.

Just then, the repeated sound of a footstep on dry leaves the exact same noise he had heard minutes before.

Jamall smiled, stopped the app, and pocketed the phone.

Amateurs.

He liked this game. Perhaps he could make it last a bit longer.

He paused at a series of muffled gunshots carried through the night from the far side of the farm where Zara had headed.

Kill them, Zara. Kill them all.

***

Hugo headed through the grove, doubling back in the vague direction of the cattle shed around fifty metres away. He paused, half crouched just for a moment to steady his breathing and then continued.

There was a plan forming, vague like the dark blocks of the supply huts up ahead, but it was the only plan he had.

A cloud passed across the moon, extinguishing his vision as if a candle had blown out. Hanna stepped out from between the two storage huts where she'd been hiding. The moonlight returned, and Hugo saw her face, expectant and calm.

"What's happening?" she asked in a whisper.

He didn't answer, his eyes surveying the large gap in the back of the first hut that had once been a window. Another glance back along the ridge towards the olive grove. Hopefully, the Mexican had lost their tracks, but if he hadn't, there was no time.

A distant snap.

"Hugo?" Her voice more demanding now. When he looked at her, she was staring back towards the grove.

"I think I heard something."

"Yeah. So did I. Come on."

He grabbed her arm and led her into the alley between the sheds, the first of the tunnel nets ahead.

Around the front was an old wooden door that Hugo eased open into the first shed. Soft moonlight through the window revealed a reel of old hose, a set of spades, and several watering cans.

They went inside, and Hanna crept up to the window to peek out.

Hugo checked the watering can with his hands. *Perfect.*

"Do you smoke?" he asked.

"That's not a great idea," she hissed back.

"Just give me your lighter!"

She did as he asked, frowning at him, and then returned to watch out in the night.

"We need to get out of here," she said, fear creeping into her voice.

"Wait here, and stay well hidden, OK, Sis?"

"Where the hell are you going now?"

"Two seconds," he replied. Before she could complain any further, he was gone into the night.

Hugo moved as fast as he could back to the cowshed and, once inside, looked around for the gasoline cans he had seen earlier.

A lift of the handle told him one was half-full.

Good enough.

At least, he hoped it was.

*****

Jamall winced as he stepped on the dry twig. It was hardly loud, but to his ears, it may as well have been a ship's horn blasting through the night.

Treading more carefully, he made his way towards the edge of the grove. A wooden fence marked the beginning of a vast scrubland that disappeared in the direction of Zafra.

Jamall crouched and waited, peering hard into the black of the night as if willing them to appear.

Only night vision would truly tell him.

The air was thick, and he listened to the crickets for a few moments.

Whatever was here is gone.

Jamall moved back through the olive trees back towards the farm.

A memory. Much younger. Running through the woods, shooting targets.

Some of it is blocked out as if photographs had been torn into strips, and there is missing information. Missing pieces of the puzzle.

He remembered his fear of the training sergeant yet, at the same time, held a gritty determination to do well, to complete the mission.

To please the doctor, his padre.

What was it he had said?

"Complete the mission. Kill the man with the bat."

That's what he had said.

And he had. Beaten him to a bloody pulp.

How many killed by his hand since? Hundreds? What did it matter? They were pictures on a collage. A moment in time.

And now the completion of this task was so close.

He would please the doctor once again and earn his place in the new world.

A volley of muffled gunshots carried through the night, shattering the peace.

Jamall smiled. Zara had found her kill.

Up ahead was the distant, dark outline of the cattle shed he had stalked them through earlier and the shapes of two huts. Directly across from him were the nets, still floating in the occasional gust of wind.

The phone had tricked him into going deep into the grove. To throw him off.

What would they do? Head back to the road and their vehicle? Or hide?

He rechecked his weapon. Couldn't afford mishaps.

Not now. Too close.

He peered across at the rows of nets stretched out into the darkness. It was a huge area of around one hundred square metres to conceal themselves in. They may have doubled back to hide in there. It's what he might do.

Just as he made his decision, his ears picked up a sound.

From those huts? Like running water. A sloshing noise?

He took a few steps towards them and caught sight of the male target stepping out between the huts.

Without hesitation, Jamall aimed his weapon and breathed in, relaxing his fingers as he picked his spot, all in under a second.

He squeezed, and a dull thud rang out. A cry of pain, and the figure fell back between the sheds.

Straightaway, the assassin was moving, closing the distance between himself and the target as quickly as possible.

Reaching the level ground, he came to the sheds, and suddenly a pair of arms jerked an object out of the window. Before he could think what the hell it was, a wall of liquid soaked his face and jacket.

Jamall fired a shot at the window in response as he passed by and turned the corner between the sheds.

He stopped dead in his tracks, realising what the liquid was. *Gasoline!*

It burned his eyes, blurring his vision.

Wiping it from his eyes, Jamall looked up.

The dark figure of his target, Hugo Reese, stood at the far end with gritted teeth, clutching his arm.

Jamall smiled, slow and deliberate. This was fun.

"Did I shoot you in the same arm, Hugo?"

Hugo spat onto the ground and stepped backwards.

"Hey, puta. Instead of guns, why don't we see some of those hand combat skills?"

The Mexican smiled again, nodding as if understanding the game had risen to a new level.

"Even on your best day, you wouldn't be any sort of challenge. Now, tell me where the tablet is, and I'll make your death quick. I may even spare your friends."

Hugo's grimace changed to a grin now, stepping back again as he held his hand aloft. A click and a spark of flame appeared. *Zippo lighter.*

Jamall frowned and raised his weapon. "You think you can

set me on fire from over there, amigo? Last chance. After I've killed you, I'll simply torture the information out of your friends."

Hugo jerked his arm downwards, and a whoosh of flame ignited like white light in front of his eyes, racing down the alley towards Jamall. In an instant, Jamall realised the ground had been soaked with gasoline.

Then torrid, flaring pain engulfed his entire body, forcing him back onto the ground.

Palms covered his face, beating flames that would not go out.

For a moment, he saw a beautiful white butterfly across his vision, its wings spread wide, and then heard his own screams.

A sound he had never heard before.

Chapter 35

They scurried around the edge of the cattle shed, Hugo clutching his arm.

Just ahead, the car they had left in a big hurry lay abandoned, doors still wide open. Hugo scanned the buildings on the far side of the road and then froze as he caught movement. Two figures, one holding up the other.

"Joe!"

Hanna ran over to them and put her hand on Joe's shoulder.

"Is she OK?" she asked

"She's fine," rasped Gianna. "Just caught one in the leg."

"What happened to the devil woman?" Hugo asked.

"She's history," said Joe.

"And the Mexican?"

"I gave him a flaming Sambuca," Hugo grunted. He had slumped down onto the ground, his hand covering a stream of blood that soaked between his fingers.

Joe gave him a quizzical look for a second.

"Shit, you've been shot again as well."

"Yeah, that fucking puta got me in the same arm...the bitch." He rocked his head, shaking it, sweat quickly forming on his brow.

A cry of pain caused Joe to turn to Gianna, and he eased her down onto the ground.

"OK, just rest it for now," he said.

"Thanks for the advice, Joe. Think I'll do that." She managed a weak smile but was obviously in agony.

Hugo managed to slip off his backpack painstakingly slowly and then rummaged around inside with his other hand. "I've still got bandages and shit; we need to fix that wound." He jerked his head towards Gianna.

"And yours, too, Hugo. Come on, Hanna. We need to get these guys off the road."

They slowly moved to a spot out of sight from the road, and Hanna crouched and tended to Gianna's flesh wound as Joe stripped off a bandage to dress Hugo.

"Need to control the bleeding. Get a strip of bandage and tie it tight above the wound. Then apply constant pressure to it," said Joe, calmly instructing Hanna.

"Got it," she replied.

"The leg's a tricky one to get wounded. You get a hit in the femoral artery, and it's game over," he added.

"Th-thanks," replied Gianna.

"Don't worry; you'd be dead by now if it was damaged."

"Double thanks."

Joe turned his attention to Hugo.

"Not having a lot of luck, are you?" he quipped.

Hugo managed a laugh through his gritted teeth. "You can fucking believe that, Bruh. Believe that."

"We need to get organised," said Joe. "I've already messaged a friend who should be here soon. We need to check the police scanner, make sure they're not aware of our position, and burn the vehicle."

"Burn them?" asked Gianna through gritted teeth as Hanna

tightened a makeshift strap around her leg.

"Yeah, there'll be a feast of fingerprints and DNA evidence for the forensic snoops if we don't destroy it."

"Sounds like a plan," said Hugo, realising for the first time that they were out of immediate danger and thankful for it. A cold sweat blanketed his entire body, and he glanced down to see his hand was shaking.

"Let's get on with what we gotta do then," he added. "I don't want to be thrown back in that cell...or worse."

Joe jogged over to the car and rooted around inside, grabbing his police scanner and backpack. He opened the boot and pulled out a small can of petrol, and placed it by the rear wheel.

"I take it you still have the tablet, Hugo?" he shouted.

Hugo lifted a thumbs-up.

"Headlights!" Gianna shouted.

"Stay hidden!" Joe shouted back before lowering himself behind the car. Just then, his phone buzzed. It was Andreas. Joe tapped a reply:

"You're close. Flash your lights twice."

Joe peeked over the car bonnet and carefully watched the lights of the approaching vehicle. They flashed twice, confirming it was their man.

Happy days.

Joe spat onto the ground and shouted over to the others.

"It's OK! The cavalry has arrived!"

Chapter 36

Gianna had her leg elevated on Joe's sofa as Hanna reworked the bandages that had been rushed earlier. Joe and Hugo were sitting at the dining table drinking hot coffee, which Joe had helpfully laced with brandy.

It had been an uneventful journey back. Joe had successfully set fire to the car left in the ditch and navigated them out of the area, avoiding the approaching police by carefully monitoring the scanner. They had approached Seville via the quieter back roads and slipped back into Joe's apartment unseen.

A huge sense of relief dominated the room, the fatigue and pain momentarily forgotten as their safety of being in the flat sank in. They sat in silence for a few minutes as they contemplated all that had happened, as well as their own individual momentous escapes.

Hugo inspected the dressing on his wound, wincing occasionally in pain. Joe took out his phone and accessed Icarus. "You have the tab, Hugo? We need to get our hacker friend to work."

Hugo nodded and reached down to his backpack by his feet, pulling out the zipped leather bag and handing it to Joe.

"I wouldn't shed a single tear if I never saw this thing again," he muttered.

Joe smiled to himself as he booted it up.

'This is gold...I'm sure of it."

***

All eyes focused on the large monitor that was hooked up to Batchman's tablet via a cable so everyone could see what was happening on the screen.

Joe had converted the room at the rear of the apartment into a basic operations centre with an array of mobile phones lying on the modest-size desk. Sitting on a brown leather sofa next to Hanna, Joe tapped at the steel-finished laptop, occasionally glancing up at the screen.

Joe opened an Icarus chat window and proceeded to type directly to Sirus.

"We've looked at all the folders and accessed them with no problems, but there's one that appears to be encrypted. Can you take a look?"

Letters appeared rapidly on the screen as Sirus responded.

"Am looking now...It is encrypted. No easy way in, I'm afraid."

"Can't you hack it??" Joe typed back, "Thought you were some sort of wiz with a computer."

"LOL; you've been watching too many movies. In simple terms, the encryptions use prime numbers, ones that are thousands of digits long. Take two of these primes and multiply them, and you get semi-primes. Now, to break in, you'd need to try and reverse engineer that multiplication. It's like unfrying an egg, easy one way, almost impossible the other. A brute force attack would take thousands of computers billions of years to figure out. Unless, of course, you had a quantum mechanics chip..."

"Looks like we're screwed then," said Hanna.

Joe sighed and continued typing.

"So where does this leave us?"

"You need the encryption key. No other way around it."

"So how do we find it? Is there a chance the professor had it on him when he was killed?"

There was a pause.

"If he took his security seriously, then no. It'll either be on this tablet, hidden amongst the other documents, or somewhere else."

The words stood unmoving on the screen for a moment.

"Fuck," said Joe, rubbing his hands over his thick curly hair.

Another message appeared on the screen.

"I have to go, and it might be difficult to maintain contact for a while. Take care."

"Thanks, Sirus."

The chat window turned blank.

"Joe, do you mind if I root around in your fridge? I'm starving," asked Hugo.

"Yeah of course. Actually, none of us have eaten for some time. Let's get something organised. Hanna, Gianna? You hungry?"

Gianna nodded, and Hanna leaned forward as if to stand up as well.

"Why don't you stay put, Joe? I can make us something..."

"It's OK, Hann. I want to speak with Hugo," Joe said, signalling him with a glance.

Hugo shrugged at Hanna. "Personally, getting some food made up for me sounded like a great idea...but hey, Joe's place, Joe's rules." He held up his heavily bandaged arm. "It's not like I'm dying here or anything."

Joe sighed. "Tell you what, there might be another beer in that kitchen. There's a trusted doctor friend heading around, by the way. To make sure you and Gianna are good."

"This doctor? Someone, you trust, I take it, vato?"

"Billy was a medic in my brigade back in my army days during the first Middle Eastern wars. We're like brothers."

"You're a veteran?" It was the first time Hugo had heard this.

"I did my time," he replied curtly.

***

Pulling out a variety of bread, cheeses, olives, hummus, and other typical tapas fare, Joe piled the food up on the kitchen table while Hugo picked at it.

"So, that was quite an adventure?" said Joe.

"Yeah, seriously. I cannot thank you enough for getting us out of there. I just gotta figure out what's next." Hugo popped an olive into his mouth and sat down at the table with a sigh.

"Except it isn't over yet."

"I know," said Hugo.

Joe pointed a remote at a small television on the counter, turned down the volume, and then took out four large plates from the cupboard.

"You did well out there. I mean, you didn't freak out like some people would. Gianna mentioned you're from LA?"

"Yeah, Florene-Firestone, South Central. To be straight up, I'm in no rush to go back there anytime soon."

"You're still a wanted man by the authorities. In fact, we all are. We're in the shit, but hopefully, whatever is on that tablet will help clear our slate," said Joe.

"You think? I can't see the feds giving up on a group 'apparently' responsible for a train bombing."

Joe nodded and pulled a couple of beers from the fridge, handing one to Hugo.

"Yeah. Well, it's amazing what happens when agendas shift, and the all-seeing eye is diverted away from you."

"Whatta y'mean? Like *Lord of the Rings*? My face is probably plastered all over Europe's most wanted lists. How's that gonna change?"

"Think about it. I'm willing to bet there's very little evidence against you. That psycho who was on your case was seriously breaking laws. It's a frame-up, sticking that train-bombing shit on you 'cos he wanted the tablet. A good lawyer could tear their case apart if they were even willing to prosecute you, that is."

Joe was powering through sourdough bread with a knife before placing the slices on a large plate.

"Vato, in case you didn't see the headlines, they don't give a shit about evidence. Won't they just put me in one of their orange suits and throw me in a hole? And what are you sayin'... that I give myself up?"

"I know things are bad, Hugo, but we still have some human rights left, even if the governments have been trying their hardest to sweep them away. All I'm saying is, let's negotiate. Sirus and maybe Gianna can do some rooting around, see exactly what evidence they have, and then maybe we can sound out a deal with the Spanish authorities."

Hugo shook his head. "I dunno, man."

Joe pointed the finger at Hugo. "And that black eye and all your other wounds? You got a serious beating by that cop?

Shot to fuck by the CIA guy? We have to photograph your injuries ASAP and give it all to the lawyer."

"Why do you wanna help me, Joe?"

"You're a good guy, Hugo. People like you are hard to come by. You've been tested today. I mean, really tested. Most people would have crumpled under that kind of pressure. Regardless of what we find on the device, we'll help you out. We're not gonna leave you high and dry, mate. In fact, we could do with people like you."

"You offering me a job, vato?" Hugo said, raising an eyebrow.

"Not exactly...a new way of life, perhaps? We are building something good, a community and an organisation. If you're looking for a new beginning, maybe we can help.

Hugo looked back at Joe, and a half smile appeared on his face.

"You talkin' 'bout some hippy colony there?"

Joe laughed. "All I'd ask is once we've got you out of this situation, spend a few days with me here. Let me show you what we are trying to do. If it's for you, great. If not, then no hard feelings. Deal?"

"I'll roll with you for a few days, Bro, but I ain't into huggin' no trees or nothin'..."

Joe burst into laughter, the sound echoing off the tiled walls.

"OK, no tree-hugging, understood."

"What about Gianna?"

"What about her?"

"Is she part of the project of yours?"

"I've known her for a few years now; she's a great girl. I asked her the same as I asked you; she has her own path to follow for now. Maybe she'll come round; she's definitely got the right mindset for it."

There was silence.

"I mean...look, it's none of my biz...just curious. You had something together once, didn't you?"

Joe seemed to let the question hang as he emptied a jar of green olives into a bowl.

"You're right. It's none of your business, but I'm not bothered. There was something...but it's ancient history now," he said quietly.

Hugo made a face of understanding and decided to let that one lie, glancing at the television in the corner.

"Hey, hey. It's that puta cop! Turn up the volume!"

On the screen was a still picture of Juan Cerezo dressed smartly in his uniform, staring out from the screen. Joe switched up the sound.

"The police chief who is said to have lost his nineteen-year-old daughter in the recent Madrid train bombing. Colleagues of Cerezo expressed profound shock at the news of his suicide after it became clear he had shot himself in his office at Zafra police headquarters."

Hugo and Joe both looked at each other.

The television filled in the background on Cerezo and then moved on to another news item.

"Fuck," said Hugo.

"They got to him; that's my guess. Must have been that guy and his charming girlfriend before he came after us," said Joe, picking up two of the plates piled with food.

"You mean, it wasn't suicide?"

"I doubt it. Come on; let's eat."

Joe put down the plates on a low coffee table in front of Hanna and Gianna.

"The police chief that gave you and Hugo a hard time just 'committed suicide,' according to the news," said Joe, looking at Gianna, who raised her eyebrows.

"Shit. Well, what goes around comes around."

"That's a bit harsh," said Hanna, looking at her disapprovingly.

"Hey, that bastard slapped me onto the ground in the cell!" spat Gianna.

"Come on, guys, eat something," said Joe, pointing at the plates. He disappeared back into the kitchen before returning with the other two plates, Hugo following behind.

Joe slumped back into his chair and looked up at the main screen on the wall.

There was a buzz on Joe's mobile. "That's Billy, the medic guy I mentioned. We'll get him to treat you and Gianna in the back room."

Joe walked to the front door and let in his old comrade. "Gianna, you'd better see him first."

"I'm good; let Hugo go first. He got shot twice," said Gianna, flashing him a mock smile.

Hugo snorted with derision. "Hey, thanks, G. Let the old man go first, huh? Now you're making me feel bad."

Chapter 37

Joe and Hugo sat in silence as they focused on the problem in hand. Gianna was with the medic in the other room, and Hanna disappeared into the kitchen, brewing a round of coffees.

No one spoke as the realisation dawned that all their running, being shot, and dancing with death on multiple occasions may have been for nothing. Joe seemed transfixed on the big screen, the chat history long since wiped or burned by Icarus as was its protocol. His fingers hovered over the keys as if readying to type commands, but none came.

Hugo examined his newly redressed arm, courtesy of the doctor. The powerful painkillers had kicked in, and despite the general gloom, he felt surprisingly good. It had suddenly hit him, a sense of belonging that he hadn't felt for some time. He missed his brothers back in LA, of course, the camaraderie, being part of something.

Yeah, of course, the gang lifestyle was a mistake, but that was history now.

When Joe had told him how he really helped them out with the tablet, Hugo had a feeling they were going to be friends for a long time to come. And he felt part of something again.

If you get through this, it ain't over yet.

Hugo leaned forward in the chair, resting his elbows on his

legs.

"So, this key, it unlocks the encryption. It has to be some-where, vato."

Joe slowly woke up from his malaise and hit the keyboard, waking it from sleep mode.

"Hmm. yeah, somewhere, somewhere..." Joe seemed to be thinking it through.

"So, as Sirus said, it might either be on the tablet on another document..."

"I'm running a search for any line of numbers on the device. Nothing so far."

"Then she said it might be somewhere else. What if he gave it to someone? It would have to be an amigo he can really trust, right?"

Joe nodded slowly. "Yeah, it's what I'd do. Someone—"

"At the conference!" interrupted Hugo. "He got spooked on the train like he recognised that Jamall character as if he'd been paid a visit before. So worried about his life's work falling into the wrong hands, he encrypts it before travelling across the country for this conference. He speaks to a close amigo before he leaves, someone he knows will be at the conference and someone he trusts. Gives them the key, so if his laptop gets stolen or he is robbed and threatened the data is safe!"

Hugo leaned back, grinning, holding his hands apart.

"Well, I like your thinking. Maybe, maybe. There's a lot of questions still," said Joe.

Hugo clicked his fingers. "There were some names he mentioned on the train, only a few. I remember Eduardo because that's what my father was called. Eduardo."

"Any others?"

Hugo squeezed his eyes closed.

"Another English guy, I think…Peter, maybe Paul. Shit, I dunno."

Hanna returned and handed out mugs to Joe and Hugo. "There you go, fellas." She sat down on the arm of Joe's chair and put her arm on his shoulder.

"Any progress?" she asked.

Before Joe could reply, Gianna, moving gingerly with a fresh dressing around her leg, came into the room with the ex-army medic.

"How's the patient?" asked Joe.

"Really lucky. They both are. The wounds have to be carefully looked after. I've given instructions, but they should really be in a hospital," Billy said, concern etched on his face.

Joe got up and saw Billy out into the hallway. There were the low murmurings of conversation before the goodbyes, and thanks were said, and Joe returned.

He stood in the middle of the room, drained his coffee, and looked down at Gianna, who had slumped back onto a chair.

"Gianna. We need you to do something."

"Sure. Just not backflips."

Hugo turned to her and smiled. "Shame."

"I'm looking through Batchman's documents that we have access to, to see if there's any hint of that key, but it's more likely he'd have stashed it with someone he knows, most likely at the conference," said Joe.

"Yeah, he said he was revealing everything there, so that would make sense, right?" said Hugo.

Gianna nodded. "Sure would. Shouldn't be a problem finding the conference and a list of attendees. But how are you going to convince them to hand it over?"

Hugo threw his good arm in the air. "Hey, G, we can just

tie 'em up and force them to confess. Use a feather," he said, grinning again.

Gianna gave him a wry smile. "Is that some gang term? Using cheese wire or something?"

Chuckles drifted through the room.

"When...if...we find them, we need them onside. If it's someone Batchman trusted, we need to convince them to work with us," said Hanna, playing with a loose blonde dreadlock about her shoulder.

"When we find them," said Hugo.

***

Gianna tapped away on the laptop, the gentle clicking the only sound in the room. Daylight struggled to spill in through the firmly shut blinds onto a sofa where Joe had sprawled out for a much-needed nap. She looked over at him and smiled to herself.

Got to figure this out. Without Sirus. Then maybe Joe would realise how important she could be to him. Invaluable.

It was straightforward enough to find out about the conference, a private event booking on the hotel website titled Virology Forum with keynotes by Nicholas Batchman, Marian Hewlett, and Leon Dubois.

Gianna scanned the page that was hidden away on the site, but there was no mention of anyone named Eduardo, Peter, or Paul.

"Hugo. Batchman didn't mention a Marian or a Leon, did he?"

Hugo shook his head without taking his eyes off the flat tablet screen.

"No, I don't think so, G."

"Then they couldn't have been speakers...attendees probably. Trickier to hunt down."

"I can't find jack shit either."

"If we knew their full names, it'd be a start."

Gianna glanced over at Hugo. "Do a search for those names on Batchman's tablet, could you? There might be a mention," asked Gianna.

Hugo shook his head and sipped on a San Miguel bottle. "I already searched, G; there's no mention of any of those names at all."

"How many of those virus guys with those names can there be?" he added, looking up now.

Gianna was already searching.

Peter+virology pulled up a list of results, mostly books with both terms connected to them in some way. She took a few minutes scrolling through the results, sipping on her bottled water, conscious of the dull pain increasing in her calf and wondering if it was too soon to take her next round of painkillers.

She tried similar searches: pathology, virologist...they all produced dead ends. Then she tried the same list with Eduardo.

The details of a Madrid-based virologist came up. Late forties, jet-black curly hair.

"OK, we have one: Eduardo Crespo."

"So, Hugo. Eduardo, Peter?"

"And Paul," added Hugo.

Gianna nodded, remembering.

She typed it in, and a result flashed up straightaway, showing the credentials and photograph of a thin but tanned-faced man in his sixties with short-cropped white hair.

"Paul Fox. An English virologist based in Lisbon, Portugal," she said proudly.

Hugo clicked his fingers. "I knew it was Paul."

"Bullshit," muttered Gianna. She gave him a look, followed by a smile, before looking back at the screen.

"Yep, it's gotta be either one of them." Hugo was standing up now, peering over Gianna's shoulder, checking out the details.

Joe stirred, slowly moving his head to face them both.

"Found 'em?"

"Yep, we have full names and a few numbers. Now all we have to do is figure out which one might be holding the encryption key."

Joe, bleary-eyed, sat up on the sofa.

"Nice sleep while we were working?" Gianna teased.

"Yeah, thank you," he said, mumbling. "The phones..."

"Huh?"

"If we can get into their phone records, make a connection with Batchman, I can get Sirus..."

"Leave her be. I got this," said Gianna. She resumed typing on the screen, a frown forming on her brow.

"Hugo, his mailbox on the tab. Can you access it?"

Hugo accessed the email icon and found himself looking at the doctor's emails. "Yep, right here."

"Can I look?"

Hugo took his time easing himself off the chair before bringing it over to Gianna. He stood and watched as she started scrolling through them.

"Here we go, Marriott Auditorium in Madrid, booking confirmations...and his mobile number on the mail sig."

After a minute, the door slammed. Hanna had returned with

supplies and easy snacks to keep them going. Hugo retrieved a plate of croissants as the smell of coffee drifted in from the kitchen.

Gianna jumped back onto the web on her laptop and, within a few minutes, knew the phone network he had been using. After a quick forgotten password request, she logged into his online account and viewed the most recent phone calls before his death.

"Shit, that's impressive, G."

"Just a bit of straightforward social engineering. Lucky he didn't password protect his email; otherwise, it would have taken longer."

He pointed at one of the numbers.

"That one. A good twenty-minute call, the day before the train."

"And other calls," added Gianna. "So, let's find out who owns that number, shall we?"

"How you gonna do that, G?"

"It's easier than you think," she said, reaching over and grabbing one of Joe's phones from on top of a bookshelf. "OK to use this burner, Joe?"

"Go for it; that's a clean phone," said Joe, sipping on his coffee.

Gianna dialled the number and heard a soft ringing on the line. It soon cut to the pre-recorded message.

"You've reached the voicemail of Paul Fox. Please leave a brief message, and I'll..."

Gianna hung up, switched the phone off, and turned to Hugo and Joe.

"Looks like this Paul Fox is a very likely contender."

Joe smiled. "Good work, Gianna. Now here's what we should

do..."

Chapter 38

1.47 PM
Lisbon, Portugal

A flock of pigeons flapped across the boulevard before changing direction and heading to the roofs of the dilapidated residential buildings where dark oblong windows encased with tiny metal balconies stared out from crumbling, peeling walls.

Apart from the occasional car and pedestrian that went past where Joe and Hugo were discreetly parked, it was a very quiet street. It was siesta time, and there seemed to be very few people around this part of the town.

They had driven across to the Portuguese capital without a break. It would have been a risk to take any public transport, and apart from having to pass the occasional road toll, they were able to make the journey undetected. They had driven across the Rio Tajo into Sacavem and then headed south.

"A beautiful place," Hugo remarked.

"I'll show you around sometime...when we're not running around like blue-arsed flies."

Hanna had taken Gianna to the Andalucia property, where they had all arranged to meet up later. It suddenly occurred to Joe that the flat in Seville may be getting too risky to hang around in after using it as a base for nearly six months, especially with recent events.

On arriving, they had driven around the block several times, looking out for tell-tale signs of the building being watched. If anyone did have eyes on it, they would have to be parked on the same street, and they had spotted no one hanging around in cars. The apartments directly opposite had a vast plastic sheet covering some scaffolding, which ruled out any prying eyes from that angle.

"I don't think this guy is being watched," said Hugo, unconsciously brushing his fingers over the thick dressing on his arm.

"Neither do I, but if there's even a 1 percent chance he's being watched and we show up...say goodbye to your life...that could be him."

They both watched Paul Fox carrying a brown shopping bag, stop at the door. He struggled with a bunch of keys for a moment before letting himself into the building.

"Same description as we have...yeah, that's him," said Hugo, studying a photo Joe had pulled from the web.

A bearded young man cycled past, and Joe watched him in the side view mirror until he went out of sight around the corner.

They had arranged a meeting, posing as journalists. Joe had used the name of a journalist from the Liberatus media world, Matt Fulford, and Paul Fox had happily obliged.

"If you see anyone more than once, it's likely they're spooks. If they're good, they'll have a variety of people, and they could be anyone: tramps, old women...you name it."

"Where'd you learn all this shit?" asked Hugo.

"My old man. He did surveillance for MI6 many years ago...

tips have been useful, to say the least."

They watched a cluster of clouds move overhead through the gap of palms.

"Looks like a summer storm."

Joe looked at his watch. "OK, let's go."

Hugo and Joe stepped out of the car, pulling down their baseball caps as they crossed the street and passing under the canopies of trees planted along the boulevard. Joe buzzed the top bell, introduced himself as Fulford, and they went inside. They climbed a few steps and crossed the black-and-white marble-style flooring in the dingy reception.

There was a dark brown door, behind which they both supposed was some vintage lift from before the dinosaur age. Joe and Hugo looked at each other briefly and headed to the stairs.

On the top floor, Paul Fox waited at his doorway.

"Gentlemen. You're a bit early," he said.

"Apologies, Mr Fox. This is Pedro assisting me on the story."

Fox took a brief glance at Hugo, who had hidden his bandaged arm in a loose shirt and nodded back with a brief smile. Inside the surprisingly spacious apartment, they sat down at a dining table. The virologist disappeared to get coffee and then finally joined them.

"I don't know if I should be talking to you, chaps. Isn't Liberatus terribly frowned upon nowadays?"

Joe and Hugo smiled and nodded, sipping coffee from dainty china cups.

Joe fished out a tablet from his bag and began tapping the screen.

"Your colleague Nick Batchman."

A look of regret appeared on Fox's face.

"Yes. A victim of that horrible terrorist attack. Such a waste..."

There was a moment of silence as the men in the room briefly contemplated the prospect of death. Pigeons cooed outside the open windows, followed by a frantic flapping of wings.

Hugo leaned forward and fixed his gaze on Fox. "I met him on the train." Fox looked at him with intent, questioning eyes.

"We talked briefly; nice guy," said Hugo. "After he went off and I found his body in the baño, neck snapped like a twig before the bomb even went off."

Paul widened his eyes in surprise before holding his head in his hands. "My god."

"The bastards killed him; they killed Nicky..." he added. "I thought he had died in the train bombing. They told me that... and I was just at his funeral."

After a few moments, the old man stood up as if needing to move around and began pacing the large room, wringing his hands frantically. "My god," he uttered again.

"We're sorry, Paul," said Joe quietly. "We're trying to find out why he might have been killed. I mean, we know he had papers on the H1N1 virus, but it's important to know these people—agencies, secret departments, however, you want to describe them—are extremely dangerous. They'll think nothing of killing hundreds of innocents in some random bombing or assassinating scientists or doctors to get what they want."

Fox finally sat back down, his eyes moistening. "Forgive me. I can't stop thinking about Nick, how he died. Yes, there was a lot he talked about, his discoveries. How the virus had been modified or mutated to have different traits, like resistance to certain temperatures or to aggressively attack healthy males, which is what happened in 1918, of course. Even races…" Fox stopped and looked from Joe to Hugo.

"I take it this is off the record."

"We just want to get to the bottom of this whole business, Mr Fox. Get justice for your friend…"

He nodded, refilling their cups from the coffee jug.

"Look, I don't know exactly what was in his research, but we had a few discussions. But if that's why he died?"

"To stop him revealing what he knew. Do you think?" asked Joe. He leaned back and let the comment hang in the air.

The old man seemed overwhelmed for a few moments. His face was confused as if unsure of how to process these new revelations. Joe held up the tablet.

"We retrieved his device…his work is on here."

Fox stared at it and then nodded and dropped his head.

"Then you'll want the key."

Joe and Hugo glanced at each other, saying nothing.

"What are you going to do with the information?"

"Our suggestion would be to get Ljungborg's and Batchman's research out there through WikiTruth. It's an encrypted, safe platform for people wanting to publish classified or secret information."

"Yes, I've heard of it," said Fox, looking nervous.

"Your complete anonymity is guaranteed doing it this way. Besides, we'll be the ones uploading it."

Joe began clicking around on his laptop. There was a female voice from the speaker.

"You are connected to your conference call."

Joe placed the laptop on the tabletop and turned it around to face the old man.

"And as for trusting us…I'll let the founder of WikiTruth talk to you himself."

Paul looked from Joe to the screen and back again. Joe could tell he was close to being speechless.

On the screen was Troy Rhodes, founder of WikiTruth, via video link. Long blond hair, combed back tightly, highlighting the face of a very young, determined spirit without fear of anyone.

"Mr Fox. Sorry for the intrusion and no doubt surprise from your POV." He grinned at the old man, who was still taken aback and merely nodded.

"First, let me assure you that you can trust your guests here. My and Joe's families go back a long way. Right, Joe?"

"That's right. Our dads knew each other briefly, and Troy's old man convinced me to work for the cause."

The young man on the screen continued.

"Mr Fox. Before he began the Liberatus activist movement, my father started Liberatus News to further the defence of freedom in journalism, a profession that has been under attack from governments and their apparatus for decades. You can see how today, Liberatus News is being accused of all sorts of crimes by those who fear its influence. The free press is being hounded and razed to the ground while the mainstream sits back and peddles the line, investigating nothing of importance.

"I began WikiTruth to open up a faster, more anonymous route for free information. It's a sister organisation to Liberatus News if you like, and a lot of our verified info is published there. Our verification process and procedures are strict about making sure documents are genuine, and sources are corroborated.

"So, Mr Fox, I believe you have something of great importance. Though we don't know exactly what it is, if people are dying over its content, then I'll bet my house it is something that needs to be opened up.

"I'll leave that to you to decide. I have to go now for another meeting, so the move is yours to make, Mr Fox. No one is forcing you to do anything. Just do what you feel is right and what your friend Doctor Batchman would want."

Troy said his goodbyes and cut the connection, leaving the room in silence.

Fox sighed and leaned back. "I'll get you the key."

Chapter 39

10.42 PM
Andalucia, Spain

Gianna rested her leg on a foot cushion in the large lounge area of the sprawling Andalucia property, one hand idly toying with her neck locket while the other cradled her glass. There were low lights that gave the white-walled room a relaxed ambience. They had both eaten a chicken salad, and Hanna had found a bottle of white wine that went down a treat.

Hanna slumped down opposite her on another sofa and placed the half-drunk bottle on the low glass coffee table between them.

"You'd better not have too much of this if you're on the painkillers."

Gianna looked at her near-empty glass and gave it a swirl.

"You're right...unfortunately," she said, sighing.

Hanna gestured at the chain around Gianna's neck. "Someone special in that locket?"

"Oh yeah. Thank god I didn't lose this." Gianna put down her glass and reached behind her neck to unclip it.

"My birth mother, who I never knew, unfortunately." She opened it and passed it to Hanna.

It was a faded sepia image of a young black woman with an uncanny likeness to Gianna. "Your mother? Oh, Gianna."

Hanna peered closely at it. "She is so beautiful. Very much like you," she added.

"Thanks. It's very precious to me, as you can imagine."

Hanna handed it back. "You'd better have it back then," she said, smiling.

Hanna's phone chirped with a message, and she glanced at the screen.

"Joe and Hugo are coming up the lane. This is going to be interesting."

Fifteen minutes later, Hugo, Joe, Gianna, and Hanna had all settled into the tech room on the lower floor that had been fitted out with various computers and monitors. Next to it was an empty room with no furniture except step ladders and pots of paint.

"We'll get this finished and kitted out soon," muttered Joe to their unvoiced question.

"OK, let's see what we have here," he whispered quietly to himself, firing up Batchman's tablet, which was connected to a bigger screen.

Everyone in the room watched the folders open in rapid succession as Joe drilled through, looking for any gold nuggets.

A folder titled Mueller caught his eye. Joe opened it up along with the lone document inside with scans or microfilm shots of a different document. A large CIA logo dominated the screen, and underneath a few lines of text from an old typewriter read:

FEB 18, 1948. 08.15 a.m. – 11.34 a.m.
Interrogation of former Gestapo Chief, Heinrich Mueller.
Interviewer: James Kronthal, CIA Bern Station Chief

For Attention of: Deputy Director of Intelligence

MUELLER: They called the 1918 flu the 'double-blow virus.'

KRONTHAL: Please explain what you mean.

MUELLER: The first blow attacked the immune system, and then the second punch was a form of pneumonia. It was your own people that originally created the strain. A US army bacteriological warfare weapon was infected into US army ranks at Camp Funston in March 1918 and spread around the world.

KRONTHAL: How do you know this?

MUELLER: Well, I was told by Gen. Walter Schreiber at a Nazi bacteriological warfare conference in Berlin around 1944.

KRONTHAL: (refers to notes) And Schreiber was...?

MUELLER: Chief of the German army Medical Corps.

Joe flipped back through the files.

"Interesting. Doesn't surprise me at all, though," said Gianna.

"Jesus, you gonna believe a Nazi?" said Hugo.

"Don't underestimate the capability of any government to play around with this type of shit," said Joe.

"Anyway, there's more here. A lot more."

Joe opened another folder titled White Horse from Batchman's trove of secrets.

"So, what have we got: scans of confidential letters, audio files, confidential docs. Looks like Batchman was going to blow something wide open. This is going to take a while to go through, though," said Joe.

Gianna. "Give me a laptop. I'll help."

"Me, too," said Hanna.

After five minutes, Joe, Hanna, and Gianna were all shifting through the documents on separate laptops.

"So, there's a group of letters. From Batchman and other doctors advising the US Army that no troops should be allowed to leave Fort Riley, let alone the country," said Joe, scanning the text.

"Here's an audio taping of a phone call," said Gianna.

"Shit." She leaned forward.

"Some secretary was due to testify that before the 1918 pandemic that her boss, Wes Helms, had talked about 'the timing of the release and subsequent projected infection rates that came with troop movements to Europe.' But guess what? She committed suicide a week before it was due to take place."

Joe sighed. "Sounds depressingly familiar."

Hanna looked up from her screen.

"So, there's this professor of epidemiology at Harvard University who studied the spread of the pandemic. They're saying that the timing of the release, how it was spread across the continent, how contagious it was, and how lethal it was, was almost the perfect formula and delivery system. The chances of all these happening together are very remote, so he's implying that it implicates human involvement."

"Hmmm, not exactly evidence...but the other stuff certainly is. This all clearly points to a flu virus modified and deliber-ately released by elements in the government in 1918. This should ruffle a few feathers," said Joe.

"So, what are you gonna do?"

Joe put his laptop aside and stood up, stretching his arms in the air.

"We get it out there via Troy as planned. Put one between their fucking eyes."

"So, then what happens? We're all red-flagged to the bull?" said Hugo, frowning.

Joe laughed. "You worry too much. Don't worry; we know what we're doing."

They all saw the file titled White Horse: Reengineered Formula, H1N1.

Epilogue

A grey sedan pulled up on the quiet residential street that led to the rear entrance of the CNI area and buildings. Two darkly dressed security figures lingered behind a barrier that blocked access to the road.

Hugo blew out a long sigh as he looked over towards the guards, rubbing his knuckles with his fingers. Joe switched off the engine and turned to him, patting him on his shoulder.

"Don't worry about a thing. Mr Cedars is a really excellent lawyer."

"Yeah, you said that."

The lawyer who was sitting in the rear behind Hugo leaned forward. "Joe's right. There's really nothing for you to worry about, kid. I've looked at the evidence that your friend..." he stopped talking and looked at Joe, clicking his fingers.

"Sirus."

"Yeah...your friend Sirus found on their systems. They've got jack shit on you and Gianna. It's all gravy. Their best option is to sweep all this under the carpet."

Hugo turned and looked at Gianna, who nodded and smiled at him. "It's alright. Let's do this."

"All right, let's just stroll into that lion's den then."

Hugo, Gianna, and the lawyer got out of the car as Joe waited. The figures walked slowly across the road towards the checkpoint, long shadows stretching across the tarmac against the low evening sun.

***

Several weeks later.

Klaus Klasfeld, known as Doctor Black to his colleagues, stared ahead through the window of the cramped black MH-6 Little Bird as it approached Plum Island. The pilot gave him an update through his headphones, telling him they had five minutes until arrival.

He had avoided all the FBI background checks that other visitors had to endure as well as body searches before boarding a ferry for the mile-and-a-half journey. No, he certainly wouldn't be dealing with any of that inconvenience after insisting that Doctor Green install a helipad if his visits to the island were going to become a regular occurrence, as it now seemed that they would be.

The island was located close to the northeast coast of Long Island within New York State and, since 1911, had housed the laboratories of the Animal Disease Center, a United States federal research facility dedicated to the study of animal diseases.

The history of Plum Island was a murky one, with a biological warfare research programme in place until, officially at least, it had been cancelled by President Nixon in 1969. It had since become the subject of rampant conspiracy theories, especially around Lab 257, since closed. The theory is that the lab was an experimental hosting ground for numerous viruses.

Doctor Black smiled at the thought. They were certainly correct on that particular conspiracy theory.

All kinds of animal-related diseases had been housed at the

lab: West Nile virus, anthrax, mad cow, foot and mouth, and of course, H5N1—the precursor to the full Spanish flu. Some of the animal-based viruses had been 'accidentally released' to test the effects in a real, live scenario.

September 11, 2001, brought the biological warfare programme back online with a jolt, propelling it up the priority agenda as the war on terror began.

Those early years of the new millennium were a major advancement for those who were truly behind what was happening. The surveillance agenda, set back in the late nineties with Operation Oculus, had been swiftly put back in place via a number of executive orders: the Patriot Act, the never-ending modification to the Foreign Intelligence Surveillance Act, cleverly bypassing Congress and subjecting the unknowing American people to a massive privacy and human rights breach.

Executive Order 13603, signed in 2012, gave the US government power over all commodities and products that were capable of being consumed by human beings and animals. It also enabled them to control and distribute all forms of energy, civil transportation, water from any source, health resources, and enforce labour such as military conscription.

The European governments soon followed suit, and it had all worked perfectly.

Small steps...

All they needed now was another crisis or massive psychological operation to test the effectiveness of their structure. A crisis was needed, big enough to test martial law and terrify the public, hitting them with a killer blow, a killer outbreak.

The helicopter touched down on the newly built helipad on the southern part of the island, greeted by a lone US Marine, who saluted Doctor Black as he stepped onto the pad. The soldier escorted the doctor to a waiting army Jeep and, without a word, drove towards Laboratory 101 on the northwest plateau of the island.

The Jeep stopped at a security checkpoint where a grim-faced military man flipped through Klasfeld's identity papers before quickly giving them back and saluting.

Inside the perimeter, they pulled up outside a white convex-shaped front building that had wide steps leading to thick glass doors. A tall, wiry man with a shaved head trotted down the steps, his white lab coat flapping behind him.

"Doctor Black. A pleasure as always," he said, offering his hand.

Klasfeld shook his hand and smiled, genuinely pleased to see him. If the reports were correct on what had come to light on the H1N1 virus, then it meant they were making good progress.

"Doctor Green. Likewise."

Klasfeld knew Doctor Green's real name was David Gertner, an ex-Israeli scientist who had been based at Plum Island for over five years.

Black looked up at the facility building behind Green.

"I hope you've got all your nasty viruses locked and secure in there, Doctor?"

Gertner chuckled and led him inside the facility without a response. They bypassed another security ring of steel through a side door, where Green led him to a lift that only activated after he lined up his eyes to a scanner on the wall. The steel doors opened with a swishing sound, and they stepped inside.

"So, was Batchman's research useful?"

Green nodded as the floor digits on the lift panel dipped into minus figures; they were headed deep underground.

"Absolutely, Yes. Very useful. The new information has saved us years. Batchman had successfully carried out reverse genetics, effectively rebuilding the virus, carrying on from Ljungborg's early work at Funston. There are a few modifications that we need to make to the genome in order to amplify the infection rate."

"Yes, it's a shame Batchman wouldn't work with us. Such a terrible end, caught up in that nasty Madrid attack. But we have the capability to turn it into the White Horse virus?"

The doors opened to a hallway that was stark in its appearance. The two doctors walked to the end of the corridor towards white doors that had black oblong slits for windows, giving it the appearance of a sinister ghost-like face.

"We have the means. We just need more time."

Green once again held his eyes against a scanner, and they walked through to the anteroom; negative air pressure sucked inside, and the temperature dropped significantly.

Along each wall were hooks where white bio suits were hanging like empty skins.

"Sorry, but as a precaution, we need to wear these," said Doctor Green, handing one of the suits to Black.

They took a few minutes to suit up and walked through another thick steel door alongside a row of transparent glass-walled lab cubicles. Through the walls, they could see scientists in the same white bio suits hunched over their work; graphs and numbers were displayed on screens.

At the end of the row of cubicles, they turned and continued along a hallway until they came to a sealed-off laboratory that had dark Perspex glass surrounding it. Inside, there was a woman sitting at a desk, looking over a spreadsheet on the wafer-thin screen. She looked up as they walked in.

"Doctor Jenner, this is Doctor Klasfeld, who is visiting today."

Black and Jenner shook hands.

"Could you leave us, please, Doctor Jenner? Thank you," Doctor Green added abruptly.

When they were alone, the two remaining doctors walked slowly up to a transparent Perspex box that housed two gloved arms for handling the dangerous unseen virus.

"Most of the viruses we have are stored in the freezers at a steady minus 150 Celsius as standard onsite protocol," said Green gesturing inside the glovebox. "But as we are working on the H1N5, we have it out today."

Doctor Black smiled with glee, peering into the box like a schoolboy looking into a cake shop as he surveyed the glass tube of liquid and the virus.

"The blueprints for how to manipulate this beauty, graciously leaked on WikiTruth by Liberatus. If only they realised what they have done," said Green.

"They, along with the world, soon will," said Black.

He was no longer smiling.

Free Thriller

Exclusive offer. To grab your FREE Novella eBook, head to:
https://jaytinsiano.com/secret-access/

PLUS, you'll get access to the VIP Jay Tinsiano reading group
for:
Free Books and stories
Previews and Sneak Peeks
Exclusive material

Red Horse: Prologue

US Army intelligence officer Wes Helms ran a finger down the edge of the manila folder to sharpen the crease. He opened it up, revealing the first page of his "Operation Paperclip" file. An operation run by the Office of Strategic Services, or OSS. His top target had been Dr Wernher Reisser, the head of the secret Nazi weapons programmes. Doctor Reisser had been overseeing some of Germany's biggest technological breakthroughs, including the design and build of the V2 rockets that had been terrorising citizens in London since the beginning of the year.

The Western Allies' intelligence agencies had all been tracking Hitler's secret programmes since the beginning of the war. Now the war was almost over, and the race was on to secure these valuable Nazi assets, but also a record of the personnel involved. Helms was determined that it would be the US that got the booty.

Helms had arrived in Nordhausen a few weeks earlier, just after the US 3rd Armored Division and 104th Infantry Division had liberated the city. They had also found the horrors of the Boelcke Kaserne work camp, which had made more than one soldier retch from the conditions discovered there.

Thousands of workers, Polish, French, Slavic and many others had been forced to work on the V2 programme. The US soldiers found piles of bodies when they arrived, too many to count, and only a handful of survivors.

Helms had been given a quick tour by a Major. Although the scenes initially repulsed him, he felt impressed by the German efficiency of the operation. After, he inspected the V2 facilities and began overseeing the US army as they prepared to take the remaining rocket parts and equipment back to the States. The information from the top Nazi rocket scientist Dr Von Braun led them to a mine shaft where they found related documents for the project.

They had to move fast as the area was due to become part of the Russian zone, and those in the know of Operation Paperclip intended to leave as little as possible for the Russians.

Now, Helms had been lured to Leipzig following in the slipstream of the US advance. The news came that one of his top targets, Wernher Reisser, was there to escape the Soviets and had given himself up to the Americans.

A guard brought in Reisser, a tall, lean man with a gaunt look as though the skin had been stretched over his skull, and he looked much older than his thirty-two years.

"Dr Reisser, please sit down."

The man did so, nervously adjusting his grey cloth suit and settling into the chair. Inexpensive attire thought Helms. A suit that perhaps a low-level official might wear. This was a man hoping to keep a low profile. It was not a great time to be a Nazi, after all.

"We've verified who you are finally," said Helms with a thin smile, looking up from Reisser's identification papers. "Let me begin with a question. Are you happy to be on our side of the line, or would you have preferred to be talking to the Russians?"

Reisser barely suppressed a chortle, waving a dismissive hand.

"I hope you don't think I would ever have any desire to work for Stalin? If that's what you're implying, then you're well wide of the mark."

Helms leaned back and smiled again more genuine this time. "Just asking the question. I'm interested."

Helms pushed over his pack of Lucky Strikes that Reisser had been glancing at and gestured for him to help himself.

"We should have joined forces and fought the Russians," said Reisser, lighting up and inhaling with satisfaction. "Germany always wanted to seek peace with the West. Hitler told me that when I received the Knight's Cross in Berlin. Churchill didn't want to know. But the Fuhrer always thought it was possible."

Reisser paused and added, "Stalin is your real enemy, Mr Helms. The Russians are your enemy now."

"Did you hear? The US 1st met and shook hands with the Red Army at the Elbe yesterday," he said with satisfaction.

Reisser pursed his lips slightly. "Yes, I overheard the guards mention it. Trust me, that's a friendship that will be short-lived."

Helms sighed and picked up the phone.

"Private, can you get more coffee in here?"

He replaced the receiver and focused on the files again.

"The Red Army will soon have control of this area. Is there anything else you can give us, Doctor? Before it all falls into Stalin's hands?" Helms asked.

Reisser considered the question for a moment. "The bases

still have a lot of equipment. The documents on how to use that equipment and the rest of the personnel are another matter. I would like assurances."

Helms jotted down a note on the file.

"We want to have everything, Dr Reisser. This is not a negotiation."

Reisser leaned back, unbuttoning his suit, and grinned.

"Yes, there is something. Something that your intelligence and Government have little idea about, and I'm not talking about the V2 project. This is something different." He looked at Helms. "Again, I would like assurances."

"You realise high-level Nazis are going to be hung after their trials. There was another concentration camp found this week. The world is appalled and horrified at the Nazi regime."

"I know nothing about that," Reisser said quickly.

"Maybe so, but that hardly gives you much to bargain with."

Reisser glared at Helms.

"Do you want the programme? Do you want the superior German technology and expertise that will take the American war machine to the next level? That is the question you should be concerned with, Colonel Helms."

Helms leaned back in his chair and stared out of the window across the ghostly bombed-out shells of buildings. Leipzig had taken the brunt of repeated Allied bombing campaigns in the previous months before the US army entered the city, leaving it a virtual wasteland. The suicide rate across Germany had spiralled out of control as the inevitable collapse of the Nazi regime came to a head.

Helms stroked the wooden desk. Indeed, the Major, who had been the former resident of this very room, had killed himself in it only days before.

There was a rapid knock at the door, and an orderly brought in a tin jug of coffee before leaving.

Helms offered another cigarette, lit them and then poured coffee for them both.

"It's not the best coffee but all we could find around here," he said.

Helms took a gulp and took a pull on the Lucky Strike.

"I can arrange your safe passage, Reisser, and new identity and accommodations. I have the authority to do almost anything I please. So, tell me about your secrets."

Reisser smiled, tilting his head slightly at Helms.

"Very well, where are your maps of the country?"

***

The Sergeant came into the major's office with the rolled-up maps and handed them over to Helms. "Get me, Captain Richards. Ask him to come here immediately," ordered Helms.

The Sergeant saluted. "Yes, Sir!"

Helms stood up and unrolled the first map and flattened it on the large oak desk, helped by Reisser, who focused his eyes on the Sowie mountain region in Southern Germany near the border with the Czech Republic.

He pointed a bony finger at the map.

"This area here," Reisser said, circling an area in Southern Germany near the Czechoslovakian border, "there is a vast network of underground bases and factories that have been working on the Fuhrer's most secret projects. Which, of course, I was in charge of until three days ago."

"There are over two hundred thousand square metres of tunnels, sixty kilometres of roads, bridges and one hundred kilometres of pipeline," he continued.

314

"Built under the mountains?" asked Helms.

"Yes, and there are others in Germany, but I don't know the exact locations. My orders were to help construct and run the entire 'Riese.'"

"Riese?"

"It means 'Giant.' The name for the whole complex."

"Is it completed?"

Reisser shook his head. "No. There are countless tunnels, and some areas are unfinished. Some have caved in."

Helms rubbed his short greying curly hair and leaned over the map.

"I want to see it or at least get an idea, a taste of it. What was the situation there when you left?"

"The whole complex was under the command of an SS unit. They guarded all of them, but they were pulling out at the same time I was leaving so I believe them to be empty."

He paused before continuing. "But I cannot discount that there might still be some SS or even WerWolf units in the area."

Helms nodded. He knew all about the WerWolf SS divisions. A force of fanatics, well-armed and highly trained, who were ready to cause chaos even after the defeat of Germany. But recently, there had been no clear evidence they were any real threat. His real worry was the approaching Russians. They weren't that far away, and he would need to move fast before the whole area was overrun.

He couldn't forget his primary mission, the V2 programme in Noshausan. Someone else could handle that, he thought. He knew plenty of competent and trusted Colonels in the US Army in that area who were more than capable of carrying off all the equipment and documents.

"So, these facilities have been abandoned by the SS? Then

they should be empty?"

"As I said, that is what I saw at Książ Castle with my own eyes. Everyone was pulling out, and as far as I'm aware, it was the same for the whole area."

"Thank you, Doctor. You can return to your quarters. But be ready for a little trip."

Reisser went to leave.

"And Doctor," Helms added. Reisser turned around to face him.

"If you're not truthful with me, I'll personally shoot you in the back of the head."

***

Two German army trucks emblazoned with Red Cross insignia followed a winding forest road set deep in lower Silesia. Tall canopies of fir trees obstructed the blue sky. Helms and Reisser were sitting in the front of the second truck. The very best soldiers had been picked from the 272 Regiment of the 69th Infantry Division, who had helped take Leipzig only days before. All of them wore civilian clothing but were heavily armed. They also had brought along an army photographer to record anything of interest.

Everyone had been briefed that this was a covert operation. If they were captured in that area by Germans, Russians or Polish alike, they would almost certainly be treated as spies. Wearing US army uniforms would be hard to explain to Soviet troops so far from the Allied lines. It was a tense time between the Allies as the defeat of Germany grew closer.

Helms had complete authority and decided to keep the operation low-key, making them all wear civilian clothing but with army-issued kit and weapons.

Leipzig airfield, now occupied by the 60th Armored Infantry Battalion, had mostly been bombed by the Allied forces or burned out by the retreating Germans. Helms was looking at the option of having to drive the 270 km or give up the idea of trying to get to see project "Riese" altogether. However, a few calls to military command, and he was able to get the use of a C-47 Skytrain, a widely used US transport plane flown down from Nuremberg. The high importance of this mission in the eyes of the US Government gave him plenty of clout.

Helms placed Colonel Wilson in charge of military planning to be based in Leipzig.

After five kilometres, the forest began to thin out and opened up into a plateau of grassy meadows; the grey mounds of the Owl Mountains dominated the horizon to their left.

Helms took out a silver box of cigarettes and offered one to Reisser.

"Beautiful views, aren't they?" Reisser said.

"Absolutely. Shame they're going to be in Russian hands soon."

Reisser looked at him with a frown, pausing the lighting of his cigarette.

"Are the Americans not going to advance any further?"

"They'll be no American occupation of the lower Silesia. According to the 'occupation directive 1067', the US army will be required to withdraw back to pre-defined lines and hand the area over to the Soviets. The top priority is getting as much information about the V2 programme in Nordhausen and whatever you're showing me now. These territories are soon to be in Soviet control."

Reisser lit his cigarette at last and blew a column of smoke into the passing wind.

"We'd better hurry then."

After another hour's drive Reisser directed the convoy towards the Owl mountains that dominated the skyline, and the vehicles slowly made their way upwards on a track surrounded by woodland.

"The Sorna complex is ten kilometres ahead. I suggest we be careful from this point on," Reisser said. Helms nodded and leaned forward to ask the driver to pull over. He beeped his horn three times and stopped. The truck ahead came to a halt a few metres ahead. Helms walked up and spoke briefly to the Captain in the front, who then got out and banged on the side.

"Take a break," he shouted to the soldiers inside.

A column of relieved US marines clambered out to smoke and stretch their legs. A couple ran into the woods to relieve themselves. Reisser joined the captain and Helms as they stood behind the truck.

"Captain Richards. Reisser tells us the complex is ten kilometres up this road."

Helms looked to Reisser, indicating him to elaborate.

"Originally, it was guarded by the SS units. I honestly do not know if there are any still around."

The captain, a heavyset man with rugged features, looked from Reisser to Helms, concern creasing his face.

"You didn't mention taking on any SS units—Sir."

"They shouldn't be there. I'm certain there were orders for them to pull out at least a month ago. At least that's what I heard," Reisser said.

"But you're not certain?" asked the Captain.

Dr Reisser shook his head.

The Captain sighed and looked around at his men. "Great,"

he muttered.

Helms took the Captain aside.

"Captain. This is of the highest priority to the US Army and Washington. Do you understand?" Helms, despite his shorter height, fixed the Captain with a furrowed stare.

"Yes, Sir. I just like to know what we're up against."

The US vehicles moved closer to the compound and, on finding no resistance, pulled off the road once again. Two groups of three soldiers made their way on foot through the trees towards a round pill box set on a hill just ahead of them. They crawled around it, and two gave the signal to the others that it was empty.

Ahead was a clearing, with a large cave-like entrance, ten metres high and just as wide, set into the side of the mountain. Two more German pillboxes stood either side. Cautiously, the two groups of marines approached. When they were certain the entrance area was free of the enemy, they signalled Reisser, Helms and the rest of the convoy to drive up.

The groups of figures entered the cave-like entrance, finding it still lit by a series of lights by cables attached to the stone walls and followed the tunnel along for around twenty metres. The man-made structure was formidable. They passed abandoned MG42 machine gun posts and other defences before the area opened up into a high archway of reinforced steel and concrete that reached up into the darkness.

They continued walking through the elaborate, tunnelled complex that never seemed to end. Finally, they came to a long platform built from concrete and set into the side of the rock with rails running along into another tunnel ahead of them.

"How big is this place?" asked the captain.

"About thirty-five square kilometres, in total. It connects

to a vast network of tunnels and areas, living quarters, and communications. There are also around five more levels below us, but much more was planned."

"And the exact purpose?" asked Helms.

"It was set up to serve many different functions. Advanced weapons research, a possible hiding place for top officials and other experimental programmes."

They moved along a new set of tunnels that were square with thick power cables, around a foot in width, running along the walls.

"This looks like enough power to run a city," said Helms, catching a glimpse of the German smiling in the little light.

"The power station is ahead," Reisser said.

They reached a set of steel doors that opened up into a vast industrial space, lit by spotlights around the stark walls. Helms looked up in amazement. It looked to him as if the height of the space could be as high as the Washington Monument. Several cranes hung overhead, still and silent, their claws hanging like dead hands in a state of rigor mortis. Away to their right side, a train track disappeared into another dark tunnel mouth. Above them, an arched ceiling, around three hundred metres high, stretched into what seemed like a deathly black sky. Pulleys hung loosely from rails that crisscrossed overhead.

Helms could only imagine the activity that would have happened here. Probably only weeks or days before. Now, it was akin to a ghost town. Abandoned and discarded.

In the central area, a circular silo constructed from steel reached up into the roof; the curved metal disappeared into the rock above them.

All around them were massive machines, engines from

aircraft, and parts from what looked to Helms like rockets. Helms recognised an aircraft engine, although it was like nothing he had seen before.

"Jesus," Helms muttered, looking around in amazement. "What is this? A manufacturing plant?"

"This is the central testing area and the construction site for advanced military prototypes. Just one of the Reich's top-secret projects," replied Reisser. Helms could detect a hint of pride in his tone as the German strolled ahead, waving an arm across the floor.

"The track is for bringing in heavy materials from the Eastern side of the mountains. The engine is part of the new Luftwaffe aircraft," Reisser hesitated and corrected himself, "—was—for a new Messerschmitt; the 163. It's rocket-powered."

"Rocket-powered?" Helms had walked over to it, rubbing his hand over the smooth steel.

"Yes, indeed, like the V2s. Capable of reaching one thousand kilometres per hour. All work on the 262 engine systems took place here. I dare say if the Allies had delayed the invasion, even by a few months, you might have been looking at a different outcome of the war."

Helms gave a short laugh. "You sound disappointed."

Reisser sighed. "Only in that the capabilities of all this might not be realised."

"I wouldn't worry about that, Doctor."

Helms turned to the soldiers who had taken up positions around the space.

"Where's the photographer?"

One of the soldiers jogged across and saluted Helms.

"Private Damato, Sir."

The private then gestured to the photographer and pointed at the engine. "Get shooting, some pictures—get everything!"

The photographer quickly walked across. "Yes, sir!" He adjusted his large camera, and a simultaneous series of clicks and eruptions of light echoed at their backs.

Reisser turned and threw both arms into the air at the strange black circular silo that stood in the centre of the space as if worshipping a great god. "And this! This is a testing space for 'anti-gravity propulsion.' If we'd had a few more years, well, the mind can only imagine."

Helms joined Reisser at his side, looking up at the sleek tube. "What do you mean by that?"

Reisser paused, savouring the moment.

"This was for creating a place or machine that is free from the force of gravity. Can you imagine? But this is a whole other project. The last device was taken away months ago."

Helms nodded, clearly impressed as he took it all in, if not fully understanding what he was looking at. He felt excitement rising within himself like a child discovering a fantastic new box of toys. Toys no other kid had access to or had seen. The significance of what this German engineer was showing him almost made him tremble. What it could mean; Helms was almost shaking at the thought of a million possibilities. This was gold in the real sense of the word.

"Did you have much success?"

"It was close—with more time—perhaps—?"

"You have the details of all these projects?" asked Helms.

"I can get some of the project documents, certainly," Reisser replied.

"Good. And it was you who designed and built this facility? The architect?"

Reisser smiled. "That's right."

Helms nodded. A faint whisper of an idea, a vision forming.

"This way!" Reisser walked across the train track towards a set of double steel doors tucked away in the far wall.

"Something else you might be interested in..." he added, pushing open the doors.

Helms followed, the camera flashing behind him. The other soldiers had split up and moved cautiously to the other tunnels and doorways that made up the maze they were in, keeping alert.

Reisser flicked on some lights inside the room and turned to Helms, who saw a line of six dummies covered in a dark leathery material and heavy vests covering the chest area. The room was long.

"A shooting range," Reisser said, answering his unasked question. "But the material on the dummies is prototype bullet-resistant material, up to 8mm for certain."

They walked up to the dummies, and Helms felt material, nodding slowly.

"A stronger than steel fibre," Reisser added. Helms turned his head. "Private Damato!"

The private and the photographer came into the room and breezed up to them.

"Get this lot," ordered Helms with a sweep of his hand.

"Alright. What else have we got time for?" Helms asked, turning to Reisser.

They walked back into the main area, Reisser leading them across the far side of the space to a larger tunnel than they had entered. Their shadows moved with them, arching across the walls and pipes that spanned across the ceiling and arrived at another set of large doors that lay half open, leading to another tunnel.

They were at the beginning of a train track that stretched out ahead of them.

Their footsteps echoed through the tunnel as water streamed down the walls and dripped from the ceiling, collecting around in pools on the ground.

The soldiers stayed alert, uttering commands to each other. Two men stayed back behind Helms and Reisser, covering their rear while the others and Captain Richards formed the core central group. Up ahead, two marines led the way.

"What is up here, Doctor?"

Reisser sighed, looking around behind him.

"You'll see."

They followed the curve of the tunnel that ended abruptly with a concrete wall. Set in the wall was a steel door, slightly ajar.

"Rogers, take a look. Be cautious," ordered the Captain. He nodded his head at two other marines who took position on either side of the door. One of the men swung open the door quickly. Private Rodgers moved into space, weapon raised.

The other two followed him in, in combat-ready mode.

After a few minutes, Rodgers came out and walked up to Captain Richards, Helms and Reisser as they stood away from the door.

"You better come and see this," he said, his eyes wide with shock.

The three men followed Rodgers through the door into another big space. A strong smell of decomposition hit the back of their throats, and they all immediately put their hands covering their mouths. Inside, the light was dimmer than the tunnels, but there were enough striped lights to see the cages.

Rows and rows of them spread out across the room like blocks in a city.

Rodgers and the other soldiers were standing around with handkerchiefs tied over their faces.

"Flashlight?" ordered Richards.

One of the men produced one from his backpack.

Helms grabbed it and pointed the light at the nearest cage. Dead children. No older than five or six. Five of them.

He looked closer.

All shot in the head.

He moved along the row and saw the same thing.

"What the hell?" someone gasped.

Helms had seen the reports of concentration camps that were being unearthed across Europe, but why would they keep their victims down here?

He continued walking. Behind him, someone had produced more torchlights and was checking the other rows in the grid.

"Hey, over here!" One of the marines. "We got some live ones."

Helms and the others who had spread out converged on the spot.

When he got there, Helms looked down at the faces of two boys staring up at him.

Dirty faces.

Dead eyes as if any life had been squeezed out of them like pips from a lemon.

They stared at the soldiers, some covering their eyes at the light. Their cage had dirty blankets spread over the floor, and the children were virtually naked apart from dirty pyjama bottoms.

Next to the cage was a clipboard resting in a wooden holder.

Helms picked it up and held a torch to it. He scanned down a column of three-digit numbers with information written next to each name.

"Sir?"

Helms looked up. Captain Richards was staring at him.

"Yes?" Helms replied.

"The children... shall we get them out of there? Give them water?"

Helms looked down at the children, the subjects.

"Yes," he said finally. "We'll need them."

His eyes immediately fell back on the clipboard and the subject information. Columns of three-digit numbers and other information that looked coded. He flipped through pages of information that he didn't yet understand, yet something told him it was important.

Richards turned to the private.

"Give 'em some water, for Christ's sake," he ordered.

One of the soldiers forced open the cage door and bent down on his knees.

"Hey, don't be afraid. Don't be afraid—" he said to one of the children.

He offered his water bottle to a boy who stared back vacantly.

"Look, it's OK, kid." The private took a sip of the water showing it was safe, and handed it through the gap. The child took a long look at the water bottle and slowly took it from the soldier.

Helms took Reisser aside, and they walked away from the other men.

"What is this place, and what has been going on?"

Reisser stared off into the distance.

"A unique programme. It started with Josef Mengele's

human experiments programme. However, this is a step further to physiological control. To control young minds, mould them to the Fuhrer's will and use them as exceptional killers or servants for the regime."

Helms stared at Reisser.

"Mind control?"

"Yes, mind control. Years of work. It started long before the war."

Helms nodded slowly.

"Do you know where Mengele is now?" he asked. Reisser shook his head.

"No, I don't. He was based at the Auschwitz camp, but I doubt he will be there now."

Helms knew the Soviets had liberated the camp back in January. He was either long gone or in Russian hands.

Helms turned and walked over to the Captain. The men were helping the children out of the cage and giving them water and rations.

"Captain. We've been here long enough. I cannot risk our capture. Gather up all the clipboards."

"Yes sir," Richards replied. "The children? Sir?"

Helms looked down and noticed three numbers tattooed into one of the boy's arms; 192. He looked back at the clipboard. The number was there in the column, along with ten others.

His eyes, somehow lacking pity but full of intrigue, fell on the boys who were looking back at him.

"Yes, bring them too."

Also Available

For updates and a full list of retailers for each book, visit:
www.jaytinsiano.com

Red Horse (Dark Paradigm #2)

ISBN: 978-1-9162397-5-3

A hacker's mission to find her missing father leads her into a deadly game of political intrigue and danger in this electrifying techno-thriller.

Haleema Sheraz, a skilled cyber hacker for the Iranian government, receives devastating news: her father has disappeared without a trace. With the authorities dragging their feet, she takes matters into her own hands and uncovers a shocking conspiracy dating back to Operation Paperclip during World War II.

Meanwhile, her brothers have joined an ISIS-inspired uprising, plunging Iran into chaos and leaving Haleema no choice but to risk everything to save her family.

As the conflict escalates and the stakes grow higher, Haleema calls in old allies Joe Bowen and Hugo Reese to help in the desperate struggle for survival.

Red Horse is a pulse-pounding, action-packed thriller that

is a must-read for fans of high-tech espionage and gripping suspense.

Black Horse (Dark Paradigm #3)

ISBN: 978-1-9162397-6-0

Zoe Bowen, a banking trader in London, is thrown into a conspiracy when her partner throws himself off his Canary Wharf balcony.
But nothing points to suicide apart from the official verdict.
As Zoe investigates further, she unravels a string of similar suicides that equally make no sense and a global plot to devastate the food supply.
As Zoe's investigation takes her down a dangerous path, she confides with her brother, Joe Bowen, and together they enlist the help of hacker Haleema Shiraz to infiltrate one of the front financial corporations of the cabal to find the truth.
What they discover is more terrifying than anything they could have imagined; that they stand at the edge of an apocalyptic event that will change the world forever.
As the clock ticks down to the cabal's devastating endgame, Zoe and her allies race against time to stop them before it's too late.

False Flag by Jay Tinsiano. (Frank Bowen #1)

ISBN: 978-1-9997232-2-4

1991: A plan to destabilise Hong Kong is emerging; the key players are being put into place, the wheels are in motion, and innocent people will die.

Frank Bowen is a Londoner on holiday in tropical Thailand. Half drunk and strapped for cash, he's the perfect bait for a political plot that will leave him running for his life with nowhere to turn.

Pandora Red by Jay Tinsiano. (Frank Bowen #2)

ISBN: 978-1-9997232-3-1

Frank Bowen's mission is to find a GCHQ whistleblower, but in doing so unwittingly risks everything, including his own family's safety.

As part of a covert team assigned to dangerous missions, Bowen believes he knows what he's up against until a team of Russian mercenaries are thrown into the mix, leaving everyone and everything hanging in the balance.

It's a race against the clock to save all that he holds dear and uncover the dark truths behind his mission.

Ghost Order by Jay Tinsiano. (Frank Bowen #3)

ISBN: 978-1-9162397-0-8

Frank Bowen attempts to piece together a fractured life at home but finds himself pulled back into the dark state once again. Only, this time, he's playing both sides.

Blood Tide by Jay Tinsiano.

ISBN: 978-1-9997232-6-2

Detective Douglas Brown transferred to Hong Kong to forget his past and the dark memory that still haunts him—Richard Blythe.

Blythe, an explosives expert gone rogue, had terrorised London and outwitted Brown, leading to the deaths of countless innocents.

Now the detective's worst fear has come true. Blythe is free from prison to wreak havoc and lead Brown on a deadly cat and mouse game in the city of Hong Kong.

Blood Tide is a gripping terrorism thriller from Jay Tinsiano.

Blood Cull by Jay Tinsiano & Jay Newton

ISBN: 978-1-9162397-2-2

A series of ritualistic killings.

A retired detective inspector desperate to save his wife.

A horrifying secret.

Detective Inspector Doug Brown has retired to Scotland, but when his wife falls ill, there is no choice but to take on a private contract offered by an old acquaintance.

Soon he finds himself on a dark path, tracking down a ritualist killer of affluent men who has so far eluded the police.

But as the merciless killings continue, Doug is unknowingly getting closer to unveiling a sickening conspiracy.

About the Authors

Jay Tinsiano

Jay was born in Ireland but grew up on the flat plains of Lincolnshire surrounded by cows and haystacks before moving to the city of Bristol, where he has lived, apart from far-flung nomadic excursions, ever since.

He is the author of the Frank Bowen thriller series and, in collaboration with Jay Newton, the Dark Paradigm Apocalyptic thriller series, Doug Brown and the shorter Dark Ops stories.

Jay is an avid reader, specifically of crime, sci-fi and thrillers, with occasional non-fiction thrown in. He can be occasionally found in a Waterstones bookshop café or perhaps a quiet pub, furiously scribbling notes and whispering to himself.

Jay Newton

Jay Newton practices and teaches martial arts, is a keen cyclist, manages a band and is an avid fiction reader.

He is currently working on the Dark Paradigm and Dark Ops series with Jay Tinsiano and lives in Bristol, UK, with his family.